Lefty and Macavity Award-winning,
Agatha
Award

#1 *Los A*
bestselling author

JERRILYN FARMER
3210 S.E. HAWTHORNE BLVD.
PORTLAND, OR 97214

Cooks up delicious mystery you'll savor."

SUE GRAFTON

"Has raised the bar for the amateur sleuth mystery in a most provocative and exciting way."

SUJATA MASSEY, AUTHOR OF *THE TYPHOON LOVER*

"[Has a] flair for original storytelling augmented by a good sense of humor . . . but she never forgets she is writing a mystery."

CHICAGO TRIBUNE

"Shows how a light mystery doesn't have to be light-weight and why the amateur sleuth mysteries can be endearing."

FT. LAUDERDALE SUN-SENTINEL

"Madeline Bean is charming, the food is divine, and the Hollywood background is juicy."

JILL CHURCHILL, AUTHOR OF *WHO'S SORRY NOW?*

"Farmer can ham-and-egg her way through a comedic mystery series with ease."

PITTSBURGH TRIBUNE

JERRILYN
FARMER

The
Flaming
Luau
of
Death

AVON BOOKS
An Imprint of HarperCollinsPublishers

AVON BOOKS
An Imprint of HarperCollins*Publishers*
10 East 53rd Street
New York, New York 10022-5299

Copyright © 2005 by Jerrilyn Farmer
Excerpt from *Desperately Seeking Sushi* copyright © 2006 by Jerrilyn Farmer
ISBN-13: 978-0-06-058731-4
ISBN-10: 0-06-058731-8
www.avonmystery.com

First Avon Books paperback printing: December 2005
First William Morrow hardcover printing: March 2005

Avon Trademark Reg. U.S. Pat. Off. and in Other Countries, Marca Registrada, Hecho en U.S.A.
HarperCollins® is a registered trademark of HarperCollins Publishers Inc.

Printed in the U.S.A.

10 9 8 7 6 5 4 3 2 1

In memory of Gary Gelt

Acknowledgments

I owe a debt of gratitude to all my hale aikāne who contributed so much to this book. Special mahalos go to Mei (May) Chen, the bravest and sharpest of young editors, and my longtime champion, senior editor Lika (Lyssa) Keusch, with a happy word of welcome on the arrival of Kanekelo (Xander) Lee. Thanks also to my wonderful literary agent, Ewana (Evan) Marshall, and the insanely gifted Pamila (Pamela) Spengler-Jaffee.

More mahalos go to Palapala (Barbara) Voron and Hekele (Heather) Haldeman, Luka (Ruth) Glass and the Wekeli (Wesley) School community, and from all across the country, the fabulous Kī Makamaka (TeaBuds).

Most inspiring of all was the time I spent on the Big Island with my beloved team of heroes: Kama, Niko, and Kilika (Sam, Nick, and Chris) Farmer. Their good humor, bravery, and support added so much to the making of this book. I could never do it without them.

The
Flaming
Luau
of
Death

Male
(Married)

A tall, willowy blonde stood silently in the doorway to my office. She was wrapped, all six feet of her, in one striking color. Bright pink flip-flops with matching toenail polish. Hot pink jeans and jacket over a tiny pink bandeau. Shocking pink sailor's cap tipped at an angle above her white-blond bangs. How long had this vision of raspberry sherbet been standing there?

"Holly." My voice sounded calm. Good. I remembered to smile. "Wow. You're early today."

"Um," she said. "I was actually kind of hoping I could maybe talk to you. Just for a minute. You know, if you have time."

I straightened a few papers absently and in the process scuttled the ocean turquoise travel brochure for Hawaii beneath the pile of chef's catalogs and order forms on my desk, where it had been sticking out like a Britney Spears fan at a Julie Andrews concert.

"Hey, then," I said to my assistant, intoning just the right casual, cheerful note. "Sit down."

"Where's Wesley?" she asked, arranging her lean legs in a puzzle of twists as she took the chair opposite my desk.

"Kitchen." I casually swept aside the pile of papers on my desk. "Doing Friday-morning stuff."

Wesley Westcott and I own an event-planning company in Los Angeles, going on eight years, which we operate out of my house. Holly has been with us almost from the start. Our firm does every kind of way-out party. Every kind. From the killer "Mock" Mitzvah we threw for the thirteen-year-old daughter of a millionaire rapper—never mind that the family is Southern Baptist—to a series of small dinners for a hip mah-jongg club of Hollywood Hills gamblers, we just kind of elevate the celebratory insanity to meet our town's taste for the lavish. For each event, Wes and Holly and I work out every detail, plan every menu option, and spend a ton of our clients' cash to achieve, as close as we ever can, a perfect party.

"Look, I know you're busy," Holly said, her manner much more subdued than her outfit. "But . . ."

"What's up?"

Holly fiddled with the enormous pink diamond on her third finger. "You know how I am, right?"

I began to pay closer attention. Aside from the standard-for-Holly outrageous wardrobe—the blinding garb and the neon-hued lipstick—I was beginning to perceive that this didn't look entirely like my usual Holly. My usual Holly was a million smiles, a pedal-to-the-metal talker. But now she was quiet. And I noticed her twisting her ring around and around. "Is something wrong, sweetie? Are you having some"—there had to be a kinder word than *doubts*—"some thoughts about your wedding, Holl?"

"Yeah. How'd you . . . ?" She looked up at me. "Well, yeah."

"Is it Donald?"

"Donald? No, no. Donald is great. He's fine."

"Okay, then. Cool." The way she was acting had me worried there.

"Donald?" she said, laughing. "He's fantastic. What a guy!"

In only two weeks' time, Holly Nichols was to have her big dream wedding and become Mrs. Donald Lake. There had been all the usual plans and festivities. I thought they were extremely cute together. But truthfully, as a couple, they'd been through more than their share of ups and downs. On any given month, frankly, it was difficult to remember if they were on or off. But for most of the past six months, they'd been on. Way on. I looked at my watch: 8:34. We had twenty-six minutes, but I really should have been in the kitchen already working with Wes, so . . . "Okay, talk."

"Maddie, you know how you help people sometimes? Not just with planning the parties. I mean how you can solve problems for people. Like you look into things and figure them out."

"I like to get to the bottom of things. Yes."

"Take a look at this." Holly unzipped her hot pink purse, a narrow leather roll hardly large enough to hold a tube of lipstick and a pack of mints. She pulled out a piece of white copier paper that had been folded, fanlike, into a tiny slip, and handed it across the desk to me.

I unpleated the paper. It held a printed message and appeared to be a printout from Holly's e-mail account. Netscape, I noticed right away, and in the subject field, it read: **Ugly Trouble Coming**. The e-mail was from: nmfchef@gotmail.com, but that meant nothing. Anyone could set up a gotmail account—they were free and untraceable—and hide their true identity. The date field said 5:02 this morning. It was addressed to Holly Dubinsky at holly@madbeanevents.com, her company e-mail account. The note read:

Mrs. Dubinsky,

　　Your husband won't be able to hide forever. And if we can't find him, we'll come and do our dirty business with you. Be smart. Give us Marvin and we'll leave you alone.

It was not signed.

"But," I said, rereading the note, "it's a mistake. You're Holly Nichols. Your husband-to-be is a screenwriter named Donald Lake. This is not you."

"Well . . ."

I looked up. Holly repositioned herself, rewrapping, right over left, long thin pink-denim legs.

"There's this other thing. And I was meaning to get to this other thing, Mad. I was meaning to. But time just sort of slipped away from me."

"This *other* thing?"

Holly tipped her jaunty cap at a slightly different angle and chewed her lip.

I waited as patiently as I could, considering Wes was presently in the kitchen just down the hall at the back of the house, receiving our secret guests all alone, and probably wondering why I was taking so long. Finally I could hold it in no longer. "Holly? This other thing?"

"This other thing," Holly said, "is kind of a goofy thing. Look, you know me. I have all the best intentions. Right? I want to help my fellow man. Women too." She stopped and looked up.

"You're a helper," I prompted.

"Thanks. And then, sometimes I can get distracted. I mean, I don't have ADD or anything like that, but you know I've never been tested for it either, and—"

"Holly," I said, with a little snap to my voice. "Please. This century."

"Okay. I think I got married when I was eighteen to a guy named Marvin. Frankly, I could hardly remember his last name."

I stared at her.

She continued. "I guess it could have been Dubinsky."

"You got married?"

"I'm not totally sure about that part. It was Vegas, Maddie. We were kids. It was after the prom."

"The prom? You got married after your high school prom?"

"Hey." She looked thoroughly miserable. "I can't remember everything I ever did, can I? I thought it was a joke."

Okay. I'm a professional problem solver. I get paid to do this—although usually the problem has to do with how to feed thirty hungry nine-year-olds when the parents told us they were only inviting ten. But still, I guess you could say I know a problem when I come across one. Holly, whose wedding to Donald Lake was only fourteen days away, was already married to another guy. A guy named Marvin. I tried to get my dear young friend to focus. "Holly!"

Under the jaunty hot pink cap, beneath the fringe of blond hair, her bright blue eyes were on me, intense. "This is bad."

No, no, no. This had to be a joke. I smiled at her. "Are you telling me that all this time we've known each other, you have really been Mrs. Marvin Dubinsky?"

Unfortunately, Holly didn't smile back. "Possibly."

"Oh, man. So you never got it annulled? Or filed for a divorce? Or talked to an attorney?"

"My bad." She raised her eyebrows, waiting for me to yell at her or something.

"Holl. You know that motto they have now: 'What

happens in Vegas stays in Vegas'? You can't really count on that."

"I'm an idiot. I know." Her eyes burned bright with anger, directed inward. "I just didn't think about it. It didn't seem for real."

She was my friend, and she was in pain, the it's-my-own-damned-fault kind of pain—the pain of consequences slowly and finally catching up.

Holly. Always so wonderfully carefree. No worries. But me, I am the yang to Holly's yin. I see the potential for danger everywhere. I check things out ahead of time. I research. I plan. I prepare. I wouldn't go to the corner 7-Eleven without thinking it through, let alone go out on a date with a guy whose last name I couldn't recall. Or to the prom. *Or to a wedding chapel in the middle of the night with a fresh marriage license in my hot little hand.* Now that, no matter where you stand on the control-freak scale, was totally flipping nuts.

But my way, the tiptoe-through-life way, was not the right recipe for everyone. And I loved Holly and the way she could charge ahead in life without worrying herself to death over six zillion things that could go wrong.

In the end, I had to laugh. "Honey, who the hell is Marvin Dubinsky?" Holly was twenty-six, and yet, in all the time we'd been buds, I had never heard that name.

"He was just some guy from high school. He was in a band," Holly said, relaxing back in her seat, smiling back at me. "The Roots. He played bass."

"Sounds like your type."

"He was the shortest guy in our senior class."

"It figures." I got a great mental picture of teenage Holly, Amazonian-tall wild child that she must have been, attending her senior prom with the most vertically challenged boy in school.

"He was really, really smart. He took all APs and had a freaking enormous brain. He ended up going to some supergeek college, I think. University of the Insanely Gifted, or something."

Holly has a certain flair for picking men. Always had. "So you married a diminutive, bass-playing genius?"

"He was a sweet guy. I think he was going to go into some agro-techy field—you know, study plants. Like aquaponics, or I don't know what."

"Botany?"

"He grew orchids and bromeliads and stuff like that."

"Holly, you are a magnet for weird males."

"I can't help it. It's like a gift."

"So what happened?"

"Well, he was like my tutor for senior bio. That's how we met. Without Marvin I'm sure I would have flunked the damned course, but he got me through. At the end of senior year, after all those Tuesdays and Thursdays in the science room after school, he finally told me he was in love with me, which, you know . . ." Holly became a bit dreamy-eyed at the memory. "Well, he was sorta sweet. So, anyway, one day he admitted to me his darkest secret; that he hadn't been able to get a date."

"To the prom?"

"*Ever.*" She shook her head, awed. "Isn't that, like, sad?"

I thought about high school. What a minefield of pain it could be for the short, smart guy. I sighed.

"So you know me," Holly continued. "I'm all heart. I just felt it was my duty to help the poor kid out. He was really a pretty funny guy when he wasn't getting all giggly. I think I made him nervous."

I nodded, picturing it all, and bit my lip.

"And I think he was gonna have a nice smile someday, you know, when he got his braces off."

"The poor boy was still wearing braces in the twelfth grade?"

Holly nodded, grinning. "He had what we might call 'appearance issues,' Maddie. And he was shy. So I just got it into my head and asked him to our prom."

"You have always been very sweet."

"My friends thought I dated him just because he gave me all the answers to the bio final, but that wasn't it at all. I mean, I was really grateful for the help with those answers, but I had always kind of liked him. He used to write me poems, Maddie. I used to go home and actually look up some of the words. They were always flattering too. Like he called me *serene*."

"Okay. You asked him to your prom. This is all fine. Generous even. But then you married him?"

"I honestly don't know how that happened. One thing led to another. I was pretty wasted, actually. Everyone gets too drunk on prom night; you know how that is. And we were having fun, Marvin and I. And I didn't have to get home right away because my parents already thought I was going to stay overnight with my girl-friends."

"So after your prom, you went to Vegas?"

"Right. He told the limo driver to keep driving. He'd been joking with me all night about how I was wearing this white gown and he was in a tux and we looked like we were getting married. When we got to Vegas he told the chauffeur-guy to drive to the marriage bureau over on Third Street and see if they were still open. It was something like four in the morning."

"And they were open, I'm guessing."

"Did you know that that city office stays open until

midnight most every night of the week and twenty-four hours on holidays, Maddie?"

"Incredible service," I said and wondered why my local library couldn't stay open on Saturdays.

"So I guess we got a marriage license. I wish I could remember that night more clearly, but I do seem to recall I had to find my driver's license for some reason. I just don't know! I mean, we were having a great time and I was smashed."

"Okay, Holly. But think hard. Did it all end in a ceremony at some chapel and then move on to the traditional wedding night . . . event?"

"I swear. It's all a hazy blur." She widened her already wide eyes. "I wish I could remember."

"My God, Holly."

"I know," she said.

"Correction," I said, in awe of Holly's entire romantic history, but this chapter taking the prize. "Make that: my God, Mrs. Dubinsky."

"It's totally twisted, for sure." Holly shook her head slowly.

"So how did it end?"

"It was my fault, no doubt," she said, with a guilty look. "I mean, it had all been a lark. We were just having fun. And then I guess I kind of flaked on poor Marvin."

"You broke his heart?"

"I never meant to hurt his feelings in a million years, but I think that's what happened. The next day, I remember I was mega-hungover. We drove back to L.A. in the limo, and I called my mom to kind of update my cover story, and to check for messages. I guess I shouldn't have squealed so loudly right in front of Marvin, but my mom told me I'd gotten a call from Griffin Potecky."

I looked at her, not understanding this turn of events.

"Griffin Potecky was a teen god, Maddie. I'd had a crush on Griffin since middle school. I'd been trying to get him to notice me forever. And he was finally calling me! But I probably shouldn't have squealed in front of Marvin, huh?"

"Hm."

"And then I got dropped off at home. Next thing I heard, my sister told me Marvin had gone right off to college, early, just like that. And I never heard another word from him."

"Wow."

"But, Mad, this was all so long ago. I haven't really thought about Marvin or the prom or any of it in years."

"Does Donald know about this?"

"No. Heck, *I* don't even really know."

Just then a muffled sound made its way from the back of the house, from the direction of the kitchen. We both looked up.

"What's that?" Holly asked. "Wes?"

"Must be," I said and quickly went back to Holly's urgent matter. "But now, about your present crisis."

"Can you help me?"

"Of course. It looks like you have three main problems, Holl."

"You are always so organized," she said, exhaling. "Thanks, Maddie. Thanks."

"First, if I had to place a bet, I'd say you probably *are* married to this Dubinsky person, because how else would these anonymous e-mailers get your name unless it was off of some official marriage record somewhere, right? Which means you need to get out of that fluky old marriage immediately in order to marry your Donald."

"Right."

"Second, you are going to have to tell Donald about your past."

Holly nodded, her face serious. "Okay. I can do all that."

"Good."

"And third?" Holly asked.

"But then third, clearly," I said, looking back at the creased paper, "since you actually knew a Marvin Dubinsky, and you actually *married* a Marvin Dubinsky, then you are actually the Holly these jerks are threatening by anonymous e-mail, after all."

"That's the part," Holly said, "that I sort of already *got*, Mad."

"And I hate to see anyone I love being bullied. So just don't worry about this anymore, okay? Some idiots using scare tactics. We'll get to the bottom of it."

"I knew you could help me."

"Do you have any idea where Marvin Dubinsky is today?"

"I have absolutely no idea in the world," she said. "Nada, none, zilch."

"Well, that's something we need to find out. Because this Marvin dude seems to be dragging you into some kind of trouble, and we have to clear that up."

"Cool."

"And we're going to need to get you clear of that marriage too, if it was legal and you really got hitched."

"Right."

"So we'll just have to do a little digging around and find Marvin Dubinsky. I mean, how hard can that be?"

Pu-'iwa
(Surprise)

I don't know whether I should laugh about this or cry," Holly said. "I wrote back to them, whoever they are, right away. I don't know Marvin at all anymore; I have no idea where on earth he might be. They must have made a mistake."

"A really big mistake."

Holly nodded. "I put in: please, please leave me out of it. No hard feelings." Then she looked up at me. "How did they ever get my e-mail address, Mad? It's been bugging me all morning."

"It's easy to figure out a person's e-mail address if they do a little investigating and find out where you work."

"Yes, but how did they hear about me in the first place? I mean, I may have gotten myself into a one-night marriage to Marvin Dubinsky, but I'm hardly his wife! I haven't heard a thing from Marvin in years and years."

"We have got to find out a lot more," I agreed. "Did they respond?"

"No. No more e-mails. Not before I left my apartment, anyway. You asked me to come in this morning at nine, but I thought I'd better get here a little early and catch you."

I looked at my watch: 8:52. We still had eight minutes

yet. "Why don't you log on to your computer and see if they replied?"

Holly jumped up, and I followed her just beyond my office door.

The reception desk was set up in the entry hall of my old Spanish-style house—tall ceilings, archways, dark hardwood floors. We'd renovated the main floor to serve as our business space, where I shared an office with Wes in what used to be the grand old formal dining room, and Holly worked close by.

She turned on her PC, and in a few seconds the screen blinked to life. A few more whirs and blips and she began receiving her new e-mail. There were five new entries, four of which promised to enlarge a certain male appendage. She quickly deleted down to the fifth.

It was from nmfchef@gotmail.com. I read it over her shoulder. The subject header read: Re: **Ugly Trouble Coming**. Nice.

Mrs. Dubinsky,
  Don't be foolish. We know where to find you. We know where you work. We know exactly where you are sleeping tonight. We can visit you at any time. Send us his current location immediately or you will see how serious we can get.

"Madeline." Holly's pale face had lost its smile. "That's a threat."

"This is just stupid," I said. "Scary and stupid."

"They know where I live!"

"I'll take care of this," I said, picking up her desk phone. My friend Chuck Honnett is a detective with the LAPD. He'd tell us what to do. "Just as a precaution. I'm not really worried, okay?"

Holly snatched her perky little cap off her head and pushed her light bangs to the side. "This is getting worse and worse. What should I do? I can't go back to my apartment. What the hell?"

I dialed quickly and, after a brief conversation, hung up. "Look, I left a message for Honnett. It's the best I can do at this moment. But don't worry. I'll figure this all out."

"Okay," she said, giving me a helpless look. "Isn't this awful?"

"Don't worry. It will be fine," I said. I have spent much of my professional life saying these same words to hundreds of hosts and hostesses. No matter what the trouble—from opening a mislabeled crate of truffles, which turned out to contain live earthworms, to discovering one of our part-time waitresses was also a part-time hooker—these magic words always work. "Everything is going to be just fine."

"I knew you'd help me," Holly said. Her confidence was touching. "Thanks, Mad."

I checked my watch. Nine o'clock on the dot.

"Hey, Holl. Why don't we go see what Wes is up to in the kitchen?"

"Sure."

Holly popped her pink sailor's cap back onto her head and rose from her desk chair to her full height, which is about half a foot taller than me. I followed this cute, willowy giantess back through my office and on through the original butler's pantry. The little hall is lined, floor to ceiling, with lighted, glass-fronted shelves and cabinets where we display our serving platters and partyware. And on past the butler's pantry is the kitchen, remodeled several years back to the specifications required for a professional chef.

"It's awfully dark," Holly was saying as she reached for the switch to the kitchen's overhead lights.

"SURPRISE!"

As the halogen fixtures flashed white light across the stainless-steel and butcher-block kitchen, the sudden blazing brightness also revealed five screaming women and one bellowing man jumping up from behind the kitchen's center island. And they were throwing confetti. Instantly, someone punched on a boom box, and Snoop Dogg music began blaring.

Holly turned to me, her mouth a perfect pink O.

"Surprise." I smiled at her. "We're kidnapping you for a bride-to-be party."

"You are? Get out of town!" Holly yelled, taking in the scene.

Boogeying down to the loud rap music were Holly's younger sisters, all four of them. Marigold, Daisy, Azalea, and Gladiola Nichols were almost as excited as Holly, as was Holly's best friend from high school, the tiny, darling Liz Mooney. They were all doing the bump, yelling "Surprise! Surprise!" and crowding around, giving hugs to the guest of honor.

"We have no idea what's up," Marigold said. She was the next in age after Holly and worked at the L.A. Zoo.

"All Madeline told us was to pack our bags for the weekend and just show up here this A.M.," Gladiola added. Gladdie was next in line agewise, about twenty-two now, I realized, and she worked as a makeup artist for Nickelodeon, accounting for her pronounced mascara and extra rosy cheeks.

I looked at them all as they hugged one another. Holly's sisters were clearly bred from the same stable—all of them fair-haired, lean, and long of leg. I could tell I'd be spending the weekend trying to remember who was who.

"We don't even know where we're going yet," Azalea pointed out, lifting a glass of orange juice and champagne. "We were thinking maybe Thanta Barbara." Both Azalea and her twin, Daisy, lisped a little when they were drinking.

"Or Than Diego?" Daisy guessed. I noticed Daisy had skipped the orange juice altogether and was taking her champagne straight up. The twenty-one-year-old twins, I remembered, were in junior college. Daisy was also big into astrology and earned money giving tarot-card readings, while Azalea taught a yoga class.

"Or maybe Palm Desert," Gladdie suggested, batting her heavily made-up eyelids while handing Holly a crystal-stemmed flute.

"You've all been great sports," Wes said as I refilled their glasses, "so I'll reveal this much: we're going to go *spa-hopping,* chickens."

"We're going to a thpa!"

This is the sort of pronouncement that was guaranteed to bring whoops of girlish glee to our half a dozen beautiful guests, and Wes smiled at me as it had its predicted effect.

The two of us had been designing and organizing this surprise Bachelorette Party weekend for months, each of us over-the-topping the other in creative party planning insanity. Hey, we're event planners. It's our deal. The big thing at the moment is the "destination" party, where you invite everyone on your guest list to meet you someplace exotic and magical and party over there—so we decided to take the ladies on a "destination" bridal shower and spring the location on them at the last second. I had pulled in several important markers, getting us comped into the amazing new Four Heavens Resort.

Our bridesmaids' beauty weekend was all about drop-dead glamour. What fun.

In fact, it was my knowledge that we were leaving Los Angeles in just a few hours and taking Holly away that allowed me to relax a little over the strange e-mail she'd received. By the time we got back in three days, I was sure we'd have plenty of ideas for how to handle it.

"So where are you taking us?" Holly asked, dimpling with anticipation.

"To the . . ." Wes said, raising his own glass of sparkling apple juice in toast, "Big Island!"

"Hawaii!" shrieked Azalea and Daisy, the twins, in unison. The decibel level of squeals set a new high.

Who says surprise parties are tough? You just have to make sure you know your guests' tastes and then over-whelm them with luxuries big and small. I sipped my own mimosa and looked over at my partner.

Wesley Westcott smiled back at me kindly. He knows how hard I try to plan things to perfection, and we both know how impossible perfection is—but this party was not just another business event. This party was personal, a celebration for one of our own. And we owed Holly big-time for her years of loyalty and friendship.

"Everything okay?" Wes asked under the din of reveling sisters and the percussive drive of the music.

I crossed my fingers and took another sip of mimosa, the wave of happy chatter sweeping me up in our guests' delighted anticipation. This big bad bachelorette party ship had left the docks, and come what may, we were on our way. Plans had been made. And confirmed. Bags had been packed. Our guests had arrived. Our surprise was sprung. And now, despite whatever fate might want to throw at us, this party weekend was launched.

Wes drained his glass and looked happy. He was, as always, well dressed for the occasion. Today, for instance, he was wearing the perfect khaki cargo shorts with the perfect light blue shirt open over a white T. What else would a good-looking guy wear on the morning he was taking seven chicks to Hawaii?

"Can you believe it?" he asked me under cover of the party noise. "Can you believe our baby is getting married?"

"More than you know," I said. I would need to fill Wes in on the recent startling developments, but for now, I let him enjoy the rewards of springing a most successful surprise. "Let me help you get breakfast going."

"No problems. It's all set."

Wesley had earlier prepared the fresh waffle batter, whisking together eggs and milk in a large blue ceramic bowl. He'd measured in the oil, vanilla extract, and coffee, hot and rich, made from freshly ground Kona beans of a medium-dark roast. He had then blended the wet ingredients with the dry, the flour and sugar mixture protecting the tender dry yeast from the heat of the coffee. It was Wes's trick; just one more instance where his chemistry degree from Stanford had come in handy in the kitchen. The coffee-flavored batter, covered in cellophane, had been rising in a warm spot for forty-five minutes now, and it looked fluffy and fabulous.

The breakfast area was at the back of the large kitchen, against the wall of French doors, and was this morning filled with flowers. Last night I'd set the pine farm table for eight, using heavy yellow pottery plates and our best silver. Now there was a carafe of freshly brewed coffee. A silver pitcher of freshly squeezed grapefruit juice. A porcelain pot of freshly brewed tea.

But as Wes and I moved over to the waffle irons, now

nicely preheated, I knew it was time to tell him Holly's startling prom-night story, and fast. Because as soon as the four cups of mini chocolate chips were added to the coffee-rich batter, and as soon as a dozen sweet waffles began steaming on the heart-shaped irons, and as soon as Holly's bridesmaids settled down from their estrogen high over the news we were all being hijacked away to a world-class luxury spa, flown to the Kona-Kohala coast on the Big Island of Hawaii for two luxurious days of girl-power bonding, prewedding gossip, aromatherapy, and upper-lip waxing, I expected our lives would no longer be the same. And we really needed to figure out what to do about Holly's other husband.

Aloha

A sweet little breeze, soft with moisture, puffed against my neck, coiling my naturally curly hair into tight corkscrews, gently lifting the edge of Wesley's pale blue shirt. Wes and I stood together at the door to our room at the Four Heavens, rolling weekend cases by our sides, happy to feel the caressing Hawaiian breeze play against our sun-warmed skin.

He inserted a key card into the slot, and a small green light flashed, allowing Wes to turn the knob and open our door. This simple drama was also being played out all along the path, down at the three doors to our left. Our party had been assigned to four adjacent guest rooms located on the lower floor of a secluded two-story bungalow, a seashell's throw from the shoreline of the Kona-Kohala coast. After our champagne and waffle breakfast in Los Angeles, and our champagne and spinach salad flight over the Pacific, and our champagne and chilled guava juice greeting as we checked into this fabulous resort on the Big Island, we were relaxed and happy, if not exactly sober.

The eight of us, freshly festooned with bright and fragrant plumeria-flower leis upon our arrival in the ho-tel lobby, had giggled our way through the resort's lushly landscaped grounds toward the beach, and turned up at our rooms in rather ragged jet-lagged roommate pairs.

"Schnitzel!" Holly semi-cursed.

Wes caught my eye and gave a nod to Holly, down at the far end of our building. She and her roommate, Liz Mooney, were simply not in a state where they could accurately insert their key card into such a tiny slot, and we could faintly hear Holly's ladylike oaths carried on the ocean-scented breeze.

Wes and I entered our room, and I let out my own ladylike whoop. This was the newest resort in the super-deluxe Four Heavens family. The gold standard. The Rolls-Royce of hotels. Quiet luxury. The room was massive, with understated Polynesian-style furnishings, two bamboo-poster beds, and a huge plasma screen TV with DVD player. Wes and I did our drill, our hotel recon mission. He checked the bathroom; I went to the sliding doors.

"Amazing," came Wesley's voice. "Soaking tub. And there's a door to a private outdoor garden with a lava rock shower." He poked his head back into the main room. "Did you hear that? An outdoor shower!"

I was just pulling back the heavy curtains and opening the sliding door. "Look, Wes. A furnished lanai." There were two heavy chaise longues outside, waiting for us with thick pads covered in the finest terry cloth. Only a few paces beyond our lanai was the dip of white sand and then the bright blue ocean, sparkling in the hazy afternoon glow.

Wes pulled a robe out of the closet. "Oh, look! They have our favorite kind."

Just as I was coming over to join him to check it all out, we heard heavy knocking and Holly's voice, loud, just on the other side of our door.

"Maddie! Wesley! Oh my God, you guys. Open up. Open up!"

"What is it?" Wes yelled back, both of us at the door in an instant, pulling it open in a rush. "What's the matter?"

Holly looked physically ill. How many glasses of champagne had she drunk? I checked my watch. Even accounting for the time change, it was still only seven o'clock Los Angeles time. Not late at all. And yet, we'd been partying pretty hard all day.

Wes was encouraging Holly to come in and sit down. She didn't look so chipper, he was saying.

"No," she said, "I can't. You've got to come and help Liz."

"What's the matter?" I asked.

"She passed out," Holly said, and tears were beginning to well up in her eyes. "I'm afraid she may have hurt herself when she fell."

"What?" Wes and I shared a brief worried look. He stepped outside our room, and I followed. "Was she sick or was she drunk?"

"Don't get scared," Holly said, keeping up with us as we walked down the pathway toward her room. "I mean it," she said, her voice getting squeaky. "Don't get freaked."

"*What* scared?" I asked.

"*What* freaked?" Wes asked.

"And keep your voices down. I don't want my sisters to hear us," she said in a loud hush as we walked past the closed doors of their rooms. "They worry about everything."

"We should call the front desk," I said, "They can call a doctor for Liz. Maybe . . ."

Whatever I had meant to suggest, in my zeal to fix yet one more little problem—our friend Liz, who may have overimbibed—remained forever unspoken, because just then Wes and I reached Holly's room. The self-closing door had been propped partially open. There was now a leg sticking out.

Liz, Holly's very best all-through-school friend, was lying crumpled on the floor, just a few steps into the room. She looked peaceful, thank God, and unhurt, her cheek pressed into the clean green carpet, but altogether too unconscious for my taste.

Wes knelt by her side, felt for her pulse. "She's okay."

I opened the door fully, hoping to help lift her up to one of the beds. It was then that I saw the broken lamp, shards of azure pottery strewn all over the coverlet of the nearest bed. And the tousled bedspread.

"You ever hear about how sometimes people check into their hotel room and get a little surprise?" Holly said, gulping air. "They go to the front desk, let the clerk swipe their credit card, and then they are given their key card."

"Holly, what happened in here?"

"You know," she continued, eager to get her point across, "stories about a time when things go a little flooey? They open the door only to discover that the room has not yet been vacated? You remember Carol McCoy, my friend from Dallas? She checked into a room in Omaha and actually walked in on a lady."

Wes and I exchanged glances. Why was Liz lying unconscious on the floor? Why was there a smashed lamp on the bed?

"I had a friend who opened the door at some big hotel in D.C. only to find someone else's stuff all over the place—you know, showing the room was still occupied."

"Are you saying there was someone already here in your room when you and Liz came in?" I asked, impatient to get to the truth. "At the Four Heavens?"

"What the hell?" Wes, the guy least likely to use a four-letter word, followed my eyes over to the nearest bed.

Atop the neat blue bedspread, embroidered with yellow pineapples, was a pattern of several stains—still wet and bright red.

"Now don't get excited," Holly said, her voice getting higher as she tried to keep us calm. "He was dressed in brown shorts and a brown T-shirt. The T-shirt had something written on it in Japanese, you know, like two white Japanese characters on the front."

"A man? Holly, are you saying there was a man here in your room?"

"Yes."

"*Who?* Who was he? What happened?"

"Just some strange guy, Maddie. Like about our age, maybe late twenties. He looked Asian-American. I don't know who he was. I mean, I never saw him before. I couldn't figure it all out; everything happened so fast. One minute Liz and I were laughing so hard we couldn't get into the freaking room, you know? Then this guy in brown was just like *here*! Inside the room. Liz finally got the key to work, and we walked in. Then, wham, this guy came from out of nowhere."

My eyes swept over Holly and Liz's hotel room, identical in every way to the one Wes and I had just checked into. It looked perfectly clean, with the exception of the mess on the bed. It looked unoccupied. I took a few steps over to the closet and opened the door. There were no personal items hanging there, only the two guest bathrobes provided by the Four Heavens. I moved to the bathroom. It was neat and clean, just like the housekeeping staff must have left it; all the fabulous designer toiletries were new and carefully laid out. Whoever the guy had been, it didn't look like he had been residing there.

"He came at you?" Wesley's voice was calm, but he had to work at it. "Tell it all, Holly. Did he touch either of you?"

"I came in first, and he sort of grabbed my arm."

I stared at her.

"I was so totally in shock at finding a man here, just waiting here in the room," Holly said, beginning to shake. "I guess I just had a reflex. I yelled. Liz kind of tripped and fell down. I tried to pull free, but he was holding me really hard. Here."

I looked at her bare arm but couldn't see much. Maybe a slight bruise starting to turn blue.

"So with my free hand I grabbed out and caught something. I swung it at the guy."

"You grabbed the lamp," Wes said, pointing out its unbroken mate, which was still standing on the matching bedside table across the room.

"I swung out. I guess it was instinct. I didn't even know what was happening."

"This is not good," I said. Our party weekend. Our plans for fun. I turned to Holly and said in as comforting a voice as I could, "I specifically reserved rooms without extra men."

Holly, bless her heart, had to giggle. How many parties had we planned together where it was only the darkest humor that got us through it all in style?

"So what happened to the guy?" Wes asked.

"He went down on the bed," Holly said, her smile fading. "I began to, well, to scream. Could you hear me?"

The walls at the Four Heavens were thick, and there were several rooms between ours.

"When he got up, he was holding his face and it looked cut pretty bad. I thought he was going to grab me again. But he just ran on out the door. I noticed he was careful not to step on Liz."

"This is not in my itinerary at all," I said.

Just then Liz began stirring, and I quickly walked over to help her up.

"What's going on?" she asked, her voice sounding like she was just waking up after a long night's sleep but couldn't quite figure out why she had been dozing on a low-pile carpet emblazoned with a bamboo motif.

"I think you had a fall," I said softly. "Are you feeling up to standing?"

"You feeling okay, Liz?" Wes asked, crouching down beside her too, and as she slowly nodded, he said, "Why don't I help you over to our room." And to me he added, "We better not touch anything else in here."

I turned to Holly. "Tell me more about the guy. Give me details. While it's all still fresh in your mind."

"He wasn't as tall as me," Holly said. "More like your height."

Five feet six.

"And he was kind of muscley, worked out, buff. You could see all this arm definition because he was wearing a tank-style T-shirt."

"Anything else, Holly?"

"He was wearing glasses and his hair was kind of long. I don't know. What else? I told you, Asian features."

I waited for more.

"You know, Mad," Holly said, "I'm not really sure anymore. Any guy looks pretty scary when he's coming at you like that."

"I think we should call the police."

"Oh, Maddie. Police? On my bachelorette weekend?"

At the door to the room, Wes returned. "Liz is fine," he said. "She walked the whole way. I don't think she hit her head or did any real damage, thank goodness. And she didn't see very much."

"What do we do now?" Holly pulled her hand through her blond hair.

"Why don't we discuss it back in our room?" Wes suggested.

"Yeah, okay," Holly agreed. Her eyes swept back over the nearest of the two beds one more time, over the white silk lamp shade with the long rip, the broken pieces of the heavy lamp base, one large piece with the intact lightbulb still attached, and the bright spatters of fresh blood on the bedspread. "You know what else is odd?"

I looked at her.

"I think the guy used my name."

Wes had been holding his arm around her, walking her back out of the room. But that odd piece of news stopped him. "What did he say?"

"Just that. Just 'Holly.' Or maybe he said 'Honey.'"

We guided Holly out of the room and retrieved her and Liz's little overnight bags, which had been left sitting outside the door. With Liz and Holly in our room, I began to calculate what this incident meant to our weekend. For one thing, it threw a rather major crimp in the whole spirit of party-party-party.

"Wes," I said, waving him out onto our beautiful patio lanai. "Can I see you for a sec?"

We left the two friends inside, Holly pouring bottled water for Liz, retelling their versions of what had gone down, the two of them phoning Marigold and Gladdie and Daisy and Azalea, urging them to hurry over, while Wes and I stepped outside into the insistently cheerful sunshine.

"Should we call the cops?" I asked.

"Hotel management," Wes advised. "They're the ones responsible for the property."

"Good," I said, relieved. "But do you think we should cancel tonight's festivities? I mean, Liz fainted. Holly's kind of a wreck. And, Wes, there was blood on that bedspread."

"I saw it."

I sighed.

"But you know, Maddie . . ." He caught my eye, and I smiled. "We have a simple philosophy."

"The party must go on," I said.

"Exactly, sweetie."

I reached out to hug Wes. He was right. Before every party, something always goes wrong. The party girl gets stress-hiccups. Or Aunt Laura in Baltimore can't overcome her fear of flying. Or the guest of honor's sitcom is canceled. Or . . .

"We're on the Big Island for exactly two days," Wes said. "We can overcome this."

We stepped back into our room, and while Wes discreetly called the hotel manager, I answered the door, admitting the gaggle of colorful and bickering Nichols sisters. They loved their rooms. They pointed fingers at the sister who forgot to pack the digital camera. They screeched that Marigold must share her shampoo that keeps blond hair from turning green in the pool. But when they heard Holly's tale the group became silent.

"You mean some creepy guy was hiding in your room?" asked Marigold.

"And you think he meant to hurt you?" Gladdie wanted to know.

"I don't know what he wanted," Holly said. "But what the hell was he doing there?"

"Could he have been a hotel thief?" Daisy asked.

"And you just surprised him when you entered?" continued her twin, Azalea.

"A burglar?" asked Liz Mooney, thinking it over.

"What could he have wanted to steal?" Holly asked. "We hadn't even moved our stuff into the room yet. If the guy was hoping to find wallets or jewelry, wouldn't he have been smart enough to break into an occupied guest room?"

We all mulled that over.

"And why did he grab me so hard?" Holly asked.

"Until we get this taken care of," Wes advised, "none of us should walk around this resort alone. Be careful."

We all nodded.

"What did he look like?" Azalea wanted to know.

"It's hard to say," Liz answered, now fully recovered from her fainting spell. "I feel so silly for passing out! I think it was just the sheer surprise of it all."

"So you don't remember anything about him?" Gladiola, the middle Nichols sister, asked Liz.

"He didn't look like a pervert. He was in great shape, bod-wise. Kind of young. He looked kind of . . ."

All the Nichols sisters waited for her description.

". . . kind of cute, really."

"Ew," Marigold said, grossed out. "Tell us more. Every detail."

"All I remember was thinking we must have walked into the wrong room, by mistake. And then this man said, 'Hi, honey' . . ."

"What did he say?" I asked.

"That was it. I just remember being startled. Then Holly started attacking the guy . . ."

"Way to go, Holl," said Azalea, one of the twins, pumping her fist.

". . . and the next thing I remember, I could taste carpet fibers," Liz finished.

"So now what?" asked Daisy.

"Since all of us are just fine, Madeline and I feel we should continue with Holly's party weekend," Wes said. "If that's okay with you guys."

"Thank goodness!" said Daisy.

"What's next then?" asked Marigold.

"I have the schedule," Wes said. Wesley Westcott always had a schedule. Holly and I smiled as he checked his watch. "And right at this very minute, we are all supposed to be enjoying a quick late-afternoon splash in the pool."

"Yippee," said Daisy.

"Yes, and then we'll have some time to freshen up in our amazing outdoor lava rock showers and you all can change into your luau clothes."

That was my cue. I pulled out a large box from under the desk. It contained packages we'd shipped ahead and which had been delivered to our room. Six large gift bags covered in shiny green palm fronds against a matte navy background were passed out to our surprised guests. Since none of them had a clue where we were taking them, we had shopped for each of the ladies.

"Goody bags."

"Oh, Madeline!" Holly said, taking a deep breath. "Wow!" She pulled lime-green tissue paper from her bag, finding a turquoise string bikini wrapped within. "It's freaking gorgeous!"

All the sisters opened their bags and began pulling out glittering new bathing suits, and loud Hawaiian-print sarongs, and custom flip-flops with the words HOLLY'S GETTING HITCHED emblazoned on the sole, and a rainbow of skimpy Four Heavens Resort T-shirts, and more,

Azalea held up the top of a Day-Glo orange bikini. "This is so me!"

I looked over at Wesley. We had definitely rounded the corner and were back to "fun."

"So go on," Wes offered. "Take a quick trip to the pool. But don't forget your swimsuits tonight because we just might do some midnight swimming."

The girls squealed.

"Tonight is our Bachelorette Luau for our Holly," I said, and we all saw Holly blush prettily. "So get ready for a full night of lavish dining . . ."

"Yay!" called out Gladiola, smiling.

". . . and flaming drinks that look like volcanoes . . ."

"Yay!" chimed Marigold, laughing.

". . . and beachboys . . ."

"Yay!" agreed Azalea and Daisy.

". . . and," I finished, "hula dancing under the stars."

Gladiola looked at Azalea, and Marigold looked at Daisy. And without saying another word, they scattered from our room, taking Holly and Liz Mooney with them down to the pool.

There was a soft knock at the door, and Wes and I went to see who was there. A handsome man in his late fifties stood outside.

"Hello," he said, his voice pleasant. "I'm Jasper Berger, the assistant manager of the resort. May I please have a word with you?"

We stepped outside our room into the bright sunshine and warm afternoon breezes. Bald men look so much better with a great tan on their heads, I noticed. He wore a navy blazer over white linen slacks.

"Hello, Mr. Berger."

"Please, please," he said. "Do call me Jasper."

"I'm Madeline Bean and this is my partner, Wes West-cott. We are here, as you probably know, to celebrate our friend's bachelorette weekend."

"Yes," Berger said. "Your party just checked in."

"Jennifer Sizemore helped set it up for us."

"Ah, yes. Mrs. Sizemore." His face remained pleasant. I had dropped a big name. Jennifer was an old friend of mine from back in the day. We'd attended culinary school together in San Francisco, Jennifer once hiding my favorite whisk so she could outperform me in a cooking assessment on meringue. Not that she was competitive. And for that matter, not that I hold a grudge.

We'd never been the closest of friends, and after school we'd gone our separate ways. I'd gone on to start my own catering company in Los Angeles with Wesley, but Jennifer had set loftier goals, going the hospitality industry route. She had advanced quickly in corporate positions. It wasn't too long before she'd been promoted to head of banquet sales for the Four Heavens chain. But she had recently moved up even further in that world. A year ago Jennifer married the company's CEO and, shortly thereafter, had been named the new president of their resorts division.

"We are aware that you are Mrs. Sizemore's guests here this weekend," said Jasper.

It had struck me as sheer good luck when I'd received an e-mail from Jennifer two months ago, announcing her latest promotion and inviting us to come to Hawaii. We hadn't kept in close touch. Still, she suggested that I come out to Hawaii and sample her latest hotel. She even offered to host our entire group. Wes made some comment about karma and the virtues of having sent Jenn an extremely nice wedding gift. I suspect it had more to do with her desire to show me how high in the world she had risen. But how could we resist? Jennifer's offer made our destination decision for Holly's bachelorette party a no-brainer.

Jasper continued, "Which is why I am here to help clear up the confusion about your friend's room."

Confusion. He was covering his butt. He didn't want this incident to get back to Jennifer. But let's get real. "What can you do?" I asked.

The assistant manager's manner remained calm. "That is what I am wondering myself. You see, I checked room 1023. Just now. And I must tell you the room is fine. Completely as it should be. So perhaps this young lady who fainted, perhaps she was *mistaken*. Had she been feeling the heat, do you think? Or enjoying a cocktail, perhaps?"

"What do you mean?" Wes asked, ignoring the man's ridiculous suggestions.

"There was nothing at all out of place in your friends' room," Jasper Berger said mildly.

We simply stared at him. "That's impossible. We were there."

"Would you care to accompany me down to the room and look for yourselves?" he asked, his voice friendly and concerned.

A chill traveled up my spine, despite the warm wind. What was going on here?

"Look, Mr. Berger," I said as we walked quickly down the path, "my assistant, Holly, fought a man off in that room. We all saw blood."

Berger nodded thoughtfully, but on a sincerity scale of one to ten, his expression rated a two.

"On the bedspread," I continued, more insistent. "This wasn't some mistake of a confused guest. Two of my friends saw the man. And Wes and I saw the damage."

Berger used his master key card and opened the door to room 1023. It was perfectly neat and completely without a trace of the mess that had been there before. The carpet was fresh and spotless. Sitting neatly on the two bedside tables was a pair of lamps. A pair.

"You are certain this was the room?" Berger asked, his voice not betraying a hair of exasperation.

"Yes." I looked around. What was going on? The bedspread looked brand-new. There was not a stain on it now. "Someone cleaned it up."

"Hm." Berger said. "I already checked with housekeeping. They haven't been in this room since the morning. And anyone else on the staff would certainly have radioed to me if they had discovered any damage to one of our rooms."

"There was a young man waiting in this room, and he frightened our friend," I said evenly, but Jasper Berger's mild expression never changed. "And she fought him off."

He nodded politely, his expression concerned but pleasant.

He was clearly an expert liar. There must be a great motivation in the hotel business to keep a lid on any disturbing events. Grim news cannot spread to the hotel guests. Berger was an experienced hotel manager. He would never tell us what had really gone on in here. But I was certain he knew.

Berger nodded his head again, not directly contradicting us, for that would be much too rude. Instead, he was a great philosopher unable to unlock the puzzle of humanity.

I sat down on the nearest bed, defeated by its crisp neatness.

"I am so sorry you have been distressed by this misunderstanding."

"Thank you," I said, my voice matching his in sincerity. My hand, however, had suddenly touched something cold, something tucked away beneath the pillow. Probably a bedtime mint.

"Tell me, Miss Bean," he said warmly, unaware I was now feeling around carefully behind me in the folds of the bedspread, "are you planning to visit our spa tomorrow?"

"Why, yes." Seated on the bed, I had been leaning back a bit, with both of my arms supporting me. Now, one of my fingers slowly probed under the nearby pillow and discovered not a foil-wrapped candy but instead something that felt much more like a thin metal wire.

"Excellent." Berger beamed. "The Four Heavens would like to show our concern for your distress. May we treat your entire party to a day of spa services?" So this was how dirty resort secrets are buried.

"Well . . ." I said, making eye contact with Berger. But as I stalled, my fingers slowly scooped themselves around the cool-to-the-touch metal wire and carefully pulled what felt suddenly like a pair of eyeglasses into the palm of my hand, the entire procedure done without Jasper Berger being any the wiser.

"Well . . ." Wes stammered, taken aback by the largesse of Berger's invitation. Wes and I were not easily hushed, but clearly we were dealing with a pro.

"Well, yes. Thank you," I said, sounding ready to let the entire matter drop. "That would be lovely."

Wes looked at me.

"Excellent," Berger said. "I understand you have special plans this evening. A private luau?"

"Yes, we do."

"I shouldn't keep you, then. I'm sure you want to get on with your celebration," he said and held the door open as we all walked out.

When Berger had walked off down the path, Wes pulled me back. "What was that?" he asked.

"I have no idea. None. But we were never going to learn anything more from him. So what the heck? Why not enjoy the spa tomorrow at his expense?"

"Okay. Fine. But I know you, my dear. Something else is up."

I held up my left hand, turned it palm up, and opened my fingers gently.

We both looked at the pair of wire-rimmed prescription glasses of vintage design. One of the lenses had been damaged.

"You are amazing," Wes said.

"Holly must have knocked that guy's glasses off when she hit him with the lamp. And maybe they got rolled up in the bed linens. Whoever cleaned up this room had to do it in a hurry."

"Amazing."

"Look at the etching on the bridge and the tiny arrows that hold the lenses, Wes," I said, examining the glasses.

He looked them over again and nodded. "You have a great eye. These look like real vintage spectacles. Probably antique frames with modern lenses."

"They're so distinctive we might be able to track down where on the islands he bought them," I said, putting the glasses into my bag. "Or maybe trace the prescription lenses."

"We can decide what to do with them tomorrow, Mad. But it will have to wait. As you know, I have a schedule for this weekend."

"You and your schedules."

"And right now," he said, looking at his bare wrist, mock watch-checking, "we are scheduled to have some fun."

I smiled.

"Don't mess with my schedule, Miss Bean."

But of course he was right. For the first time, Wes and Holly and I were going to get to be the pampered guests at one of our very own parties. So if I couldn't save the world or get the manager of the Four Heavens Resort to make sense, the least I could do was remember the whole point of this weekend.

We were going to celebrate our little bride-to-be, Holly Nichols. Damn it.

Male'ana Kuana Lū'au
(Wedding Shower Feast)

*T*he beauty of nature is so powerful it can even shut the mouths of a couple of carloads of overamped bridesmaids. And we were, all eight of us, awestruck into silence. Even me. It's funny. Sometimes, amid the plans and the problems, a stray peaceful moment catches you by your heart. Sand. Seashore. A setting sun. A billion gallons of blue liquid washing up at your bare feet in gentle lapping waves.

Your inner scrapbooker begs you to make a mental page, now and fast, before the glory gets away. File it away under *H* for Hawaii, memories of. Preserve it for future gray-day reflection. Such were the demands of this incredibly beautiful nightfall, with its flower-fragrant breezes and the soothing rush of waves.

And suddenly, this traffic-weary, shopping-mall-maddened L.A. girl's brain became giddy with metaphors. The sun was now a distant glowing beach ball riding the edge of the glassy Pacific. We waited, eyes on the horizon, to catch the instant it dunked into the surface, each of us facing seaward, our toes in the warm sand. So mesmerizing was this spectacle that it quieted our banter, all worrisome events of the day erased.

How quickly Hawaii worked her magic on us. We had

roared over to Anaeho'omalu Bay in a couple of rented Mustang convertibles, convoy style, riding with the tops down and Coldplay cranked on the radio. We'd parked in the public lot and hiked down to the secluded beach, calling out to one another, making jokes. But now, a whole other show was on. For a few extravagant seconds, it seemed like nothing else mattered in the entire world except for the vastness of the sky and the gentle rotation of our planet and the wide, wide sea.

"Your luau will be ready whenever you are," a young woman's voice whispered in my ear.

I turned briefly from the sun's swan dive into the deep and met a pair of pretty dark eyes. They belonged to Keniki Hicks, our luau leader. "Great," I said, when I could find my voice. "Thanks."

She smiled. Perfect white teeth behind very full lips. Did they encourage all the lovely young women in the state to grow their hair down to their butts? It must make finding employment at tourist attractions much easier, but then, as my brain always wanders off to worry about the underdog, whatever became, I suddenly wondered, of the unlucky wahines who were found folicly wanting? Did all the girls with short hairdos have to work in supermarkets?

At any rate, not Keniki's problem. Her hair was smooth and dark and wavy, with an orchid tucked behind her ear, while mine, thanks to the humidity, was a heavy mass of wild curlicues, somewhere between reddish and blondish, and came down only below my shoulder blades. Keniki was barefoot, wearing fresh flowers around her ankles, which matched those in her Hawaiian print dress, a one-shoulder affair. She had the details exactly right.

I watched her turn, her long hair swishing, and step away to check that our cordoned-off section of the beach was properly set up for our private party. This was the very reason I'd hired Keniki to run the party. A close friend of mine had recommended her, promising she would look out for us. Keniki Hicks, I'd been told, was a gracious and energetic worker. She held down two jobs, in fact. She served cocktails on the beach of the Four Heavens during the day and freelanced at night, orchestrating private parties, like ours, on the side.

"Ready to luau?" Wes asked. He kept his voice low in order to preserve our guests' reverie over the sunset, but his eyes sparkled.

"Brother, am I."

Now let me explain. Despite its touristy reputation, a luau does not exclusively refer to one of those huge, professionally cheesy shindigs. For the people who live on the Hawaiian Islands, a luau is just a gathering of family and friends, a time to enjoy good company, good food, and good times. So, on this Friday night, in lieu of us joining a thousand other tourists at one of those ubiquitous culture-in-a-can affairs held on the grounds of some overcrowded hotel, it was that more intimate Hawaiian luau that we intended to experience while celebrating our dear bride-to-be.

But at this point I was having trouble keeping a single thought in my head for very long. I wondered if this was what people called relaxation. I thought maybe it was!

As we stared at the ocean, the first of our evening's entertainers began to play. A traditional Hawaiian song plunked out as a cheerful ukulele solo was played for our party by a dear old island "uncle."

The sun was dipping lower now, half submerged in the big blue, but clusters of tiki torches had been arranged here and there around our luau-decorated section of beach. The torch flames flickered, casting dancing shadows on the sand. And the shift in the evening's light was so magical it made me imagine some cosmic hand was slowly lowering a celestial dimmer switch. The sky and ocean darkened to deepest navy blue while the tiki lights brightened our faces and illuminated the white foam of the incoming waves. Unlike Los Angeles, the temperature did not dip with the setting sun. The soft air remained balmy and warm, even in the deepening night.

The sea. The sunset. The waves. The soft chirping of the musical theme from *Queer Eye for the Straight Guy*. *Things just keep getting better . . .*

I turned my Hawaii-drugged head. Holly jumped to get her cell phone. She dove into her beach bag and found it, flipping it open.

"Hello?"

The old ukulele master finished his strumming and we all clapped. While the small beach at A-Bay was not private, it was far enough from the grand hotels to be fairly uncrowded. The few folks who had hung around to enjoy the end-of-daylight ritual began to pack up and leave as the sun, now completely swallowed up by the ocean, had truly set.

"That was Donald," Holly said, joining me. She gave me a smirk. "He had no idea where I was. Am."

"You mean in Hawaii?"

She nodded. Holly's fair skin glowed from her afternoon playing in the sun. Her evening attire, a smidge of a bikini top—really, if we're being honest, just two tiny crocheted triangles held together with string—displayed her small bosom, now just a shade too pink. Her very white short shorts revealed equally oversunned thighs.

"Wait!" Man. Donald didn't know we'd absconded with his fiancée. "I left a note in his mailbox. Don't tell me he didn't get it."

"He's not home yet. He was calling from his car. Anyway, he's really surprised."

"Let me tell you, Holl, that was one really cute note I left Donald. He's going to be freaking *charmed*." I grinned. "If he ever finds it." Not every detail quite right. I made a mental note for the future. "Is he pissed off?"

"I think he is more like stunned," she said, smiling. "Men think they know everything. You're always gonna be right where they think you are. Doesn't hurt for them to get a clue."

"Okay then."

"Girl power!" She raised a fist into the night sky.

"Go girl power!" I raised mine too.

"Right on!"

Nothing like a little feminist bonding on the beach to the musical backdrop of an old Hawaiian gentleman crooning tunes in falsetto along with a bouncy ukulele strum.

I wondered again about the two lovebirds, Donald and Holly. Marriage is so complicated. Were they going to make it? Who knows what makes a match work and what doesn't? Certainly not *moi*.

"Maddie. I think Donald sounded . . . well . . . *odd*."

I checked out her expression in the dancing torchlight. Despite the Hawaiian music (the elderly gentleman had now moved on to the sliding steel guitar), the sunset, and all our cares and woes rushing sievelike from our happy brains, I detected some concern there. Holly didn't look as calm as she might have. "Did you tell Donald about that guy you found in your room?"

"No, no, no. I'd never." Holly was wearing her hair swept up and held with a big cubic zirconia–encrusted clip. Her fluffy blond wisps took on a halo-glow when backlit by so many tiki torches. "That's over. That's done. Why worry him?"

"So everything is okay?"

"Pretty much," Holly said. "It's just, well, remember what we were talking about this morning? About my three problems."

"Oh, right."

"When I heard Donald's voice, I figured why put it off?" Then she lowered her voice to a whisper. "You know. About Marvin. And the prom. And the . . ." She ran out of words.

I offered ". . . fact you might be married?"

She nodded.

I hoped, for Donald's sake, they'd at least had a good cell connection. "Wow."

"I figured," Holly said, off of my reaction, "he could mull it over, you know, over the weekend."

"Mulling is good."

"Right," she said, sounding much more cheerful to get my agreement. "And then when I get home, we'll figure it out. He'll be fine. I told him to chill." Holly grinned and gave the Hawaiian hand signal "hang loose!"

I hoped really hard that Donald Lake was finding it in himself to be the hang-loose type. He was a nice guy and all, but a little midwestern-suburbs, parents-belong-to-a-friendly-church, iron-his-own-shirts kind of nice. And Holly was not making it easy on him, what with this other husband.

"Okay, sweetie," I said, trying not to sound stressed.

"You hang loose too, Mad." Holly grinned down at me, looking quite happy.

Well, I'd try. Really, really hard.

For one thing, I was finally a guest at one of my own

über-parties, and it was really fun just being along for the ride. My work was done. I had arranged all the details of Holly's luau from the mainland by calling on a few caterers I knew on the Big Island and getting their advice. Wes and I had hired a lot of help, and I had nothing to do now but take my own party advice and leave the work to the pros.

"I mean this, Mad," Holly said. "You need to catch the aloha spirit here. You gotta let yourself go. Do something crazy. Why not?"

Just then the photographer we'd hired to shoot the party came up with her camera and smiled.

"Madeline," Holly said, draping her thin sunburned arm across my shoulder in a girlfriend hug of good cheer, "look at us." She squeezed me.

"We look hot," I said.

"And where are we?"

"In freaking Hawaii."

"This is the most amazing party you have ever pulled off, Mad. Ever. I can't believe I'm here. I can't believe you and Wes brought all my homegirls to Hawaii! I can't believe all this fabulousness is just for me!"

"You deserve it, Holly." My eyes suddenly had tears. She was so sweet. And at that exact moment, me misting up like a dork, the photographer's camera flashed.

Looking around the beach, blinking out the dark ghosts from the bright flash, I just had to smile. Among the glowing tiki torches, several tables had been swathed to the ground in yards of white hibiscus flowers splashed on red cotton. The tables were topped with ti leaves, soon to be graced with platters piled high with hibachi-grilled mahimahi and steak. In the gentle breeze, the heavenly scent of grilling meats was everywhere as two steamy chefs kept the food turning on the spit.

Holly released my shoulder and ran off, laughing. She joined her sister Gladiola, who was flirting with one of the tanned men working the grill. Five sisters. All blond. All over the age of twenty-one. All single. It was a miracle Holly's dad wasn't in some quiet mental facility by now.

More as a guest, now, than a party queen, I checked out our party scene. Surreal orchid arrangements were placed everywhere. At the far side of the beach, a master sushi chef was preparing the freshest seafood into butterfly rolls to order, and a vintage bamboo bar was set on the sand nearby, the cute bartender blending outrageous fifties-style tropical drinks and pouring them into hollowed-out coconut shells and pineapples. It was all exactly as I had designed it in my office back in Hollywood. Only better. Much better.

It seemed to be a night made for hugs. Wes came up and put his arm around my bare shoulder. "Warm enough?"

"It's perfect," I said. I was wearing a gauzy black dress with spaghetti straps, but I wasn't even chilled.

"I love seeing you enjoy your own party," he said, sipping something potent through a long orange straw, his nose close to the foliage atop a huge pineapple.

"Wes, we simply have to get ourselves invited to more of our parties." A good-looking waiter stopped by with a tray, and I was soon nibbling a large coconut-crusted shrimp.

"The shirtless thing for the waitstaff?" Wes said, watching the server as he moved along. "That was a stroke of genius."

I checked out the stage. We had hired a rather large array of musical entertainment for the evening, following our general life philosophy that "more is more," but also, when planning a long-distance luau, it's easy to get carried away with the variety of options. I mean, who could resist hiring a group of men called the Fire Dancers of Death?

After the ukulele performance, four handsome beachboys had set up their island drums on the low stage. As soon as these guys began playing, beating out a passionate Polynesian rhythm, the Nichols sisters and Liz, who had been sampling from the appetizer buffet with gusto, perked right up and started bopping along—even Holly.

"Hula lessons!" called our hostess, Keniki.

In a heartbeat, all of us, even Wesley, were lined up behind Keniki, kicking off our sandals, waiting for instructions. Azalea retied her sarong lower on her hips. Marigold and Gladdie had stripped down to their bikinis. I'm sure the men playing the stirring island music didn't miss a beat—but only by dint of their staggering professionalism.

"This step is *'ami.* Bend your knees like so," Keniki said. "To the right, move your hips clockwise, see?"

All around me hips were swiveling.

"Good! Now, *hela.* Point your right foot forward, like this, and bring it back. Good. Now your left foot. Good. Okay, now *huli.* Rotate around, swaying your hips. Keep going all the way around."

The drums began to beat faster and, if possible, louder, and we all concentrated on throwing our hips around just like Keniki. Daisy, with all her yoga training, was the hands-down best at undulating her stomach, but then her identical sister, Azalea, was laughing too hard to get her stomach into motion at all. By the time Keniki finished running us through the steps for *kaholo, ka'o,* and *lele,* we were all feeling pretty proud of ourselves.

But then she said we were ready to learn what our hands and arms should be doing. Oh, man. Hands and arms? While it was fascinating, sure, to see the graceful motions of the dance that told the story, I was not strictly confident that I yet knew my *hela* from my *ka'o*. I stepped behind Wesley, who was having no trouble keeping up with the lessons at all. The song stopped, and we all took a second to catch our breaths. Then Keniki brought out a pile of authentic hula skirts, thick with ti leaves and beautiful beading on the hip-circling belt, and told us to try them on. How cool was this?

"Watch me," Keniki instructed. "Hands cross at chest to show embracing love." She demonstrated while keeping up the *haholo* side-to-side step in rhythm with the live music.

I tried my best, but I was just about done in. But not Wes. Wesley was one mean hula girl, swinging his grass skirt in perfect sync with the pounding beat, crossing his arms to perfection. I cast my eye around our hard-hulaing group. Liz and Holly, along with most of the sisters, were more like me—a little off beat. We could do the *haholo* step but not while moving our hands. We could cross our hands over our chests to show "embracing love," but then we lost our step. Who knew the hula was so freaking hard?

Keniki showed us the hand movements to represent a man and a woman. "This is our Holly," she said, and we all giggled. "In Hawaiian, we say the name the same. Hali. And here is her man." She made a gesture. "Her Donald. In Hawaiian that is Konala. So all together now. Sway your hips, remember? Keep up your *ka'o* steps. Good. Now make a woman with your hands. That's Hali. And now let's make her man, Konala."

We were all trying very hard to get it right, but then laughing harder at ourselves the more we got it wrong, each of us taking medicinal sips of spiked fruit juice from our pineapples and coconut shells to keep properly "hydrated" during our extreme efforts. Marigold had been doing a rather nice job of the hula until she accidentally stepped into a deep depression in the sand and lost her balance. Down she went in a pile of grass skirt fronds. Liz also showed a certain flare for swinging her hips, a talent one might not have guessed from observing the quiet young woman at work in L.A. at her CPA firm. And, by the looks of her, Gladdie was having a fabulous time too. Awash in mai tais since the sun went down, Gladiola was now using hand signs to represent Hali and Konala that were much more suggestive than the lovely "hands crossed to show embracing love" that Keniki had demonstrated.

"You need a private lesson," a male voice coached.

I looked up and met the dark eyes of a very tanned and completely gorgeous man.

"Pardon me?"

The guy smiled and gestured to my hips. "I can't help but think private tutoring could help here."

Come on! Some wayward surfer dude, probably just off his board, had wandered onto our beach and was hitting on me. At my own luau. How cool.

"I'm not exactly single," I said, smiling up at him.

I was totally tickled. What a compliment, really. There were any number of sweet young blond Nichols girls on this beach, all swinging their hips and touching their chests with much more grace than I had done. And this big rock-hard shirtless man was offering his private hula lessons to me. Wait. Was he one of my employees? A waiter? No, I decided. Absolutely not the type.

"When a beautiful woman says she is 'not exactly' single, it leaves a little room for negotiation," he commented.

I laughed a slightly piña colada–enhanced laugh. Had I said "not exactly"?

"So are you or aren't you . . ." he asked, "single?"

I tried to keep my hips going to the beat, showing I was a serious student of the art form. "I'm staying away from men right now."

"So you can't talk to me?"

"No." I felt myself blush. Damned Polynesian rum! "I mean, yes, I can talk."

"Can you sit with me and have a drink?"

"Yes, I can do that too." I stopped dancing and led him over to our bar, and he asked for a Coke.

"Thanks," he said, taking a swig from his glass.

I watched him drink and found him utterly fascinating, so confident and comfortable on the beach. And the no-shirt thing really worked for him too.

The band was swinging on a new Polynesian drumbeat. "How about dancing with me? Or would that cross the line? Since you are staying away from men."

"Well," I said, smiling despite myself, "that's probably not a problem either."

He smiled back. "I'll leave it up to you to tell me when we get to the part you're staying away from. Okay?"

I was following him out to the center of the sandy dance area, but then put up my hand to grab his arm. "But I can't dance to this."

The drumbeat was getting more and more intense as the boys in the band turned making music into an aerobic workout. About ten feet away, Wesley was still in rare form. While all the women had dropped out, there was Wes in his grass skirt, out on the sand, hips flying, keeping up with Keniki, doing the hula. Just then he looked up. He performed a neat series of *lele* steps to work his way within hearing range of me and the handsome stranger. Wes was such a snoop. When he had just about made it over to us, the music stopped all of a sudden in a burst of drumbeats. We all applauded wildly.

Keniki gave us each encouraging compliments as we shed our hula skirts, then most everyone made a mini-stampede for the bar, since learning to hula is thirsty work. My shirtless Polynesian god seemed in no hurry to depart. How nice.

The musicians, all four tan and young and a little sweaty from playing hard, took their break and joined the rest of us near the bar on the beach. After a day of nonstop girl talk, Holly's sisters seemed delighted to mingle with the boys in the band.

"I should introduce myself," said my mystery companion.

Normally, I would find his suggestion a very good development. I always liked to know the details. Name. Rank. Serial number. But tonight, I felt all those details were unnecessary. I felt ready for an I-hardly-know-you kind of fling. I smiled myself silly thinking that thought. So what if my love life at home was a mess? I wasn't at home now, was I? My inner Hawaiian was flying free. I was . . . oh, my God. I was hanging loose!

"My name is Ekeka," he said, pronouncing it like *Ay-cake-a*.

I looked back up at him, and I thought for a minute the stars in the sky above our heads were beginning to swirl. With the drums in the background, it sounded like the name of some ancient island deity.

"Really?"

He had dazzlingly white teeth, and that was just by the glow of the torches on a dark night. His sun-streaked hair must have started out light brown to begin with but was almost white at the tips, and he wore it down to his shoulders. "Well, yeah. That's my Hawaiian name. If you prefer to get mainland, you can call me Edgar. But my friends here call me Cake."

I smiled down the image of having a boyfriend called "Cake" and enduring witty commentary about having your cake and eating it too.

"This is quite a party," he said.

"Thank you. We do try."

"So I guess I'm crashing," he said, looking pleased with the idea.

"I was wondering about that . . ." I tried to call him Cake but just couldn't get the word out. I clearly hadn't consumed enough spiked pineapple juice to take a man named Cake seriously yet. There was time. "I mean, how did you appear at our little luau? Are you one of the performers?"

"No," he said, grinning at my guess. "No. I live right over there and heard your drums."

I turned and looked toward the nearby cliff where he was pointing. It was off to the side and above our small beach, overlooking the ocean. It featured a mammoth-size building, whether a resort or a lodge I couldn't tell in the dark.

"Is that a hotel?"

He smiled again. "No, no. That's my house, actually."

I had to look back again. Man, it was huge.

"So," he said, "you're having a luau."

"For Holly. Over there." I pointed her out. "She works for me, but we're more like friends for life. She's getting married in a couple of weeks and . . ."

We both looked over at Holly. At the moment she was sitting on the sand with the well-toned arm of a good-looking beachboy wrapped around her bare shoulder.

"Bachelorette party," I said, smiling. "What about you? What are you doing here tonight?"

"When my personal beach is invaded by a pack of fabulous women, I must come down and check it out."

"Your personal beach?" I arched a brow. We both knew all the beachfront was public, secluded though it may be.

"Sort of like," he said. "Just tell your friends to be careful to stay on the path back to the parking lot. My staff is pretty good."

"Your staff?"

"Security," he said. And then he changed the subject. "So you know who I am, but I don't know your name."

"Ah, names!" I said, chuckling. "I'm such an easygoing type of person, I just laugh at all the conventional boy-meet-girl stuff. But if you're into that nonsense—"

"Like learning the name of a beautiful woman? Yeah," he said, smiling, "I'm uptight like that."

"Madeline Bean. Or I should really use my Hawaiian name. If I had one."

"Oh, everyone has one. You know our island history? The missionaries came by here in 1820 and gave the Hawaiian people a written language that has only thirteen letters. Did you know that?"

I decided it wasn't a good time to admit I had read James Michener's *Hawaii* more than once, and instead, I just smiled demurely.

However, out of the corner of my eye I caught Wesley, who was eavesdropping outrageously, rolling his eyes. Wes appeared unimpressed with my new admirer. But the thing was, I was breaking in the new, hang-loose Maddie. I liked trying the totally new her out on a totally new guy. Wasn't this the essence of vacation romances? This was my party, and flirting was certainly allowed, so

I studiously ignored Wesley's pained expression and asked Cake, "Only thirteen letters in the alphabet?"

"They thought the natives couldn't learn any more than that, isn't that sad? But anyway, to figure out what your name would be in Hawaiian, you just have to know how to transpose the alphabet. Madeline would be Makelina." He said it *mah-kay-leena*. "That's nice."

"Or you could just call me Maddie," I suggested.

"That's good for me," Cake said.

From across the sand I could hear faint non-Islandy musical notes. It was the *Queer Eye* theme, ringing out again. Holly grabbed her beach bag and found her cell phone. I swear! Why did that girl bring her phone along to her bachelorette luau? Didn't she want to have a bit of privacy? I had left my phone back in the hotel room.

"Mad!"

I looked back across at Holly.

She was gesturing with her tiny cell phone, and I pretty much guessed she meant it was for me.

"I'll leave you with your friends," Cake said, starting to leave.

Holly walked up to us, handing me the phone as Cake put his hands on my hips. "Remember to swing them counterclockwise. Slowly. Think of having sex. It always works."

"What . . ." Holly asked, jaw dropped as she caught Cake's last words, "was that about?" She looked at me, her face a mix of astonishment and admiration. "Hang loose, Mad."

I nodded, so pleased with myself. I could be wild. Oh, yeah. I pressed the phone to my ear in order to hear better.

A restrained male voice asked, "What is that guy talking about?"

I realized at once the voice on the cell must be coming directly from Los Angeles, and it belonged to my former boyfriend, Chuck Honnett.

"Hi, Honnett."

One was never truly free, even on a tiny lava speck in the middle of the ocean.

Inoa Kapakapa
(Nickname)

I'm taking hula lessons."

"Did you say"—Honnett's voice came over the cell phone, deep and full, with equal parts gravel and Texas twang in it—"hula?"

"So what do you need, Honnett?"

"You were looking to talk to me, Maddie. Right? They said it was important, so I've been trying to reach you all day long. I've called your house and I've called your cell phone. Don't you check for messages anymore?"

Oops. Right. I had left him a message a million years ago, this morning. "That's not like me, is it?"

"That's what I thought."

"I think I'm actually relaxing, Honnett. Neat, huh? It must be Hawaii."

"Did you say Hawaii?"

"We're throwing a luau. You've got to try it, Chuck. It's better than Xanax." And then I continued, ". . . is supposed to be."

"I don't recall you mentioning a trip to Hawaii. Was I not paying close enough attention?"

As Wes and I were keeping this surprise for Holly really tight, and as Honnett and I hadn't been staying in really close touch these days, he was not in on the secret.

I tried to read something into the pattern of static coming across on the line. How would he react—me jumping on a plane and disappearing 2,160 miles from where he was sitting at the moment?

Not that he owned me. And not that we even knew where our relationship was going.

I waited, but Honnett let the silence run on. He was pissed. He was pissed, but he didn't want to get into it right now, over a cell phone.

I sighed. This was his trick. He knew me too well. I have this talent for seeing both sides of every issue, even the side that isn't mine, so he didn't really have to say a word. I got his point. I could see how a woman, even one in a muddled quasi sorta relationship, who keeps big secrets and shoots out of town without a word could annoy a guy.

But I figured since he wasn't going to fight about it in words, I didn't need to apologize in words. Instead, I offered a truce-filled explanation. An event-planner factoid: "It's kind of like the latest trend, Honnett. Destination parties."

Give a cop party advice, and you get a chuckle. Guaranteed. With guys who keep their emotions in check, like Honnett, you really catch a break. "So you're on a beach . . . at this very minute." After the shock of my Hawaii trip sank in, he'd gone back to his dry cop's manner of keeping his voice perfectly even.

"You ever been to Hawaii?"

"Not yet."

"You should come sometime. It's wonderful. We're throwing Holly a bachelorette party, just Wes and the bridesmaids and me. A luau."

There was a pause.

I put my hand up to my ear to mute the background party noise; loud Don Ho music was pouring out of the speakers on the beach, mixed with lively conversation as the gang grabbed dinner. "Honnett," I said, "you starting to think you should have never gotten involved with a girl like me?"

"Did you say *starting*?"

I had to laugh. Just when I was beginning to make some decisions about what to do about Honnett and me, like we should put our troubled history to rest, end our relationship, and move on, he goes and acts all good-natured and cool and adorable. I hate men. Really.

While some women, Holly as a prime example, apparently have no trouble committing to any number of husbands, I am quite the opposite. For me, work is easy but the world of boyfriends is difficult. I have been getting tangled up with Chuck Honnett for almost a year now, and I had the feeling I'd never figure out what I truly had going on with him. I pushed my hair up off my shoulders with my free hand and pressed Holly's little cell phone harder against my year.

"Here's the thing," I said, putting the business first. "This morning Holly got an e-mail that freaked her out. An anonymous threat."

"What kind of threat?" His voice remained even.

"Someone is trying to get information on an old boyfriend of hers. From eight years ago. She hasn't seen the kid for all this time, but the e-mailer claimed he would find her if she didn't tell him where the old boyfriend is now. Which, like I mentioned, she doesn't know."

"How specific was this threat?"

"Not very," I admitted.

"I'm not sure what you want me to do."

"Isn't there some way to trace that e-mail? If we knew who sent it, maybe we could convince them to stop bothering her."

"Well, I'm not an expert on Internet crime, Madeline, but if the sender doesn't want to let you know who they are, they have ways to keep their identity a secret."

"Oh."

"Yeah. It's pretty rare we get a case where the creeps are so technically lame they can't hide their tracks."

"We saw the sender's return e-mail address, though. It was nmfchef@gotmail.com." I repeated it more slowly, figuring he was copying it down.

"Look, forward the e-mail to me with the full headers. I'm no expert about tracing e-mail, but I've got a few pals around here who might know what to do."

"Oh, well." I bit my thumb, annoyed at myself. "It's not here, Honnett. It's on Holly's home PC and the one at work. I'll have to send it to you when we get back home on Monday."

"Okay. In the meantime, I'll look into this e-mail address you gave me, but don't get your hopes up. Chances are it's some blind account, or more probably spoofed."

"Oh." You don't have to know a hell of a lot about computer stuff to figure you've come to a dead end.

"But see here, Maddie, cyberspace is filled with venom. Nasty e-mails are a dime a billion. People send all kinds of garbage."

"So, basically, you're saying you can't help Holly." How depressing.

"With vague threats from an unknown e-mailer, probably not as it stands." Honnett didn't sound happy about it. But it was just about what I'd figured.

"You still there?" Honnett sounded like he could read my mind. "Better give me the name of the old boyfriend. I might have better luck trying to track that guy down."

"You sure you have the time?"

"I'm not working this weekend, Madeline."

"Right. Okay, then." I quickly told him what little I knew about Marvin Dubinsky.

"Hey, Mad." His voice was husky, and I remembered his face, his strong jaw and his habit of not shaving for several days. "Any chance you and I can talk about what's going on with us?"

Ah. The emotional price tag. No favor comes without one.

I held the tiny cell phone out in the air to be sure Honnett caught the last chorus of "Tiny Bubbles." "I'm kind of right in the middle of the luau, but . . ."

"You'll call me when it's quiet?"

"I'll call you, Honnett." As I may have mentioned, it's hard to know what to do with an old boyfriend who wants you back.

We had always been an odd pairing, Chuck Honnett and me, a homicide detective and a Hollywood party person, the straight arrow and the liberal. The age difference was a factor too, I guess. Honnett was forty-four and wary about dating a much younger woman. But our good points had always outweighed the bad. He was so strong and intelligent and sincere. We meshed in the best sort of ways, mentally, emotionally, physically. He admired me. He took me seriously. I lightened him up. I drew him out. We were great together in bed.

But then it turned out that he wasn't, in truth, quite as divorced as he'd led me to believe. There were reasons why Honnett hadn't left his sick wife completely in the lurch. Sure. There are always reasons, aren't there? But he had lied. And our relationship went to hell. I told him I needed some time to think about where the hell we were going. And I still needed time. And space. And distance.

So we ended our call. He asked me to please stay out of trouble, and I promised I would, but as I pressed the

END button, I had a brief flash of the broken lamp and the bloodstain on Holly's bedspread.

What if the two events were connected? What if the jerks who sent the threat to Holly knew she was coming to the Big Island and staying at the Four Heavens Resort? It's not like we didn't have reservations in our names. It's not as if I hadn't made several thousand plans, all with an e-mail trail of confirmations and receipts. And what if they sent that man to attack her?

Or what if I was just getting completely paranoid?

I spotted Wesley talking to Keniki, perhaps quizzing her on more advanced hula techniques. Azalea and Daisy were seated at one of the round red-and-white hibiscus-print-topped tables, daintily sampling skewers of grilled delicacies, surrounded by all the beachboys. Holly was sitting cross-legged up on the bamboo bar, laughing with the bartender. I shook my head and tried to get back to the "no-worries Maddie" I had been only a few minutes before.

Taking a hand-glazed plate, I walked over to our sushi chef and checked out his offerings. The name tag on his clean black apron said MORI.

"Hi," I said.

"What can I make for you?" he asked, alert. He was an older Japanese man with lively eyes.

"You decide." My father had a theory. Whenever he took our family out to dinner, he told us to order the house specialty. He figured if they sold enough of it, you had a good chance that it would be fresh. My dad, the pragmatist.

"You like tako su?" he asked.

"Yes," I said, smiling. "I like everything."

I watched as he prepared the octopus, cucumber, and seaweed in vinegar. I took a taste and said, "Fabulous."

Next, he expertly prepared a small dish of chilled puree of edamame, creamy steamed soybean, with flash-fried lotus root garnish topped with a sprig of shiso leaves. "This is heaven," I told him.

Wes walked across the sand and sat on the stool next to me. "Holly is too excited to eat," he reported, looking her way.

"She isn't too excited to sip, though," I pointed out. We both watched as she accepted another large coconut from the bartender down the beach.

"Ah, well. Youth," he said.

"You have to try some of this. Our sushi chef is a master, Wes."

The gentleman behind the counter smiled modestly. We watched as he worked on a beautiful presentation, making a fresh plate featuring Toro, Hamachi, Kanpachi, Hirame, Aji, Tako, and Anago. He completed the dish, a traditional Japanese arrangement marked by the Zen ideals of simplicity, harmony, and restraint, and presented it to us with a slight bow.

"I'll share some of hers," Wes told Mori, looking at my huge plate.

"This wasabi is excellent," I said, taking another small, perfectly prepared mound of rice, topped with a sparkling fresh piece of raw yellowtail. "It has a fiery yet sweet aftertaste. It's fresh, isn't it?"

Wes bit into a matching piece of sushi and relished the subtle flavors. "I think this is the best wasabi I have ever tasted."

"It must be from Japan," I decided. Wasabi is the spicy hot root, or actually a rhizome, which is traditionally grated and served with sushi. But despite the huge popularity of Japanese restaurants in the U.S., the delicate and pungent flavor of fresh wasabi is practically unknown to Americans. Almost all the wasabi served in the United States is actually a mixture of mustard and horseradish that's been dried and then reconstituted, because wasabi is a highly controlled crop. It can only be grown in the Izu Peninusula and in the Nagano region of Japan, and the growers there guard the plants like gold, not wanting anyone anywhere else to grow them.

"In Japan, we have many nicknames for wasabi. You know one nickname for wasabi?" Mori asked. "Namida."

"Tears," Wes translated for me.

"Yes. Very good," Mori said. "Tears for the fire of the taste!"

"Do you get it flown in?" Wes asked Mori.

"You like?" The chef looked at Wesley, approving his compliment. "I get from my nephew. I get you some."

"It's amazing," I said, trying another kind of sushi, my tongue feeling the spreading warmth from the tiny dab of wasabi that flavored the piece.

"I get you some," he repeated for me, grinning at our reaction.

"Nowadays, sushi is known as raw fish on a slab of rice," Wes explained to me. "But actually sushi means vinegar-flavored rice that is rolled with vegetables, fish, or pickles, then wrapped in nori—dried seaweed—and sliced into rounds, or Norimaki."

"You know too much," I said, popping another perfect piece into my mouth.

"There are different sushi formats: Nigiri (hand-shaped), futo (thick), maki (rolled), temaki (hand-rolled), and chirashi (scattered on top of the rice)."

Our chef behind the counter kept grinning his wide grin, nodding his head.

"You are my favorite teacher, Wesley," I said with affection. "And you cannot beat the atmosphere here." We were seated just ten feet from the waves, with a curtain of stars overhead.

Just then the drums began beating again, loud and slow.

We turned to the stage.

"Will the fabulous bride come up on stage, please?" The bandleader, a very cute Hawaiian boy, was at the microphone. He called out, "Holly! We need you now." Lots of furious drumming came from the three guys on percussion.

The rest of our gang stopped whatever we were doing, here and there along the beach, and headed toward the stage, whooping it up for Holly. We jostled together, sitting on mats on the sand down close to the performers, clapping along to the beat.

This was Holly's special moment. She was all smiles as she made her way to the stage, joining the boys in the band. In her cute bikini top and hip-hugging shorts, she danced a little hula for our entertainment.

We all howled our approval.

"Holly, you're getting married in two weeks, we hear," said the head beachboy, Matt.

"Yes!" Holly yelled.

We all cheered.

"That is bad luck for us boys," Matt said, and we all laughed and catcalled from the audience.

"But now the time has come!" he said to her.

"For what?" she asked, her eyes wide.

At the back of the stage, two of the musician/dancers put down their drums and picked up sets of pu'ili, a Hawaiian instrument like a split bamboo rattle. They produced rhythmic rustling sounds by tapping the pu'ili against one another's bare shoulders and arms.

"Ah," said Marigold, "they are acting just like bull elephant seals." Her sisters all giggled. "The strong males battle for dominance, for the right to rule the harem."

Meanwhile, the other musician picked up an ipu and began pounding it on the mat, getting a variety of haunting, primitive sounds from the traditional Hawaiian dried gourd instrument.

Matt looked at Holly as she danced onstage for us, clowning around. "Maybe you're not too sure you should settle down yet," he said and winked. "So here is something to help you decide. Do you have a man at home like one of these boys?"

Three new dancers, bare except for loincloths and the leaves encircling their ankles and wrists, made their bold entrance. Their chests and arms and legs were tough and muscular, their faces and bodies painted in primitive symbols. They held long knives in the air, fire covering both ends. Holly took one look at the blades and the flames and the almost-naked men and rushed off the stage. We all screamed with laughter.

"At last," Wes whispered to me. "Here are our Samoan Fire Knife Dancers."

"Those are not knives so much," I commented to Wes, "as flaming batons."

"They're swords," he corrected. "With, you know, two flaming ends."

I eyed Wes, wondering if I was about to be treated to the entire history of the Samoan Fire Knife Dance, but he left me with just the basics. "Popularized by Uluao Letuli Misilagi in the forties and fifties. They called him 'Freddie' Letuli after Fred Astaire."

"You can't make this stuff up."

Wes looked taken aback. "No, of course not."

Onstage, the dancers were doing all sorts of outrageous things with their fiery swords. By now they had two flaming knives each and were performing some intensely crazy maneuver where they placed one blazing knife in their mouth while jabbing and thrusting at each other with the other. The drums beat incessantly, pounding a furious rhythm. We all felt the heat of the fire each time a flaming knife swung by, as we were seated so close to the stage, and with just enough alcohol in one's blood, one could imagine one was on a primitive beach in ancient Samoa, enjoying a night out with the tribe.

"Maddie?"

I almost jumped. Holly was speaking close to my ear.

"Yes, Holl?" I smiled up at her. "You enjoying your Fire Dancers, sweetie?"

"The most," she said. "Who could not like flaming sharp things?"

Wes and I beamed. A few feet away, blazing knives were being thrown to and fro.

"I wanted to show you something, okay?"

"Of course," I said. "What is it?"

Holly unfolded a paper napkin. I had ordered some custom-printed ones, and they had turned out rather well. They were yellow, with hot pink lettering. They featured a little picture of a skewered shish kebab on fire, and the words said: HOLLY NICHOLS'S FLAMING BACHELORETTE LUAU, and then the date.

"You like?" I asked.

"I love," she said, "but look at this." She turned the paper napkin over, and I noticed she had drawn two small sketches. By the dim light of the flickering tiki torches, I wasn't sure I could make out what she had drawn.

Wes pulled the napkin closer and looked up at her, surprised. "What's this?"

"Maddie asked me to think about that man. She wondered if I remembered anything else about him."

Wes flashed me a glance, but asked Holly, "Where did you see this?" he asked.

I pulled the napkin close and saw two symbols: 山葵 It looked like Asian writing of some sort.

Not far from us, there were swords of flame twirling high into the air. We couldn't help but look up, even as we chatted back and forth about Holly's napkin, pausing until the dancer caught the baton and we heard no hiss of singed flesh.

"It's the design I saw on that man's T-shirt. The one who grabbed me in my room."

"You're sure?"

"I'm positive. There's a car parked out near the road that had a sticker with the same exact symbols. I'm good with design, Maddie. I copied it down to show you. I know these are the same marks that were on that guy's T-shirt."

"Those are kanji characters," Wes said. "These two are pronounced *yama* and *aoi*."

"Really?" Holly looked relieved. "It makes sense to you?"

"*Yama aoi.* It translates," he continued, "to mountain hollyhock."

We looked blank.

Wes said, "It was on the guy's T-shirt, you say. I guess it could be the name of a business."

The fact that Wesley knows how to read Japanese and is familiar with kanji is just something we have learned to take for granted. In fact, it is easier to think of the handful of things the man doesn't know than to catalog all the ancient arts he has mastered.

"Mountain hollyhock?" I was puzzled.

"Mountain Hollyhock," Holly repeated, but her voice was shaky. "Well, that's impossible." Her face looked pale in the low light. "That just can't be." She was beginning to sound pretty upset.

"What is it, Holly?"

"It's just . . ." She stammered, looking the worse for wear. "It's just that *that* was my nickname."

I stared at her.

"Yes. I'm telling you! Mountain Hollyhock."

"What? Somebody actually called you Mountain Hollyhock?"

"Yes. Years ago. Like a private nickname. The super weird thing is, it was Marvin's nickname for me. All through senior year."

"Marvin *Dubinsky*?" I asked, floored. I had to speak up louder, because the drums onstage were working up to their finale. "Your *husband* Marvin Dubinsky called you Mountain Hollyhock?"

"Let's just refer to him as my prom date, okay?" Holly suggested, her voice strained. "Anyway, listen. Marvin used to write me little poems in haiku. He used to joke that I was as tall as a mountain."

"That's romantic," Wes said.

I smiled. Boys were so clueless.

Holly added, ". . . and my real full name is, well, you know. Hollyhock. So . . ."

This whole thing was extremely, blazingly, scarily weird. We looked at one another, thinking it all over.

"Mountain Hollyhock," Holly repeated, looking fairly spooked. "I guess it could just be a coincidence, right?"

What are the odds that a random creep is gonna show up, hide in a girl's hotel room, and pounce on her while wearing a T-shirt bearing a Japanese phrase that refers to this same girl's obscure high school nickname? And all on the day she received a threatening e-mail trying to track down the high school dude that gave her that nickname.

Just then a sword, which was on fire, went shooting out across the stage, but this time it wasn't caught by the waiting dancer it had been aimed at. This time it came sailing out into the audience, sort of straight at us.

With some unsuspected hidden primitive island instinct, my hand jutted out at just the right second.

The men on the stage stopped drumming, aghast. The Samoan Fire Knife Dancers stopped in midstep.

I caught the fire knife, no problem, and our entire party just clapped their merry little brains out—Gladiola wildly whistling with two fingers in her mouth—absolutely sure this had been part of the grand finale all along.

And that's when the creepiest idea came to me in a flash of smoky inspiration. What if Holly's missing maybe-husband Marvin Dubinsky was actually here on the island?

Like
(Liz)

No matter what was going on with Holly's former prom date, Marvin Dubinsky, I refused to let it interfere any further with our luau. We'd deal with everything that needed taking care of tomorrow—the threatening e-mail, the glasses I'd found in Holly's room, and even the Mountain Hollyhock kanji. So I kept my suspicions to myself, and the party went on. A few hours later, Wes and I sat together, and this time he needed consoling.

"So now I am totally bummed," Wes said. "I didn't need to hear from my freaking neighbor back home. I don't want my everyday L.A. madness to seep into this groovy Hawaiian escape. The lesson is: no cell phones in Paradise."

"A lesson *some* of us already know," I replied, looking up at him.

It was midnight in Hawaii, but 3 A.M. L.A. time, and I was beat. We had resisted Daisy and Azalea and the rest of the sisters urging us to join them in an impromptu midnight swim. The ocean is just too big and dark at night. I shivered, contemplating deep-water oogie-boogies, watching Holly and Marigold and Gladdie frolic in the surf by moonlight. Dainty little Liz was out there too.

Wes and I had pulled canvas beach chairs right up to

the edge of the water and faced the dark sea. We sat together and watched the flow of the tide bring forth gentle wave upon wave, racing up the sand. One with the gumption to lap our bare feet arrived only about every seventh or eighth wave. Behind us, the beach had been cleaned up. Keniki and the party crew had packed up the tables and chairs, the platters and grills, and called it a night.

Wes knocked coconuts with me and took a final swig. "I'm going to leave my cell phone off from now on."

"Your neighbor left a message?"

"Elmer is really angry at me, Maddie. You should hear him yourself." He tried to hand me his little silver phone, but I put my hands up, shielding my face.

"Bip-bip-bip!" I chirped. "Remember the lesson. Remember the lesson."

"Right. No cell phones." Wes shook his head. "I need a twelve-step program."

"Like, what's this guy Elmer's problem?" I asked, commiserating.

"He hates me."

I had never liked this neighbor, but he and Wes had seemed very chummy since the day several months ago when Wes bought the house two down from Elmer's. This house was in a particularly cool section of Hollywood, up on a hill behind the Hollywood Bowl. The only access to the homes in this neighborhood was by an old elevator in a tower, and atop the hill, there were no roads, only sidewalks. When Wesley moved in, he had brought his new neighbor, Elmer Minty, a basket of fresh baked goods, and the old guy had lent Wes a power tool. It was that sort of friendship.

"He heard you might be moving?"

Wesley bought fixers. Wrecks. Houses no one else

wanted. He'd find an aging, run-down, distressed jewel of architecture in one of L.A.'s old neighborhoods and then, after doing careful research, he'd commit his money and hard work to recapturing its glory days. He insisted on preserving all the period details. He and his work crew restored the broken fixtures and cracked tile work and moldings. They replaced missing items, when necessary, with authentic chandeliers and drawer pulls and whatnots that Wes scouted out from his favorite antique salvage dealers. He would devote days to hunting for authentic period replacement pieces rather than just rip it all out and install something easy to find and cheap and new. What Wes was really passionate about was more like fine historic home restoration rather than just gutting and rehabbing, and in a city with lots of cash-heavy superstars looking for a special nest and a ten-year boom in real estate prices, it had developed into a lucrative side business.

"I told the old guy I intended to live in this house forever," Wes said, his voice low. "I meant it, Maddie. It was going to be my forever house. I love the house."

I knew this story. Wes, with his fabulous eye for finding just the right blemished gem, plus his elegant improvements and terrific good taste, had worked his magic on the house on Alta Loma Drive. He had uncovered and refinished the hardwood floors, used a razor blade to scrape old paint off a hundred panes of glass to restore a dozen French doors, and cleared the hills and landscaped until he had revealed the true beauty of a home that had been embarrassed by decades of neglect and tacky remodels. The house was now pristine. The property's 360-degree views of Hollywood could now be seen clearly for the first time in fifty years. So it wasn't surprising that Wes was regularly getting calls

these days from interested parties. A guy wanted to photograph it for a feature for the Sunday *Times*. A location
scout asked if the perfect 1920s-style kitchen might be
available for a Bounty commercial. So even though the
Alta Loma house was not officially on the market, offers
were arriving.

All the realtors knew Wes. They had buyers. And as
the purchase bids went up and Wesley's restless creative
eye wandered to other distressed properties across town,
it was only a matter of time before he'd be moving
again. And if I could figure this out, I was sure his neigh-
bors were getting the same feeling. Elmer must have
heard a rumor that Wes had said yes to a buyer.

"He was vicious," Wes said. "He left a rambling message. He hates what I did to the house now. He used to
say he loved it, but not anymore. He accused me of de-
stroying the historical authenticity of the property. He
says I ruined the house."

"Now, Wes—"

"I moved the front gate. That was it."

"Elmer is an older guy. Late sixties, early seventies?"

"Something like that."

"And he's lived in that house of his for fifty years,
Wes. He is getting emotional. Maybe he liked you.
Maybe he figured you'd look after him in his waning
years."

Wes smirked at that thought.

"Maybe Elmer got attached to your handyman ways
and your fresh baked croissants and now he's upset because you might leave him."

Wes shook his head, concerned. "You should have
heard him, Mad. He called me names."

"You're kidding me. What did he call you?"

"He yelled on my machine. He said, 'Flipper! Flipper!'"

I would have smiled right then and there—flipper! Someone who buys homes and turns around and sells them for a big profit. But I knew Wes was sensitive to this whole thing, so I kept a straight face.

"I don't just slap a coat of Cottage White on the walls and then turn around and jack up the price a hundred grand. I think I have integrity in the work I do, but—"

I had to stop him. "Wes. Get a grip, honey. This is an old angry guy. Forget about it. Okay?"

"Why do people get so nasty?"

I shrugged.

"But if I do sell it, Mad, you might like this house. It's pretty perfect for you."

"Oh no," I said, smiling big. "You can't get out of this trouble with Elmer by getting me to move in and take care of him."

"But you're looking for a new place, right?"

"I love your house, Wes, but I don't want another great old house in the Hollywood Hills."

I had my own emotional real estate issues. A few months ago, the upstairs rooms of my house had been the scene of a pretty terrible crime. After the police had come and gone, Wes took over, bringing his work crew along with him. They had reworked the three small bedrooms, expanding the master bedroom and building a walk-in closet and a new master bathroom. The house was now much more wonderful than it had ever been, but I still couldn't forget about what had happened there and feel truly comfortable.

However, it was complicated. The main floor still worked well for our business, with the huge industrial kitchen and workspace for Holly and Wesley and me. It was just that I simply didn't want to live there anymore. I had made up my mind. I intended to rent out my old living quarters to some nice, friendly, solvent, easygoing tenant.

For my own dwelling, I needed a clean start, a new perspective. Time to change things up. I had fallen in love with an odd building right in the heart of Hollywood and I was working on the owner to let me lease the space I was after. I hadn't told Wesley yet. He would fight me. He believed in owning real estate.

"Look! Here comes Lizzie."

In the water, like a slippery and tipsy mermaid, Liz Mooney was splashing through the shallow surf and stumbling her way toward us.

"Tonight," I said to Wesley quickly, "would you mind staying in Holly's room so Liz and Holly could stay with me? Not that we should expect any more trouble, but . . ."

"Of course. No problem," Wes said.

"Hi, you two," Liz called as she spotted us and changed course. The water dripping from her iridescent yellow tankini shimmered in the moonlight.

Wes stood gallantly. "Come on over here and sit down, Liz. I'll go back to the car and get you a fresh towel."

"Thanks, Wes," she said, tumbling out of the ocean and into the chair in one almost graceful move.

"Aren't you cold?" I asked, watching her hold her arms across her chest, droplets of water streaming off her trim legs.

"No," she said, smiling. "I mean, yes. It's colder out of the water."

"I was so happy you could come this weekend," I said. "After all, you're Holly's oldest friend."

"Holly and I met in second grade," Liz said, nodding, sending water dripping down to the sand from her long dark hair. "St. Anne's."

"And you went to the same high school, right?"

"Holy M."

"Holy Mother." I knew it was in the Valley. "Isn't that an all-girls school?"

"It used to be. They went coed a few years before we got there. Thank God!" She began giggling, and I joined her. "I mean, can you imagine Holly in an all-girls school? She'd freak."

Liz yawned, and I could tell the chill in the air against her wet skin was probably the only thing keeping her awake.

I asked, "Holly had a lot of boys interested in her, I'll bet."

"Tons," Liz said, nodding. "Tons."

"Tell me Holly stories."

"Oh, she just attracted boys. They always liked her, even though she was taller than almost all of them. Didn't matter. Holly was like flypaper, and the boys were like bugs."

I nodded. "Did she go with anyone special?"

"She went steady all the time. Lots of different guys, of course, but one at a time. You know."

That I did. "Do you remember the guy she went to your senior prom with? I'm thinking of making up a song for tomorrow's dinner and we could use some great names from the past." Never bother with the truth if an easy story comes to mind.

"Oh, how funny!" Liz smiled and closed her eyes. I

looked over and wondered if she was dozing off to a pleasant dream of high school.

"Liz?"

"I could tell you stories," Liz said, opening her eyes. "Holly has never been restrained when it comes to boys. She would get very interested and then it would pass."

"Names?"

"Where do I start?" she asked. "Okay, take these down. Barry Zeman in ninth grade. Then David Deutch. Chris Pantone and Dennis Fogerty and Brian Kim—they were our fencing team. Then Jason Martz in tenth. She dated Zack Wheeler from Loyola for a few months. Then Jordan Bunzel, Donny Yamaguchi, Andy and Kenny McNeal . . ." Liz stopped reeling off names for a few seconds to put in a side comment—". . . the twins"—and went right on. "Then there was Gabe Cummings, Billy Evashwick, Jesse Perlmutter, Tim O'Bannion, Michael Childers, and Joseph Allen."

It had been quite a recitation.

"Wow. You have great recall for names," I said.

"Madeline, I had to hear about every single one of them and how she was going to marry each one. And then how she wasn't. Usual high school stuff."

"Wasn't there another one?" I asked.

Liz thought it over. "Did I mention Marvin Dubinsky?"

"No." Hot damn. "Tell me about him."

"Really fabulously brainy dude," she said. "Totally off-the-map nerd, though. You know how that goes. Our Holly took the ultimate pity on Marvin."

I'd say so. She married him. I wondered if Liz knew about it.

"Did Holly tell you about what happened with Marvin after the prom?" I asked.

Liz looked at me and smiled. "I do believe she fulfilled his teenage fantasies. You should have seen the dress she wore to the prom. It was white, strapless, cut down to her navel, and skintight. All that and a white feather boa. As I recall, poor Marvin's eyes only came up to Holly's chest level, due to their height discrepancy, but I don't think he was complaining."

"Did you ever hear what happened to Marvin after that?"

"He went off to college, I think. He had scholarships to anyplace he wanted to go, I remember that."

"And what about you, Lizzie? Do you have a list of broken hearts that long?"

"Me? Oh good God, no. I didn't date at all during high school."

"No one?"

She shook her head and smoothed her wet hair. "I was the quiet type. You know, all honors classes and a big math brain. Real Future CPAs of America material."

I looked at her in her tight bathing suit with skepticism.

Liz still looked serious. "I know what you're thinking, Maddie, but back then I was just skinny and flat-chested. No boy would look at me."

"Lizzie, you're gorgeous. Boys are such imbeciles."

"Don't I know it," she said, smiling. "Even the smart ones are perfectly stupid."

"Say, about that Marvin guy," I said. "Do you know what happened to him?"

"Marvin Dubinsky? No. I haven't heard anything about him since high school. But he was a really intense guy. He was totally fixated on Holly too. Devoted. He wrote her sonnets. I wonder why he never kept in touch with her."

"Good question."

"Say, Maddie, do you think Holly's going to live happily ever after with Donald Lake?"

It was a perfectly valid question, noting Holly's effervescent past. But it was not a totally reassuring thought that the young woman who knew Holly best was asking it.

Palekaiko Lilo
(Paradise Lost)

*T*he phone in my hotel room rang. I pushed a hand out from under the fine Italian linen sheet and swiped for it. Mid-second-ring I got it off the hook, my eyes still closed.

"Miss Bean?" said a lovely lilting voice. "It's seven o'clock. This is your wake-up call."

"But I didn't leave instructions," I said, my voice so low and raspy it would make gravel sound perky, "for a wake-up call."

"My most humble apologies, Miss Bean," she said, sounding truly sorry. "I believe Mr. Westcott requested the call."

My brain was foggy, but I did recall that the always early-to-rise Wesley had been my roomie until I rearranged our group. Great.

"I also have a note to remind you that your entire party has been scheduled for our Day of Beauty package in the Sports Club and Spa. All complimentary, as you are guests of the hotel manager. The first appointments start at eight o'clock."

Eight? What sadist came up with this blasted crack-of-dawn schedule? I took a breath to reply, but it may have sounded something more like a snore.

The lilting voice continued, gently, helpfully. "If you'd like to inquire about changing these times, I can put you through to the spa."

The thing was, if I had to wake my brain up enough to think about rescheduling aloe vera wraps and frangi facials for eight people, I might as well get out of bed right now. I was done sleeping. Besides, I meant to dig around and find out more about what was going on around the hotel, maybe get some information that would make sense of the break-in in Holly's room. And I felt I had a shot if I could talk one on one with some sympathetic hotel employee.

"No, that's okay. We'll be there. Thanks." My eyes still closed, I tried to put the receiver back on the hook. I missed. The handset of the phone clattered off the bedside table.

"What's up?" came a pillow-muffled voice beside me. I was sharing one queen-size bed with Holly. Liz was on the other.

"We're getting up," I said. "Rise and shine. Our day of beauty awaits."

I heard a groan from the direction of the other bed.

"Or," I said, finally opening my eyes and propping myself up on one elbow, "if you both want to sleep in, you can. This is not mandatory beauty. No one will hold a gun to your heads and insist you exfoliate."

"Free massages," moaned Holly into her pillow. "I cannot pass that up. It's against my religion. I think we should just throw on clothes and get some breakfast. We can shower and whatever at the spa, right?"

"I'm with you," I said. "Liz?"

From the other bed we heard a long groan. The covers were pulled up over her head.

I turned to Holly. "I believe that's a pass."

I picked up the phone and dialed Holly's original room, the room where Wes had stayed for the night.

"Wes?"

"Yes, Mad."

"Did you get a wake-up call?"

"At five-thirty, as I requested, yes. And I asked them to call all of our rooms at seven, which is now."

"You woke up at five-thirty? Are you insane?"

"Honey, five-thirty in Hawaii is *eight-thirty* in L.A."

"Oh."

"Are you awake enough to do the math?" he asked.

"No."

"Okay, I'll tell you. That means it's really ten o'clock California time right now."

"Oh."

"Feeling a little less tired?"

"Yeah. I am. Are you coming to the spa with us?"

"Of course," he said. "Who can say no thanks to a free salt scrub?"

"That's what Holly and I have been asking ourselves. Liz seems to be able to resist."

"I'll round up the sisters and meet you for breakfast," he said and rang off.

It turned out only five of us could manage to get it together for the eight o'clock beauty spa treatments. Daisy and Marigold could not be roused. Liz was still motionless under the down comforter when Holly and I tiptoed out of the room. But lined up in front of the spa reception desk at the appointed time were Azalea, Gladiola, Holly, Wes, and I, all a little luau-ed out, but present and accounted for. The receptionist had us each add our names to the sign-in book and then handed each of us a key to our assigned lockers. We split up at that point,

Wes going off to the men's locker room and the four women going along to our own changing room.

The interior of the changing facility was like a tropical retreat. There were mirrors on almost every wall. Indirect lighting and thick pale-green carpet added a luxuriously muted note to the light-colored wood lockers. Restful New Age music flowed around us, coming from tiny speakers hidden in every corner of the spa. Down the hallway were showers and also a separate area for putting on makeup and blow-drying one's hair after one's treatment was over. A door led to the steam rooms. Another led outdoors to a palm-shaded lanai area with a large whirlpool. Here again the decor was uniquely Hawaiian, reflecting the aloha spirit of the islands' golden age. The lap pool, whirlpools, saunas, steam rooms, and cold plunges were all set amid lushly landscaped tropical gardens.

I found my locker, number 22, and quickly undressed. I put on the brown and black batik-print cotton robe and disposable black flip-flops that were waiting for me. The key to my locker was on a sort of coiled plastic bracelet, so I put that on as well.

The four of us were the only women present in the locker room at the time, but our lockers were spread out throughout small elegant rooms, designed for privacy.

"I am so loving this," called out Gladdie. "We're like ancient Hawaiian princesses."

"Princesses who had access to peroxide," chirped up Holly from another corner of the locker room, fluffing her hair in a nearby mirror.

We met up in the inner waiting room, each of us in our identical batik robes, wearing our identical flip-flops, and our key bracelets.

"Do you think Wesley is wearing the same thing?" asked Azalea.

Just then, a door opened and a few of the spa's aestheticians entered the waiting room. They were young women of various cultural backgrounds, but each wore a long sarong in a pale-green-and-tangerine-colored jungle print and a fresh flower lei. One by one, they called our names, and we split up and followed them out to our individual treatment areas.

"Okay," I instructed. "Nobody panic. When next we see each other, we shall be beautiful or we get our money back."

"Madeline?" A soft-spoken island woman who looked to be in her early thirties spoke up. She pronounced it correctly, *Mad-a-line*, like the little girl in the storybooks.

"Yes, hi," I said. It was my first time in a spa, and I was intrigued by all the manners and rituals.

"Good morning. My name is Pualani. In Hawaiian it means 'heavenly flower.'"

How lovely. And my name, Mad, means completely off one's rocker. Could anyone need relaxing spa treatments more than me?

"We have you starting out today with our Dead Sea Mud Mask Body Treatment. Is that correct?"

"It sounds fascinating," I said. "But to be honest, I'm not sure what I'm signed up for."

"Oh, you'll love this one," Pualani said. "It's my favorite. It's a total body treatment designed to detoxify and tone the skin. Very luxurious. Very restful. You'll see."

I so needed this. Wes had been addicted to luxury spas for years, but I had resisted. The idea of strangers and massages had turned me off. But that was just silly. Look at Pualani, my first masseuse. She was darling. She was wearing hibiscus flowers around her neck. This was all too great.

Pualani asked me to follow her to my individual treatment room, and we went down a small hallway, past several identical doorways, and entered a room that was kept dimly lit by a dozen scented candles and very low lighting. The New Age music was also piped in here, coming from hidden speakers.

Pualani continued speaking in low, soothing tones. "We'll start with a dry brush exfoliation, is that okay with you?"

"Sure."

"Wonderful. And after we rid your body of any traces of dead skin, the body will be painted with a rich mixture of mud. The mud mask is followed by a warm wrap and a neck and scalp massage. How does that sound?"

"Dreamy."

"Wonderful," said Heavenly Flower. She held up a giant leaf green–colored towel. "Please take your time. You may take off your robe and hang it on this peg. Then get onto the table and cover yourself with this towel. I'll be back in just a few minutes. All right?"

I nodded.

It occurred to me, a few minutes later, that I, Madeline Bean, was lying naked on a table, under a piece of terry cloth, on an island in the middle of the Pacific Ocean, waiting to be painted with mud that had been flown in from the Dead-freaking-Sea, and I felt wonderfully sanguine about the prospect. I went on listening to the gentle string music and breathing deeply the candle-fragrant air, truly letting my mind go blank for the first time in, well, years. When Pualani noiselessly reentered the treatment room, she adjusted a small pillow under my head, carefully arranging my wild curly hair so I was comfortable, and then she took out a brush with short, soft bristles. All her movements were careful and graceful, like a dancer in slow motion. With a light touch, she took my right arm out from under the cover sheet, and with a circular motion, she began to briskly rub the brush over my shoulder, working her way down my arm to my wrist.

"Is the pressure too hard?" she asked, her voice filled with concern for my comfort.

"It feels fabulous." And really, how often in the last few years has anyone been so happily dedicated to my comfort? It was generally the other way around. I was the one putting on parties for everyone else, worried about their comfort. I was surprised to find how quickly I could relish this turnabout.

Pualani finished with the brush-down, having carefully withdrawn each arm and leg from beneath the green terry cloth drape, one at a time, and then, holding the large towel just so to preserve my modesty, had me flip over onto my stomach. She then worked on the back of my legs and over my shoulders, each step professionally designed to treat me like royalty while sloughing off all this alleged dead skin. I felt a warm glow as my blood began circulating in the past half hour as never before.

Next, Pualani got out a thick paintbrush, the size you might use to paint the molding strips around your door, and began laying on thick, warm, dark gray-brown mud in smooth strokes down my back. She was tidy and didn't miss a spot. This is definitely the woman you'd want to call if your armoire needed a quick coat of varnish. The smell of the mud was earthy but clean. How did they manage that?

"Our brushes are made from sable hair," she explained.

Of course. I allowed myself to breathe deeply, relax further, concentrate on the sensations. The brush felt smooth and silky, while the mud was rather hot and thick and wet.

"What exactly does the mud do?" I asked, my eyes closed, so relaxed at this point that I didn't even think twice about the brilliance of my conversation.

"Mud is wonderful," Pualani said, sounding perfectly happy to talk about the goo. "We are all part of the earth, of course. So this takes us back to nature's elements. Mud has curative properties, you know, Madeline. It's all the minerals that are contained in it. This morning, for your treatment, I'm using mud from the Dead Sea, which is the highest quality mud available; very mineral rich."

And to think, before this morning, I'd had no idea there was a hierarchy of mud.

Pualani went on. "It actually has a nice anti-inflammatory action that helps to draw out any impurities and metabolic wastes," she explained, going through her spiel. "As it heals and soothes sore muscles, the mud replenishes the body with nutrients and minerals."

"Ahh."

For most of the next fifteen minutes, that was about all I could respond. But as Pualani was wrapping me in a warm sheet and beginning the scalp massage portion of the treatment, I began to feel a little chattier.

"So have you been working here since the Four Heavens opened?"

"Oh, yes. We've been open a year. It's a beautiful hotel, isn't it?"

"Yes."

"Is this your first time with us, Madeline, or have you stayed here before?"

"First time," I said. "We are having a party for my assistant, Holly. She's here somewhere too. We're celebrating her upcoming wedding."

"How nice!" Pualani said. "This is a special treat, then."

"Yes."

"You have chosen the right spot. All of our staff are trained to make sure you are pampered here."

"Everyone has been fantastic. Do you know Keniki Hicks? She works at the resort, I believe, during the day?"

"I know a Keniki," Pualani said and stopped rubbing my scalp for a second.

How quickly one can go into spa withdrawal. More scalp massage, please. "She works as a waitress," I added. "Out by the Orchid Ponds."

Pualani went back to rubbing my neck. Heaven regained.

"Yes. All the staff get to know one another like a family," Pualani said, but her voice had changed. Her breathing had become audible, and her hand was shaking a little bit.

"Pualani, what is it? Something is wrong."

"It's nothing," she said quietly. "I can't go into it here. This isn't permitted."

"What isn't permitted?"

"The guest must not . . . I'm so sorry, Madeline. I must step away for just a minute." Pualani stopped rubbing my neck.

"No. Tell me. What is going on? Is something wrong with Keniki? I am really concerned. She helped us run the party last night," I said.

"That was your party?"

I was lying on a table, slathered in a coating of mineral-rich mud, wrapped tightly in hot, wet sheets, and yet I felt a sudden chill. "Please tell me what has happened to her."

"Nothing happened to Keniki, thank God. But it's her boyfriend. He works at an orchid ranch down the coast. He works there at night. I think he's a watchman, but I'm not sure. They found him very early this morning. He's a very good swimmer. Everyone knows that. But how did he get in the water?"

In my mummified configuration, I couldn't prop myself up on the table. I could barely move. I simply had to ask again, "What happened to Keniki's boyfriend?"

"He was found this morning. Dead. The waves were pushing him up against the rocks."

Poor Keniki. So beautiful and happy last night. I remembered her laughing at us, trying to teach us the hula. I remembered her bonding with Wesley and showing him some advanced moves. Keniki was a young woman, and I imagined her boyfriend must also have been young. And now he was dead. "Oh, no."

"I'm so sorry to be the one to tell you this, Madeline."

"Was it an accident?" I asked, hoping to get a little more information before Pualani pulled her professional act together and realized she must stop upsetting the spa guest.

"It's just a terrible thing," she said, shaking her head, still shocked by the news. "Kelly was her fiancé. Kelly Imo. He was strong, a very strong swimmer, but anyone can get knocked over by a wave. You must never turn your back to the ocean, not even for a short time. Maybe he hit his head on a rock."

"Is that what happened?"

"They say no one saw him go into the water. He was wearing his work clothes, they said, so how could he have meant to go swimming?"

"I see."

"It is so sad for Keniki."

All of a sudden, being wrapped in warm towels and entombed in a mud-crusted cocoon began to feel oppressively confining. That state of blissful relaxed mindlessness, a state I had only just begun to discover for the first time, was, of course, completely shattered. All I could think of was "Poor Keniki."

"Yes. And with your party right there," Pualani agreed.

"Right where?"

"Right there at Anaeho'omalu Bay. Didn't I say? That's where they found poor Kelly's body this morning. He was washed up against the rocks near Anaeho'omalu Bay."

Ki'i
(The Photograph)

I finished showering and drying off and then wrapped my squeaky clean, mud-free, detoxified, and completely exfoliated self up in a fresh version of the brown and black batik robes all the guests wear around the Four Heavens Sports Club and Spa. When my eighty-minute mud mask treatment time had been up, Pualani had left me at one of the private shower rooms, all glass and slate tiles, and, apologizing again, hurried away to her next appointment.

I walked over to the mirror-lined room that held the hair dryers and other accoutrements of beauty prep, and began the endless process of combing out the tangles in my long hair.

According to the large clock on the wall, I was scheduled for the next luxury treatment in my Day of Beauty in twenty minutes. But it could wait. First, I would go see Keniki Hicks. And the thought of Keniki, her long hair swaying, spreading Hawaiian cheer at our luau only last night, and now suddenly thrown into such anguish, made my eyes sting. Why had fate brought such tragedy to this nice young woman?

An array of sprays and lotions and creams and ointments were displayed in a row of glass jars along the marble countertop before me. One of them promised to detangle and condition. I had been making little progress through the thicket of hair, and so I gave a few spritzes to my unruly curls, and then a few more spritzes for good measure, before going back to work with the comb.

And I couldn't help thinking of Keniki's boyfriend—his body found right there at our own Anaeho'omalu Bay. Just hours after our luau, it must have been. Just yards away from the beach upon which Keniki had distributed hula skirts and taught us all how to make the hand motions for "a man" and "a woman" and "enduring love." It was an irony of such bitterness.

I turned away and tried to concentrate on some facts. Keniki's boyfriend had been washed away, no one yet knew how or from exactly where he entered the water, and then found early this morning among the rocks at Anaeho'omalu Bay. He was wearing his work clothes. Had he been working late at night on some misty path and fallen into the ocean, becoming injured in the fall? Had he been out on a beach, perhaps walking out on the lava rocks that jut into the sea? People got swept away by an unexpected surge all the time, Pualani had warned me.

I looked again in the mirror and was surprised to see the spray-on detangler stuff had actually helped. I picked up the can and checked the label. Perhaps I would have to buy some of this. It smelled faintly of grapefruit. Nice. I gave my head a shake, and corkscrews of red-blond hair fell gently into place on the left side. The right side was still a bird's nest, so I went to town, giving several additional spritzes, and began working out the tangles with the comb.

And yet, I thought again, I knew almost nothing about this couple. Had they been happy? I hated to give words to this question, but having dated a cop, I know how they think. An accident? And so close to where the girl-friend was working. Could there have been something sinister going on? Had the couple been fighting? I hate this sort of thinking, but I know how predictable investigators could be. In an unexpected death, they would wonder, who had something to gain? Who held a grudge? And always, look to those closest to the victim. Poor Keniki.

What a shock, to have your life planned for happily-ever-after and discover one fresh morning that it simply will not be. It was all too familiar to me, stirring up old memories too difficult to remember.

I've had a few shocks of my own, enough to remind me how little control we truly have over the course our lives will take. I thought about Xavier and the pain I'd felt when he left me. And here I was, nine years later, doing just fine, thanks. Doing just great.

I padded over to my locker and then realized I had somehow misplaced the key. Probably left it in the treatment room. But when I made my way back down the hallway, the door to the treatment room was locked.

I tried a few other nearby doors. Several must have led to additional treatment rooms, but they were locked as well. I stood in the dimly lit, narrow hallway and thought it over. There were no spa attendants in view. And the tinkling New Age music was beginning to get on my nerves.

The one door that wasn't locked was marked: STAFF ONLY. I peeked in, looking for help. This room was also empty. It appeared to be a plain-wrap version of the guest locker rooms down the hall, and much larger than I'd expected. I walked in. On a bulletin board were employee notices, including warnings from Workers Comp and OSHA, along with the week's work schedules for the spa as well as the staff who worked at the hotel's three restaurants.

The room must serve as the rest lounge for all the resort's female employees. The colors were muted, just as in the guest locker rooms, but the lockers for the staff were smaller. A watercooler stood beside a table that held a basket of tea bags and sweetener. On the wall across from the bulletin board was a chart. In the left-hand column was a list of names, presumably the names of each of the employees. I scanned the list and noticed that Pualani Santos was listed. I also saw the name Keniki Hicks.

"Pardon me," said a female voice from behind me. "This room is for the staff. Can I help you?"

I turned and faced a young woman with a long braid coiled on top of her head.

"Sorry," I said. "I left my locker key in one of the treatment rooms. Pualani was my aesthetician. My name is Madeline Bean."

"Don't worry, Miss Bean," she said, smiling warmly. "We have a master key to open the lockers. Just a moment and I'll get someone to help you."

"I didn't notice any attendants out in the spa," I said.

"No. We are very short staffed today. My apologies. We have had three of our girls cancel on us. Very distressing, I can tell you, with a full appointment calendar. Let me take you to your locker and use my own master key." She led the way back to the luxurious guests-only locker room.

"Staff members haven't shown up to work? Is that because of what just happened to Keniki Hicks's boyfriend, Kelly?" I asked.

The young woman's expression changed. She lost a little of her smooth guest relations veneer and became just a little more human. "Well, yes." She looked at me with open curiosity then, and sighed. "I'm surprised you have heard anything about it so soon. I suppose all the guests will be talking about it."

"Maybe not quite yet. But I am a friend of Keniki's. She helped me with a luau last night."

"I see," said the young woman. We now stood in front of locker 22. She pulled a key from a ring hidden somewhere in the folds of her sarong—did those things have pockets? And used it to open my locker. "There you are."

"I'm on my way over to her house right now. I want to offer my help if there is anything I can do to help her."

"How very kind of you, Miss Bean. Keniki is a friend of mine too. It's her sister Cynthia who didn't come to work today. She is one of the masseuses here, one of our best specialists. And also two other girls who are Keniki's best friends. So here is your locker. Is there anything else I can do for you?"

"I should cancel my next appointment," I said.

"I believe you were scheduled for a manicure/pedicure next. No problem. I am happy to cancel that for you. With our staff shortage, it will be a little bit of a relief, actually. Is there anything else?"

"I have Keniki's address in my room."

The young woman hesitated only a moment and then said, "I'll draw a map for you. I'll be right back."

As she left, I quickly got back into my shorts and T-shirt, and traded the disposable plastic spa flip-flops for my own beach-worthy pair of flip-flops. Hawaii, gotta love the dress code.

By the time I was tossing the spa's batik robe into a nearby wicker laundry basket, the woman with the coiled braid had returned, carrying a bright green shopping bag from the gift shop of the Sports Club and Spa.

"I was wondering if I might ask you to do us a favor?" she asked, speaking softly.

"Of course."

"I am not sure when Keniki will be returning to work." She looked sad, and I could imagine that each of the young women who worked at this resort must empathize greatly with one another. They must all have boyfriends or young husbands. How could they not wonder what it would be like if something this awful had happened to them and their loved ones? "These are the items that were in Keniki's employee locker. There may be something here that she'll need. If you don't mind, could you take this bag out to her? I hate to ask you to do it, but the rest of us are going to be working double shifts today. I'm not sure . . ."

"No, no. That's fine." I reached for the bag. "I'm happy to help."

"Thanks. You'll find the directions on a slip of paper in the bag."

I pushed the door out to the main reception area and signed myself out in the guest book.

"Are you leaving us already?" asked the pretty girl behind the desk.

"I'll be back," I said. "Is there any way I could leave a message for my friends? They're all still in the spa, I think."

"Of course. Just a moment and I'll look up where they are right now. Can you give me a name?"

"Holly Nichols." I didn't want Holly to think I'd abandoned her. I'd leave her a note and let her know I was coming back soon.

"Holly Nichols is currently getting a Lomi Lomi massage."

"What's that?"

"Lomi Lomi is a traditional Hawaiian massage that connects the heart, mind, body, and soul," she recited flawlessly.

"Is it as good as the Dead Sea Mud Mask Body Treatment?" I asked, ever the comparison shopper.

"Oh, it is quite a different experience," she said, smiling. "But each is magical. The Lomi Lomi is quite popular here, as it is a sacred healing art, passed down from generation to generation in Hawaii."

"Ah." I wondered if there would be time enough when I returned to get me one of those. I might yet find relaxation possible.

"Yes, the Lomi Lomi utilizes rhythmic strokes integrating the use of the forearms and elbows."

"Pardon?"

"The masseuse uses her forearms and elbows. Very relaxing."

Indeed.

"Your friend, Miss Nichols, will begin her Lomi Lomi in five minutes. You might actually be able to catch her in the inner waiting room if you want to try."

I thanked the receptionist and went back into the women's locker room, walking straight through to the spa waiting area. By now I was thoroughly accustomed to the scent of spicy herbs that saturated the air and the sound of tinkly sitar music over the sound system. Three other women were seated, reading magazines, awaiting their treatments. The clock said 9:55. Just then Liz and Holly came in, both wrapped in the standard batik robes.

"Mad!" Holly yelped, happy as a pup to see me.

"Hey, Madeline," Liz greeted me. "I finally woke myself up. I'm usually an early bird, but what a night we had last night!" She shook her head. "I am now ready to get spa-ed. So how come you're dressed? Where are you going?"

"Must run a little errand," I said, raising the large green shopping bag in some vague reference to "things to do."

"We're both getting Lomi Lomi–ed," Liz said, speaking softly so as not to disturb the other spa patrons, who were trying to relax.

"Wonderful."

Holly looked more blissed out than ever. "Oh, Mad! I'm having such a good time."

"Excellent. Perfect. I'll be back in an hour or two. Don't worry about me."

Holly pulled me over to the side of the room, away from Liz and the other women. "Where are you off to? What kind of errand?"

I held up the bag. "Remember Keniki from last night?"

"Of course."

"I'm just going to run something out to her house. No big deal. I have the rental car and I'll be back before you know it."

"Oh, okay." Holly smiled. "Sounds good."

She didn't need to hear all the grisly details of Kelly's death quite yet. After all the time and effort these good spa people were putting into relaxing us, I felt it wasn't fair to undermine every one of our states of bliss. Liz and Holly took seats and waited to be led away to another hour of beauty.

I took a few steps away and opened the bag I was holding, making sure I had the driving directions I needed. Inside were several small items. A hairbrush. A makeup bag. A bottle from a local pharmacy, half filled with pills. A framed photograph. I couldn't help but notice it was a picture of Keniki with a young man. Kelly. I pulled it out of the bag.

The room began to sway. Or maybe it only felt that way. I stared at the picture. Keniki Hicks's young man was a nice-looking guy with Asian features. And in the photo he was wearing glasses. I looked closer. The oval lenses were held in place by tiny silver arrows. The exact same wire-rimmed eyeglasses I'd discovered in Holly's hotel room bed.

"Holly," I said, my voice a little sharp.

She looked up from her magazine.

"Could you come over here?" I whispered, toning my volume way down.

"What's that you're looking at? Is that Keniki?" Holly asked, turning my hand so she could view the picture.

I nodded but almost lost my grip on the frame when Holly let go of it abruptly and stepped backward.

"Oh my God, Maddie. Oh my God!" She was still whispering, in deference to the soft tinkly music and spa manners, but her expression had completely changed. She now looked extremely stressed, her blue eyes wide with disbelief.

"This is the guy that was in your room, Holly, isn't it?"

She stared at me. "He's the one who grabbed at me. The one who scared the living daylights out of me yesterday."

"Look at the T-shirt," I told her.

"It's the same exact one with the kanji for Mountain Hollyhock. And the wire-rimmed frames. *It's the guy!*"

It couldn't be. It couldn't be. "This is terrible, Holly."

"Who the hell is this guy, anyway? And how does he know Keniki?"

"I'm taking a guess. But I think he could be her fiancé."

"Keniki's boyfriend was hiding in my hotel room?" Holly asked, completely befuddled.

"Hey, you guys, what's up?" Liz asked, joining us.

I turned the frame around and showed her the picture. Liz let out a strangled little yelp.

"Liz, do you remem—"

"Oh my God, Maddie!" Holly screeched, her voice much louder than spa courtesy might dictate. "*Catch her! Catch Liz!*"

It must have been too much for Liz, the shock of seeing the hotel-room guy again. Damn. Just as Liz Mooney started to swoon, I managed to get my arms around her. Off balance, I began to topple myself, but then Holly got her arms around me. Still, gravity had its way.

"Oh my goodness!" murmured one of the waiting women seated nearby, her copy of *Town & Country* slipping.

"Dear God!" said another one sharply.

The three of us—Holly, me, and an unconscious Liz—landed in a dog pile on the center of the light-green carpeting, a most unexpected lady wrestlers–style floorshow for the waiting spa-sters.

From the bottom of the dog pile I quietly announced: "Got her."

And Holly just giggled uncontrollably on the floor.

Ni-ele
(The Busybody)

I pushed on the heavy doors of the spa facility and stepped out into a perfectly gorgeous island day, feeling better the moment I emerged from the darkened building into the bright daylight. The Hawaiian sun warmed my skin.

Liz had already recovered a bit, ministered to by Holly and several spa attendants. The young woman with the coiled braid had taken charge, bringing ice water, calling an ambulance. I waited to make sure Liz was really all right and then I slipped out. I longed to breathe fresh, un-candle-scented air. As I left, I heard Liz protesting she didn't need to go to the emergency room, and Holly gently insisting, *no, she really did*.

Each step I took away from the spa building gave me that much more resolve to take action. I now had two tasks this weekend, and I didn't see why I couldn't succeed at both. I would continue hosting Holly's party extravaganza, of course, but at the same time, I would get to the bottom of what had happened to Kelly Imo.

My plan was to return to my room and pick up the keys to the Mustang and then sort out all the new and disturbing information during the drive out of town on my way to pay my call on Keniki Hicks. Driving helped me think straight. And then, from Keniki, I was pretty sure I'd be able to uncover the answers to much more.

I turned right at the path to the beach bungalows and went over the odd events again. None of it made sense. Just what had Kelly been doing in Holly's room? Was he a disturbed young man, a sexual predator? I looked across the beach, my view filled with the gentle blue of the sky, the gentle aqua of the ocean, the palm fronds barely swaying in the slight breeze. A man filled with dark intentions in such a beautiful paradise? Was it possible?

Whirls of new questions washed over me. Had his death really been an accident? If Kelly Imo fell off a cliff in the middle of the night and died in the surf, had somebody pushed him? And really, how the hell did Kelly connect to us?

A family with two small children passed me on the path. The mom, her oversize plastic tote filled with beach toys, waved. The dad, his exposed white gut betraying a certain desk-bound mainland existence, said hello. They were here looking for fun; I was looking for telling details. I smiled a busy, distracted, I've-got-work-to-do smile. We were headed in different directions, and for me the beach could wait. Relaxation, frankly, is overrated. I would much rather solve a puzzle than doze.

The family turned back and looked at me, their faces showing surprise—or was it concern that I wasn't wearing a resort-mandated laid-back expression?—and then walked on. But really, I wanted to tell them, I felt energized by all the things I planned to do. Workaholism gets a bad rap.

I still had a few questions that needed answers. Important questions. I stopped walking, pulled the framed photograph out of the shopping bag, and studied the two happy faces. Keniki Hicks, our hula instructor, was wearing a sarong, pale yellow with pink and blue orchids in the print, smiling at the camera. The young man with his arm across her shoulder was athletic looking, clean-shaven, his features handsome. There was no mistaking the wire-rimmed spectacles he was wearing. I had held them in my hand last night. Studied them. I clearly remembered their unique nose bridge, an odd retro style. So what had Kelly Imo been doing in Holly's room?

His face shined up at me from the photo.

Perhaps he was connected to some illegal schemes on the island. Burglaries at the Four Heavens, for instance. Maybe he had taken his girlfriend's resort master key and made a copy.

The whole idea got me irritated. It seemed completely unfair that there should be crooks and con men in Hawaii. It was positively un-state-like. This wasn't California, for heaven's sake, where a person must wear daily her skepticism like armor against all the genial liars and scam artists and fakes. This was Hawaii. The Aloha State, for pity's sake. Sure, back in L.A., I'm prepared for deceptions. It's a town where "reality" is produced and edited. It's a town where everything and everyone must be suspected of being artificial until you can prove otherwise.

But here in Hawaii, couldn't a con man thrive just as well? I traced the outline of Kelly Imo on the eight-by-ten photo. That clean-cut exterior could be just the image he wanted to project, the good-looking camouflage to cover up a heart filled with schemes.

So what the hell was Kelly doing in Holly's room? And how had he gotten mixed up with the people who had sent Holly the nasty e-mail, the ones looking for Marvin Dubinsky?

I put the framed photo back into the bright green shopping bag and began walking again. I would think it over later. Driving around the Big Island with the top down on the Mustang would blow some new ideas my way, get things straightened out. I realized just then, walking next to that pristine sandy beach, that I missed the traffic in West Hollywood. Six lanes across on Santa Monica Boulevard. Stopped at red lights, waiting for the left-turn arrow, I seemed to get my best inspirations. How about that?

The neat path was lined with leafy bushes abloom with perfect yellow hibiscus, and I followed it to our row of hotel rooms. As I approached our bungalow, I suddenly remembered Holly's two sleepy sisters, Daisy and Marigold, and wondered if they had ever managed to get out of bed. It was almost ten-thirty, which—not to sugarcoat it—was actually one-thirty in the afternoon, West Coast time. And with that realization I instantly snapped right back into my party-planner mode. The girls might sleep away this golden day and miss the fun.

Marigold had room 1025. I turned up the little walkway and noticed the door was not fully closed. That was odd. As I got closer, I realized Marigold had stuck a small trash can in the doorway to keep the door ajar, perhaps to encourage breezes. She must still be inside.

Or maybe she had gone next door to room 1027, visiting her other late-rising sister, half of the twin-set, Daisy. I stopped for a second, wondering if I should go to Daisy's room first, when the sound of a female voice caught my attention. It was coming from Marigold's room. She was there after all. I was just about to call her name when her words began to register.

". . . never again. That's Holly! I mean I love her to death and all, but she doesn't deserve the attention, Daisy."

Well, well, well. It appeared that Marigold was gossiping—maybe on the hotel telephone?—to her sister Daisy, next door.

"Why did he fall all over himself?" Marigold's voice sulked.

Was this sibling jealousy I had inadvertently (I swear!) eavesdropped upon? Was Marigold dissing Holly's fiancé? Holly and Donald seemed like a pretty cool couple to me.

I should have called out to Marigold right then. I should have said, "Yoo-hoo! Marigold!" or in some other way made my presence known. I realize that. But before I could, Marigold's voice piped up again from inside the room, sounding defensive and a little whiny. "But what about me? He never knew I was even alive. I've waited and suffered, Daisy."

What was this about, then? *Marigold* suffered and waited? For whom? Holly's Donald? No way. That just wasn't right. I was struck with a sudden thought: how lucky I was that I didn't have any sisters. How could five sisters ever get through life without invading one another's most private feelings?

"Hello!" I called out before another secret could be spilled. "Are you here, Marigold?"

"Who is that?" she asked, and then, a second or two later, her blond head appeared in the open doorway. "Mad? Omigod! You scared me! What's up?" She cradled the phone between her ear and her shoulder, the trick of a habitual phone marathoner, as she opened the door all the way.

"Hey, there," I said, all smiles.

"Come on in. I'm just talking to Daisy. We're always on the phone. She's taking forever to get dressed," Marigold complained. "Normally, I wouldn't mind waiting a couple more hours for Daisy to get ready," she continued, her humor always taking an affectionate potshot when it could, "but today we're going down to the spa, where she'll just have to get undressed again."

We both laughed. Marigold was dressed and ready. She was wearing a lime-green T-shirt and very short shorts in the same hue, and her makeup was perfectly done.

"Wait a minute, Daze," she said into the phone. "I'm asking Maddie about the spa." Then, without taking a breath, she asked me, "Did you get a massage? Was it *très* cool?"

"I loved it." I did. And the party planner in me wanted to shield my guests from any hint of unpleasantness, so I stuck to that.

"Daisy," Marigold scolded into the phone, "Maddie's here checking up on us, for goodness' sakes! She thinks we're the worst sort of slackers. Listen to me, now. Wear the tangerine tank, the shorts with the word HELL-CAT on the butt, and come on over here. Right away." Marigold hung up on Daisy and giggled at me. "Little sisters."

Looking at Marigold, away from the pack of Nichols sisters, I had to say that aside from the blond thing and the height thing shared by all the girls, she didn't really look like Holly at all. While Holly has a delicate pointy chin and tiny nose, Marigold was all about big strong features. If Holly was the ballerina of the family, Marigold was the linebacker.

"It's exciting to think about your sister getting married, isn't it?" I asked. I mean, what's the use of eavesdropping if you can't press your advantage?

"The wedding?" Marigold said, raising an eyebrow. "You mean *if* Holly actually goes through with it."

Marigold was jealous. Holly's Donald was a nice-looking guy, in that sort of corn-fed from the Midwest, great cleft in his chin, hunky in a pair of Levi's way. And certainly he had achieved fast success in Hollywood. His first screenplay had been a wild hit. But gosh, there were other attractive men in Los Angeles besides just Donald Lake, so did Marigold have to go pining away for the one guy in the big city who was soon to be married to her sister?

"I'm just saying," she said coyly, "it's not that Holly is all that predictable when it comes to men, you know? I sure hope she gets married. Mom and Dad have spent a fortune on the wedding, so it would be really nice if she goes through with it."

Hm. What was she really saying? Interpretation of sister-speak was an art perhaps best practiced from within the family.

"You two talking about Holly and Donald?" asked Daisy, pushing open the door and entering Marigold's messy room. The beds were a jumble of fine sheets and fluffy comforters, with several pillows tossed here and there on the floor. Marigold and the absent Gladiola had apparently just opened their suitcases and goody bags any old where, and seemed to be grabbing clothes as needed.

"What else?" Marigold smiled a tight-lipped smile.

"I think they are a cute couple," Daisy said. "I really do. And if Donald can put up with Holly and all her scattering around, they should be very happy."

"I was just telling Maddie that. But you know our Holly. She is so all over the map when it comes to men."

Sisters.

"Like you're any better," Daisy teased.

"Shut up," Marigold said, tossing a stray pillow across the room at Daisy's head and missing. "We're late, as usual."

I ducked, just avoiding a goose-down whap in the mouth, and followed the girls out of the room.

"You coming?" Marigold asked me.

"I can't right now," I said. "I'm taking off for a while, but you two go and enjoy!"

I could multitask better than anyone I knew. I had gathered the last of my tardy guests and was herding them off to the day's activities. Now it was time for me to go after some answers, and I knew the place I had to start.

A visit to Keniki Hicks.

Kipa Wale
(Dropping In)

*T*he address I had been given was about a thirty-minute drive from the Four Heavens Resort. Keniki Hicks lived in a rented house that was located outside the old sugar town of Hawi, at the northernmost tip of the Big Island, near the spot where the Kohala Coast turns the corner onto the Hamakua Coast.

Out on Highway 250, I left the ranch town of Waimea behind and steered the Mustang convertible—top down, baby—through lush jungles north to Hawi, which I soon learned was pronounced *Hahvee* by the instructive locals I stopped to ask for directions, probably retired grammar teachers, all of them.

I looked around as I drove, spotting historic markers hidden here and there among the thick foliage, marking remnants of the island's exotic past. While the Hawaiian Islands are the textbook example of natural beauty, their history is less than lovely, steeped in island-against-island warfare and blood and kapu. Even before the Europeans and Americans began to covet this land, the island people fought and battled among themselves. And then, of course, the missionaries arrived in 1820. Had I traveled straight up the Kohala Coast, on Highway 270, I'd have been tempted to stop and visit the

Kalahikiola Church in North Kohala, founded in 1855 by an old Maine missionary, Reverend Elias Bond.

I had studied Hawaii's past while planning our trip. In addition to the inter-island skirmishes and wars, the islanders' interactions with their earliest outside visitors was at best ambivalent. As a prime example, there's Captain Cook. In 1779, an English captain named James Cook sailed along the Kona Coast, where today the best resorts, including the Four Heavens, were located. As it happened, Cook anchored there during an island festival, one that was ruled by the god Lono, and the islanders mistook the sails of Cook's ships for the banner of Lono. Stories about parties naturally capture my attention, so I remembered the details of this one quite well. It is recorded that the Hawaiians mistook Cook for the deity. So far, this was a fairly typical tale—simple, trusting native people; weird white dude with strange technology. But the story goes on.

After a pleasant visit—hey, they treated the guy like he was Lono—Captain Cook sailed north, where, alas, he encountered trouble. A severe storm broke the mast on one of his ships. Limping back to the bay, Cook returned to his new friends, expecting a reverent welcome once again. But this time the Hawaiians were suddenly skeptical. Big storm. Wrecked ship. What kind of god couldn't control a few waves? Of course they now questioned his godliness.

Small items began disappearing from his ships, and when a skiff was stolen, Cook got fed up. He took a local chief as hostage, setting off a skirmish in which Captain Cook, ultimately, was killed. So the moral of the story: Just because the island people are gracious at their luaus, don't assume they cannot add two plus two, especially once they have sobered up the next day.

A local guidebook describes a white obelisk at the north end of Kealakekua Bay that marks the spot where Cook is believed to be buried. A pointed reminder indeed for anyone visiting from L.A., where we can take ourselves a little too seriously.

Before long, I had reached the town of Hawi, and soon I found the turnoff to Kamakana Place, Keniki's street. Just one block from the main road, I spotted her house.

Everywhere I looked, up one street and down another, was landscaping so lush it could bring tears to the eyes of a mainland gardener. The grass was incredibly emerald here and seemed to shimmer a brighter green than was altogether natural. In front of Keniki's small home, a splashy carpet of bright green rushed up to the deep pink stucco of the house. Three stubby sago palms hugged the home's walkway while two coconut palms stood tall out by the driveway, shaggy fronds scraping the light blue sky.

I pulled my Mustang up to the curb across the street from Keniki's house, not wanting to take up prime parking space; her relatives and friends would probably be arriving throughout the day. Perhaps I shouldn't have come. After all, we hardly knew each other well. And yet, perhaps there was something I could do to help. And, equally urgent, perhaps Keniki could answer some of my questions.

At the front door, I rang the bell, and in the seconds that followed had a brief moment to reconsider. Who knew how Keniki would be taking the news of her fiancé's death? And yet I was certain she held keys to the puzzle.

After about a minute, a young woman opened the door. Very long dark hair. Slender build. She looked so much like Keniki I almost thought it was her, but when the woman didn't recognize me, I started to notice small differences. This woman was taller. And her eyes were smaller, rounder. At the door, beside her, squirmed a yellow lab, his tail wagging, his head pushing her aside to sniff the new visitor.

"Aloha," said the young woman pleasantly, greeting me at the door. "You must be a friend of Keni's. How good of you to come."

"Thanks. We haven't met. My name is Madeline."

"Oh, hi." She stood there, lost in thought for a moment. "I'm sorry. I've forgotten my manners. I'm Cynthia Hicks, Keniki's sister."

"I heard about Kelly and . . ." I started over. "I wanted to check with Keniki to see if I might help out, if I could."

As we stood there at the open doorway, I patted the lab's head, and he gave my legs a frenzy of good, strong sniffs.

"Who's this fellow?"

"Let me introduce you to Dr. Margolis," she said, smiling at the dog.

"Hey, Doc." His nostrils quivered. He was in love with my scent. I wondered if he could pick up any remnants of Dead Sea Mud. Just then a white van pulled up in front of Keniki's house and stopped, half in the driveway, half out in the street, rap music spilling out of the open windows. On the side of the van, *Best Coast Florist* was written in green script under a picture of purple orchids.

The driver of the van, a kid in jeans and an OutKast T-shirt, hopped out and went to the back of his vehicle, soon coming up the walk with a large arrangement of tall, stalky birds of paradise amid a lush tangle of greens.

"More flowers," said Cynthia, reaching down for her dog's collar as his curiosity transferred from me to the new guy and he strained to get some new whiffs.

"Why don't I take these for you?" I asked, holding my arms out to the flower van driver, a skinny guy with braces.

"Hey, I've got two more," he said, relinquishing the flowers to me.

"Thanks," Cynthia said vaguely. "But what do we do with all these plants?" She held the screen door open, and I walked into a bright living room, decorated in vintage bamboo furniture and 1950s-style prints. Wesley would love this place.

I set the flowers down on a low table, next to two smaller arrangements that must have arrived recently, just as the kid from the florist's van came to the door with two more. Dr. Margolis had trailed the driver from house to van to house again. There was some jockeying of bowls and vases, but we managed to situate the gifts, creating a small jungle of indoor flora. I noticed many of the arrangements featured native plants.

"Keniki has been resting, lying down in her room," Cynthia said after the young man had left us.

"I don't want to disturb her."

"It's okay. Just a second. I'll tell her you're here."

Dr. Margolis sat down so close to me he actually sat on my right foot. And he rested his chin on my bare knee. "Hi, guy," I said, rubbing his forehead. "Are things kind of sad around here today?"

While I waited, I stood up and looked about the room. A painting of two young Hawaiian girls dressed in hula costumes, flowers circling their bare feet, was hanging over the sofa. It had been painted in an artful primitive style, which I liked, and I wondered if it might possibly be of Keniki and Cynthia as children.

"My mother painted that one," said a soft voice. I turned to see Keniki, still wearing her resort uniform, a sarong with the Four Heavens' hibiscus print, her long hair hanging on both sides of her face.

"It's really beautiful."

"Forgive me," she said, "but I'm surprised to see you . . . here. Was there a problem with last night's luau?"

"No, no. Everything about the luau was just perfect. I brought some of your things from the Four Heavens."

She noticed the bag I had carried into the house and nodded.

I continued, "I hope you don't mind that I came to see you. I just wanted to offer my support."

"Have you heard about what happened?" Her eyes were wide, but little comprehension could be observed in them.

"I did. I felt—"

"The luau last night *was* wonderful, wasn't it?" she asked brightly, cutting me off. I was a little surprised she was holding herself together so extremely well. "You're sure you were happy with everything?"

"At Holly's luau? Of course. It was amazing. Thanks to you."

"It was my pleasure. Come and sit down," she said, gesturing to the sofa and a matching bamboo armchair. So calm. Dr. Margolis stood up and walked in a complete circle, then laid down at Keniki's feet.

I checked her out. "How are you doing?"

"Fine. Really." She smiled at me.

I tried to smile back.

She must have read my thoughts because she said, "It's probably odd, I know. But . . ."

"Who can say what's the right way to react? Whatever way you feel is right."

"I just keep asking myself, how can this have happened? Kelly and I were engaged, you know? We hadn't set our wedding date, but we were waiting for him to save enough money to . . ." Her voice trailed off.

We sat there as the silence stretched out. I had so many questions to ask her about Kelly, but I wanted to be sure she was comfortable.

"Look," I said, "about the luau, I know we arranged to pay you the balance at the end of the month, but I want you to have all your money right now. There are sure to be expenses." I rummaged in my bag and came up with the check.

She looked at the crisp rectangle of pale blue paper. "This is too much," Keniki said, handing it back to me.

"No. This is fine. You have enough to deal with right now, Keniki. Bills need to be paid, right? And if there is anything else I can do to help you, please just let me know."

"You are truly a kind person," she said, her eyes dreamy.

I noticed her sister, Cynthia, was standing in the hallway, listening to us but not joining us in the living room.

"We're a little lost," Keniki said, apologetic. "We aren't sure what to do. Kelly's family is in California. They were called by the police or someone. His dad is flying in to take care of everything. I think they plan to take him back to Oakland."

"Oh."

"But all his friends are here," Cynthia said, coming a step into the room, into the conversation.

An opening. I asked my first question gently. "How long has Kelly lived on the Big Island?"

Keniki answered immediately. "Two years. But we only started seeing each other about six months ago."

I noticed she held a fresh tissue in her hand, but she didn't seem to need it. She must still be in shock. Or perhaps she had been given a pill and it was working.

"Do you feel like talking about him?"

"I don't mind," Keniki said, meeting my eyes. "Everyone is so upset. Everyone else seems afraid to talk about Kelly now."

Cynthia shed a tear. "I'm sorry, Keni. I'm not sure what is right and what is wrong."

"This is a hard time," I said, and then turned back to Keniki and tried another question. "I don't think I heard how you two met."

"At a party," Keniki said, and she smiled a shy smile. "Kelly was there with a guy that he works with. I went with Cynthia. It was a very posh party, but I took one look at Kelly and he looked at me. We knew. Neither one of us belonged at that party, but we knew we belonged together."

"Where did he work?" I asked.

She looked at me and blinked. Her boyfriend would now and forever be referred to in the past tense. "Over at a horticulture center," she said. "He was in love with plants. That's why people are sending us all of these. And these." She gestured to the forest of shoots and stalks erupting in pots in front of us. "This one is *B. nutans*. And here is a *T. siamensis*. Kelly taught me all the plant names."

"Kelly could grow anything," Cynthia said softly.

"It's true," Keniki agreed. "He could. But these plants are just for show, Cyn. These people weren't his friends.

Not his real friends. They are all such . . ." She took a deep breath. "They're hypocrites."

"I know," murmured her sister.

I looked up. "What do you mean?"

Keniki plucked the card from the tallest green arrangement and read it aloud. "We will miss our brother, Kelly. From The Bamboo Four. Can you believe their nerve?"

"Kelly had enemies," Cynthia explained to me quickly.

"What sort of enemies?"

"He was very political. And there were factions that were working against him—like those four. I guess he was threatening the wrong people, and they were not too happy."

I paid very close attention. Were Keniki and Cynthia implying Kelly Imo's death was tied in some way with politics? But they sounded so calm. "Can you tell me what sort of politics?"

"Oh, Kelly had radical ideas," Keniki said, smiling at the thought. "And not everyone here on the island was too happy with that. Still, they all sent gifts, didn't they? The Four! The jerks."

"The jerks," Cynthia agreed, her soft voice bitter. "I hate them."

And then Keniki's head fell into her hands. That eerie force, which had somehow managed to restrain the terrible storm of emotions up to this point, could hold it back no more. Anger set it free. And a primitive moan racked her slender body. Then another. And there were tears. Tears came pouring, torrents of tears. Dr. Margolis stood up but stayed close to her as the tempest of sorrow and anger was finally unleashed in that small living room.

"Oh, Keni." Cynthia, her own tears flowing once more, sank down on her knees on the floor in front of her sister. Their graceful arms entwined around each other. "That's okay. That's okay."

Witnessing their pain was difficult, but you don't have to be Dr. Phil to know such a release is necessary, healthy even. Now she would be able to move through her grief. It was all about feeling her true feelings, giving herself up to the truth. But man, the truth in this case was hard.

And it was more than time for me to leave, despite the fact that so many of my questions would remain unasked. I whispered, "You can call me for anything," and stood to go. Keniki would know how to reach me at the resort if she wanted to talk later.

Cynthia caught up to me at the door, put her hand on my arm. "Thank you for this. This is right. We needed this. It's for the best."

By now, everyone has watched enough *Oprah* to figure out what is best for everyone. I swear, that woman on TV does the world a great service.

"Look," I said. "I'm wondering about something Keniki said."

"Yes?"

"Can you just tell me what sort of politics?"

Cynthia stared at me, not comprehending, but I had to know just this little bit more. Just this one thing. "Kelly's politics?" I stood with the front door open. "Local? Federal?"

"About the future of Hawaii," Cynthia answered, still perplexed.

Our conversation had caught Keniki's attention. She grew quieter, calming herself down. She called to me at the door, "They're all probably meeting right now."

I turned back to her, facing her red and swollen eyes. "Where?"

"At Bamboo, of course."

"Oh, no. I think they probably canceled their meeting," Cynthia said, but she didn't say it with conviction.

Keniki shook her head, her long wavy hair shimmying. "They sent me a lovely plant, but I know these friends of Kelly. They are still having their filthy meeting today. Kelly should be there too. My Kelly . . ." But she couldn't go on. She began choking on a new rush of tears, and Cynthia turned and went back to her.

Through it all, Dr. Margolis had stayed right by Keniki's side, but he looked up at me as I put my hand on the doorknob, his dark brown eyes giving me a warm good-bye. And then I let myself out of the house, more confused about Kelly Imo than when I had arrived. Everything I learned about Kelly seemed to contradict everything else. But now I had a lead—a meeting at someplace called Bamboo. So I would have to keep digging for more. And if I was very lucky, I thought I might find it soon.

Kahua Ho'olulu
(Meeting Place)

Of course I still didn't know if Kelly's death was natural or not, but his death had to be considered suspicious. And it seemed Kelly had been involved with the people who were making threats to Holly. It was possible that they could be the same political people that Keniki had mentioned. The Bamboo Four. I was certain I could discover everything I needed to know if I could just find the political meeting that the Hicks sisters said might be in progress.

I pulled the rented Mustang out onto the main highway and decided to cruise through town. Hawi is an old city. Once bustling with growth in the 1800s and early 1900s, during the sugar boom, and then almost extinguished when the sugar plantation shut down in 1970, the town was now recast as a small artists' way station. This same dismal economic theme played throughout Hawaii over the past thirty years, as the world price of sugar had plunged and the one industry that had sustained many island workers became extinct. Unemployment, depression, suicides. That was the legacy of a local industry gone bust.

Today, Hawi was trying to keep its original Hawaiian history intact, and many of the original buildings had been preserved. I slowed down as I drove along the three blocks of downtown Hawi, noting a Kona coffee shop and a handmade-ice-cream shop amid a few other tourist-oriented stores, all set in mildly refurbished structures.

And right across the street from the ice-cream shop was a ramshackle three-story building from the old days. The pale green clapboards could use a fresh coat of paint, but atop the open double-door entry was a beautifully kitschy sign. Brightly painted bent bamboo, the yellow letters proclaimed: BAMBOO.

Isn't that interesting?

One had to love a small town. Could Kelly's political meeting still be in progress, as Keniki had predicted, despite the loss of one of its important members? Or perhaps because of that loss? I had to stop and check.

I found a parking spot on the next block up and walked back. Bamboo, it turned out, was a charming restaurant and bar situated on the ground floor of an authentic plantation-era building from old Hawaii, with art gallery space upstairs.

I was greeted by an elderly hostess, but my eyes were scanning the place, looking for anyone who might fit the vague description of The Bamboo Four.

"Just one?" the old island auntie asked again.

I focused on her finally and spoke up clearly. "I was told there was to be a meeting here today. But I'm not sure I got the time right."

"A meeting?" she asked, checking me out. I was wearing a neat pair of short white shorts with a pale lavender T-shirt, along with the de rigueur flip-flops. Lots of tan skin, my hair doing its corkscrew thing in the constant soft humidity. Not the sort of getup one would wear to attend a Republican caucus, I grant you, but I still had no idea into what sort of radical politics

Kelly Imo was mixed up. This was Hawaii. Everyone was laid-back, no?

"You mean HBA? No, no, you don't want them, miss."

"HBA?" I grabbed on to it. Hawaiian Birchers of America. Ew. Hawaii Break-Free from America? Hm. "My friend told me to come."

"Well, that's the only group here," she said, smiling. "You like bamboo?"

I looked around the twinkle-lit interior, so charming, with old hardwood floors, framed Hawaiiana on the walls, and vintage bamboo decor. My kind of restaurant in an old refurbished building. I was dying to read the menu. "I love it," I said.

"You love bamboo?" The woman, dressed in a floral muumuu, looked startled. "Then you come with me. HBA for you."

Whatever that meant.

I followed her around the corner to the far section of the main dining room. There, a large round table held eight or nine people, all deep in serious conversation. They looked up as we approached.

"Who's this, Mary?" asked a large, tan white man in his fifties. "You thinking of hiring a new waitress?"

"She with you HBAs," said the hostess, pulling another chair over to their table.

I sat down and faced the stares. Eight men and one woman. All wearing aloha shirts in various hues and patterns. They had no idea who I was, naturally, but I just smiled. "Hello. I'm Madeline Bean. Keniki Hicks told me you would be here."

"Keniki sent you here?" asked another man, this one very wiry but equally overtanned. "But why?"

"She was touched by all the plants and flowers that you sent. For Kelly."

"Ah," said the female member of their group, putting down her pen. "She's here to sit in for Kelly. Is that allowed?"

"Not in our bylaws," said the first man, sounding grim. "Absolutely not."

"Earl," said the woman, a trim blonde, in an exasperated voice, "we don't have any written bylaws. I've been trying to get you guys to recognize how important it is to—"

"Thanks, Claudia," said the man, shutting her down. He didn't sound thankful.

"You can't vote in Kelly's place," said the second man, the wiry one. Everyone else seemed to be alarmed by the idea as well, and I heard a lot of whispering as cross conversations sprang up at the far end of the table.

"Why can't she?" asked Claudia. "We have no written bylaws, so—"

"This Modlin woman," said Earl with a grimace to the wiry man beside him. "This is all she keeps harping about—"

"Look," I said, trying to get their attention. "I have something to say."

Claudia shushed them all.

Now what exactly could I say? I still had no flipping idea what this group stood for or why Kelly was at odds with them. "But first, can a girl order lunch around here?"

"Jeez," said Earl. "Get this young woman a menu, will you, Claudia?" And then to me, he said, regaining his charm, "Look, we don't mean to sound heartless. Jeez. I mean, no one here is sadder than I am that Kelly had that terrible accident. We even considered rescheduling our board meeting today."

Ah. They considered it.

"But a lot of our group come over for this meeting from the other islands. We were already here this morning by time we got word of what happened. If I rescheduled, we'd lose a month, and none of us thought Kelly would want us to do that."

I'm sure they were thinking of Kelly Imo foremost when making this decision.

Claudia returned to the table, holding out a menu. "Here you are, sweetie," she said. I could tell she must be a great mom; she had that sort of offhand caring competence about her.

"Thanks. Say, why don't you just continue on with your meeting while I get settled? We can talk about Kelly a little later, if that's okay."

I saw one of the men at the far end of the table nudge a buddy and whisper, "That Kelly. He had great taste in females."

"Okay, let's go on," said Earl, figuring, I suppose, that making me leave would be too much of a disruption. Such a fuss would hardly be tactful, since I was invoking the name of a very recently deceased member. A member of *what*, I was dying to discover, but I figured if they were willing to hold their meetings out in public, they weren't planning to overthrow the U.S. government. Most likely.

"Where were we?" he asked Claudia, who then consulted her handwritten notes.

"You were talking about Panaewa."

"Right."

I looked over the menu, wanting to take it all in as I always do, while at the same time trying to keep an ear out for mention of what this group's politics really were. In truth, I was starving. The list of pupus, or appetizers, was heavenly. I considered quickly the chicken sate pot stickers, the Margaritaville prawns, or the kalua pork quesadilla. The prawns were herb-grilled with fresh papaya, drizzled with a spicy tequila lime sauce. Yummy. While the pork was smoked in a traditional Hawaiian imu, or underground oven, and tucked into a grilled flour tortilla along with jalapeño jack cheese and topped with tropical fresh fruit salsa and sour cream. Equally divine.

A waitress, a young girl with her hair swept up tight on her head, materialized. Decisions, decisions. I looked up, and Claudia Modlin met my eyes. She whispered, "The kalua pork."

I smiled and ordered.

Meanwhile, the gang of Hawaiian-shirted men was deep in discussion. When I heard the word *dying,* I paid keen attention once more to the conversation.

One of the men, a very old Asian fellow with white hair, was speaking with a froggy voice. "This is why they die," he was saying. "He chews and he pisses."

Ahem?

"Yes, Ike," another man said, as if he had been down this road before.

Who dies? Who chews? Who . . . well, who? I sipped my water and tried to become invisible as I waited for my food.

"The *T. siamensis* has been chewed, true," said Earl, sounding weary. "But it's still hanging in there."

"Maybe yes," said Ike, "maybe no. But the *B. multiplex* was not so lucky. It's dead!"

"The fern leaf again," Earl said. "Yes, we know all this, Ike. We need to move on now. What do you expect? It wasn't planted on the tiger's path, but a tiger cannot be controlled. It's going to chew. It's going to piss. We can't control that."

I must have looked as perplexed as I felt. What sort of political group was this?

"The zoo," Claudia explained, correctly interpreting the furrows in my brow, "over near Hilo. We planted bamboo in the new white tiger habitat. There's been some worry about how well the plantings may thrive with the tiger taking such a keen interest in them."

"Ah." My kalua pork arrived before I was expected to react to this news. Thank goodness. I mean, what could I possibly add to a conversation about tiger piss?

"May we move on?" Earl asked the group.

So their big topic of conversation was dying plants? HBA. Hawaiian *Bamboo* Association?

I ate as they moved on to discuss sales of T-shirts. New association T-shirts that featured a stylized block print of . . . I waited as one of the club members fumbled with a drawing and then held it up. Bamboo. Oh! I was so good. I was so right.

But hey, what was really going on here? Had I in fact just boldly crashed a luncheon for avid bamboo lovers? Or was there possibly something more sinister involved? Keniki Hicks had come unglued when she talked about Kelly's political foes. Were these folks them? Could all of Keniki's anger really have been aimed at a group of bamboo fanciers? I had expected some answers here, possibly as to why Kelly wound up dead. I nibbled my insanely good quesadilla and figured, at least until I got my butt kicked out of the meeting, I might as well continue listening.

"And now, finally, we are up to the new business," Earl stated, looking at me warily.

"About time," said a muscular man who was called Brian. "I've got a proposal."

"No, you don't," argued Earl. "You never sent me notice of any new business, so it will not be—"

"Now, maybe I didn't," Brian said testily, "but you know damned well Kelly did. He was going to raise this issue today, and so I am doing it in his place."

"That's out of order," Earl said. "You are not recognized, Brian."

"Is that right?" Brian asked, his voice going up half an octave in outrage, looking over at Claudia.

"We need to have a set of written bylaws," she started up again, sounding pleasant between the loud bickering.

"To hell with that," said Brian. "If I can't raise the issue, then let this girl do it. She's sitting here for Kelly. He's the one who got the motion together, right? So let her do it."

I had just raised my lovely half-eaten quesadilla to my lips as I noticed everyone at the table had now turned to me. "Me?" I asked, talking around the tortilla.

"It's unheard of," fumed Earl.

"Go ahead, sweetie," suggested Claudia, her pen up.

What the hell had Kelly been going to propose to this group of agitated bamboo fiends? A new planting in the zoo? Not likely, because I noticed old Ike was less interested now. What, then?

"Let her finish her sandwich in peace," Earl suggested. "We can take all this up next month."

"No!" yelled Brian.

"Let's all just be patient," said Claudia calmly.

I swallowed. "Look. I am not a regular member of your group, um, obviously."

They looked at me, waiting.

"But let me say this. I feel it would be best if Brian put the proposal into actual words, as it were. And then, you know, to satisfy Earl here, I can make the official motion on Kelly's behalf."

"That's right," Brian said, standing up, "that's fair." And then he launched into a ten-minute description of Kelly's master plan for how bamboo could save the Hawaiian Islands.

Ka-kau
(The Secretary)

I'll say this for the plan. It was as brilliant as it was wacky. Kelly Imo had apparently figured out a way to save Hawaii from its almost total dependence on tourist dollars—in other words, rescue the state from economic crisis—by introducing a new agricultural business to the islands. In place of the dismal commercial disaster that befell sugar, he proposed developing plantations of *bamboo*, which he intended to be harvested and processed for use as building material. A similar plan was showing promise in the Philippines and in Vietnam. Bamboo, apparently, was amazing stuff. His research showed that bamboo had a tensile strength greater than steel. Steel! Who knew?

Of course, our part of the globe has not yet taken much to using bamboo in construction, so Kelly's scheme required some deep-pockets investors who would build processing plants and mount a stunning PR campaign to somehow convince the Western world to get with the bamboo. New businesses would be developed to turn the raw bamboo into construction and building materials, such as bamboo poles, bamboo thatch, bamboo molding, bamboo fencing, bamboo weave, bamboo mats, bamboo board, bamboo flooring, and probably six or seven other utilizations that flew right over my head.

"But you have a problem from the start," the wiry man seated next to Earl interrupted. "Which variety are you proposing to grow?"

"Stop getting bogged down in the details, Pete. We'll grow the best kind," said Brian, flushed, waving off the question, not wishing to be pinned down. He had bigger ideas to share.

"Does 'the best' mean the *strongest*?" the wiry man challenged, just as hot about his bamboo. "The *straightest*? The most *durable*?"

"Pete—"

"I'm not finished! The most *flexible*? The most *bug resistant*? Does it mean the most canes or tonnage per acre? Do you want to use the bamboo 'as is' in the round? Or do you want to mill it for composites or laminates? Or do you want it primarily for furniture?"

"Pete!" Brian raised his voice, trying to stop him.

"See," the wiry man continued, his voice strong, "you have not done your homework, Brian. And neither had Kelly, God rest his soul. So don't go taking this group off the edge of the cliff. We could get ourselves into real deep doo-doo if we follow this madness without thinking it through. That's all I'm saying."

"Yes," Claudia said in her calm, cool voice, taking rapid notes. "Out of order, every word, but that's all you're saying."

What rabbit hole had I fallen down? These men and a woman were getting hot and bothered over a cockeyed plan to introduce bamboo plantations to the economy of Hawaii. Somehow, pros and cons be damned, it didn't sound like the makings of a motive for murder. After all, no matter how heated the discussion, I couldn't see any of these bambooists killing over it. I mean, really. Except . . . I surveyed the table. Maybe Earl.

I pulled three fives out of my purse and put them on the table. I had learned a lot about bamboo, without a doubt, but I'd learned practically nothing of any real value about Kelly Imo or why he had been in Holly's room. I knew even less about why he might have died so suddenly.

The closer I got to knowing what made Kelly tick—his sweet girlfriend, his green thumb—the less he seemed a likely player in any sort of a deadly game.

"You're leaving?" Earl asked, startled.

"Not without making the motion," Brian demanded. "Come on, now. Just make it."

"Okay," I said, still standing.

The rest of the group quieted down. Claudia Modlin, her blond hair neat, held her pen ready.

"I move that the HBA advocate Kelly's proposal, as stated by Brian."

"Time has come we stand up," said Ike, putting a fist into the air. "We show the whole world. We can save people here. Many will get jobs. Let's share our secret. Let's tell the world about the power of bamboo."

"Hell," said Earl. "You're supposed to second it, Ike, not make a speech."

"I second it, then," Ike said, his froggy voice loud and clear.

The noise level at the table rose, each HBA member disagreeing again with his neighbor. "Settle down, now," Earl said. "We'll have plenty of time to discuss the motion further at our next meeting." As they bickered, I quickly made for the exit.

When I got to the front door, I had another thought. I scribbled a note and asked the young waitress if she would mind taking it. I wrapped it in a five-dollar bill, a healthy tip, and then walked out into the Hawaiian sunshine.

Two minutes later, Claudia Modlin joined me on the bench out in front of Bamboo.

"I just wanted to thank you for helping me back there," I said.

"It was fun to see Earl squirm." Her tanned face was unable to hide a hint of satisfaction. "It was horrible of him to railroad this meeting after what just happened to Kelly. We usually have two dozen members in attendance, but Earl knew many of us would stay away out of respect for Kelly. I almost didn't come, but I'm glad I did."

"Were you close to Kelly?" I asked. She was in her young forties, I guessed, but looked wonderfully fit. Perhaps living in Hawaii gives one great skin.

"He was a dear boy," she said, her voice softening. "My husband is a doctor on this island, and Kelly and he used to go surfing together, along with my sons."

"I see." Again, I was reminded of how strong a swimmer Kelly had been, how comfortable in the ocean.

She looked at me and said, "I'm surprised we haven't met you before. How long have you known Kelly?"

It's amazing how much you can get away with in life if you just practice the art of ignoring the questions you don't want to answer. I'd learned this from watching politicians on TV. Instead of admitting I didn't actually know Kelly from Adam, I came up with a distracting question of my own. "I'm concerned about his death," I said, lowering my voice. "Aren't you?"

Claudia Modlin sighed. "It's very rough, the surf here. People don't realize how dangerous."

"You think he was swept off into the ocean?"

"It's certainly possible."

"Really?"

"There was a tourist couple visiting Kauai not very long ago. From Indiana, I think, or Illinois. They were walking out on some rock outcroppings with their eleven-year-old son while the tide was very low. People think that's safe to do." She shook her head. "I imagine they were having a wonderful time, a great family holiday in Hawaii. But then a wave came—a rogue wave, very large and unexpected—and it swept the parents off the rocks. Isn't that tragic? Right in front of their boy. And they were gone. They were dead. Drowned just like that. It was on the news for days. There were dozens of witnesses on the beach nearby, all shocked, of course. A kind man took the son back to shore. Can you imagine? That's the ocean. Never turn your back on it."

Again, a story about death in paradise.

"That's horrible. But tourists from the Midwest might not know any better. Kelly was a local guy. He was a surfer, a man who knew these waters very well. Aren't you at all surprised that such an athletic guy would die this way?"

She looked at me, and something behind her eyes shifted. "I know we're all shocked that Kelly is gone. But are you saying you don't believe it was an accident that killed him?"

"Well." I looked at her and made a quick decision. "Yes."

"I see."

"Only, I have to be truthful with you, Claudia. I did not actually know Kelly. I know his fiancé, Keniki." And as she kept her very wise eyes on me, I told her all about what I suspected regarding the Four Heavens incident as well.

"I wish I knew what to say." Claudia pulled her sunglasses out of a straw bag and began to polish the lenses with a special tissue. "I'm sure more information will come to us. There's sure to be an official investigation. But it makes absolutely no sense to me. I loved Kelly, and I can't imagine who didn't."

"What about Earl?" I asked.

"Yes, the two of them were often at odds," she said mildly, "but surely you can't suspect Earl of being involved in Kelly's death?"

I shrugged.

"And how do you feel about bamboo? Are you a plant lover, my dear?"

"Well, I don't know if I'd say we're lovers. More like just good friends."

"I have always loved botany. Passionately. It was my major at UCLA. Kelly and I both found bamboo completely fascinating. We talked about bamboo most of the time. And then he hit it off with the men in my family. They all love the ocean. But I agree with you, it is certainly a mystery. And now I'm afraid I have got to go."

"Did Kelly have any trouble at work, do you know?" I asked, realizing my final lead had led exactly nowhere.

"He seemed very happy," she said, shaking her head and standing up.

"Where did he work?"

"Down the coast," she said, pointing southward. Then she put on her sunglasses. Of course, at this northernmost point on the Big Island, almost everything was located in that direction. "Say," she said, turning to me, "do you need a ride somewhere?"

"No, thanks. I have a car."

"Well, then. I wish you luck, my dear." Claudia Modlin, secretary of the Hawaii Bamboo Association, opened the door of a spiffy late-model Mercedes parked near the restaurant's entrance and pulled away from the curb like a bat out of hell.

I turned to leave, and out of the front entry of Bamboo Restaurant walked Earl, the heartless leader of the HBA.

"Hey, little lady," he called to me. "Hey. Thought you had gone already."

"Just talking to Claudia for a minute. Well, bye-bye." I backed away.

"Say, wait a sec!"

Damn. I had almost pulled it off. As an impostor bamboo fanatic, I had done pretty damned well. I had managed to implant myself into a fractious horticultural society meeting at which I had absolutely no credentials. And then, knowing nothing at all about plants, I had stood up and made a motion to support a bamboo viewpoint that heretofore I had never even heard of. And in the process, I had gleaned a bit more knowledge about Kelly and his enemies. So it seemed to me, my work here was done. Now all I had to do was get the heck out of Dodge pronto before I blew my own cover.

"Miss!" Earl was walking fast. He would catch up with me in just a few more strides. "What did you say your name was again?"

I didn't want to tick the guy off now. I had done so well up to this point. No one hated me yet. No one was yelling. I was only half a block from my car, but I hesitated to break into a sprint. Instead, I stopped and turned back while Earl caught up with me in one long step.

"Miss . . . ?"

"Bean."

"Friend of Kelly's, right?" he asked, looking me over.

Note for the future: when impersonating a plant enthusiast, it is much better to quit while one is ahead. Run like hell after the meeting is over.

"Horrible damned thing," Earl said. "Boy like Kelly getting washed up onto the rocks at A-Bay. I would never have believed it, great swimmer like Kelly. Terrible thing."

"It is."

"You live here on the island, Miss Bean?" He pulled a golfer's cap out of one of his pockets and put it on, shading his pale eyes.

"No. No, I'm just here for a few days."

"I see. Well, maybe you don't know it, then, but me and Kelly have been buddies for a while. I'm the one who brought him into the HBA, in fact. He had a genius for cultivating plants."

"I didn't realize you were friends," I said.

"Oh, hell, yes. He was a great kid."

"You didn't agree with his plan for bamboo to take over the world, though."

"Well, now." Earl was not a tall man, about my height, and he smiled at me, eye to eye. "We had differences, sure. He was a young man, and perhaps I'm an old one." He paused.

I work with men like Earl all the time. I knew what Earl wanted to hear. "No," I said, "you're not!"

"Okay, then, not too old. But I respected Kelly a lot. I think he was on to something very big. Bamboo is an amazing material. You know that. But the enterprise had to be approached the right way. We need to proceed very, very cautiously. Line up investors. Get some construction giants from the mainland to come over here. Junkets. You know what I mean. Sponsor seminars on bamboo and how to use it in building. Stuff like that."

"That sounds pretty well thought out," I said, taking the shortest route to Earl's heart.

"Sure. I worked as a lobbyist in Lincoln, Nebraska,

before my wife and I decided to move here. It takes a special talent for getting key interest groups to back a major new industry. And that takes time. Kelly was much too impatient. He wanted us to go right to the state legislature. Right now. Get the state to subsidize test bamboo plantations, pay for brand-new processing plants, the whole nine yards. Before we developed a market! He'd drawn up maps, marking out abandoned cane fields and selecting ideal sites, all located on state land. Kelly had lots of grand plans. I told him to take it slowly, but would he listen? Hell, no."

"You fought about it. Kenicki said—"

"Sure, we had quite a few late-night phone calls, Kelly and me. I'm sure his girlfriend would rather have been canoodling with Kelly, instead of listening to him argue all those times Kelly called me. But Kelly and I enjoyed getting a rise out of each other, getting into the nitty-gritty details of our plans. Jeez, I can't believe he's really gone."

What Earl said made sense. And so, I had to reconsider everything. Looking at it all from this angle, it wasn't plant politics gone deadly. It was a couple of bamboo enthusiasts disagreeing about the finer procedural points of a pie-in-the-sky, altruistic plan that could mean work to men who really needed it. A gallant plan to save their adopted home state by cultivating the vegetation they loved.

I'd run clean out of ideas and subtlety. I held up a hand and shaded my eyes from the glare of the steady sun. "Earl, do you have any idea why Kelly would have been in a vacant hotel room at the Four Heavens Resort yesterday?"

"Not a clue. Was he?" he asked, smiling down at me.

"Yes."

"Well, let me guess. Meeting up with his girlfriend, maybe, for some afternoon delight?"

Now, that was something I hadn't thought of. Keniki worked at the Four Heavens, of course. Maybe once in a while, they borrowed a free room to take advantage of her work breaks. Could Kelly have been waiting for Keniki yesterday afternoon?

"Well, if you have any other questions, you just let me know," he said, handing me his business card. Earl Maffini, North Coast Real Estate.

"Thanks," I said. "Actually, there is one more thing. I'm trying to find out where Kelly worked."

"You don't know where he worked?"

Okay, I could read his mind here. If I was such a close friend of Kelly's that I would show up and put forward his master bamboo-conquers-the-world scheme before the board of the HBA, how was it I didn't even know where he worked?

I shook my head. When stepping through such a narrow maze as the one I'd built, I always stick to the strict truth. Well, as close as was possible. "I've been thinking about what I might do to help Keniki, and I thought I could gather up his personal things at work—just to save her the sorrow. Only, she was pretty upset this morning, as you can imagine. I didn't want to trouble her for the address."

"Well, you were just talking to Kelly's boss. I'm surprised you didn't just ask Claudia."

"I beg your pardon?"

"Sure. Kelly worked for Claudia for the last year or so."

"I wonder why she didn't mention it to me."

"Well, now," Earl said, smiling again, "it was on the QT. But it wasn't like they were very good at hiding the secret. They thought their project was pretty hush-hush."

"Did it have something to do with bamboo, Earl?"

"Hell, no. Nothing as cool as bamboo, Miss Bean."

I smiled at that.

"But they were growing something there down the coast. Everything grows best in our volcanic soil, you know. From what I could gather, they thought they would get rich from it."

Had Kelly come up with another brilliant idea, a second cash crop to make a fortune in Hawaii? Was he growing something illegal? Marijuana, maybe? And if he was mixed up in drugs, there could be a lot of reasons Claudia wouldn't want to talk to me about it. "You know where their office is located?"

"No office that I know of," he said. "Just a field."

"Where?"

"Near the water. Right down the coast aways. Not far from where they found his body, poor guy."

So Kelly had been working on some secret project with Claudia Modlin, which my active imagination was now convinced had to be cultivating the Big Island version of Maui Wowie, and I, great genius at discretion that I am, just told the woman that I was suspicious of his death.

Nice one.

Haru Wahine o ka Lomi
(Mistress of the Spa)

*T*he difference between Wes and me is that Wes truly enjoys turning off his brain once in a while, and I have a hard time finding that switch. I stopped back at my room at the Four Heavens, hoping to find Wes, but it looked like he hadn't come back. Apparently he'd been gobbled up in a marathon day of beauty, and the lure of free treatments had turned his head completely. I needed to see him, though. Preferably now. We needed to sort through the layers of information.

I noticed as I stopped into the room that the message light on the desk phone was glowing. Maybe it was from Wes.

I dialed the message center and heard a pleasant automated female voice state we had four messages.

The first one was from the front desk of the resort. The man at the business center was calling to say they had received a package addressed to Wes and me. Hm. I would go pick it up in a few minutes. The second message was from Liz.

"Hey, Wes and Maddie. I'm over at the North Shore Medical Center, but I'm grabbing a cab back to the Four Heavens. Don't worry, I'm fine. They did tests. They took my temperature. Nothing wrong with me at all.

"Holly came out here to the emergency room with me, but I told her not to wait around. I'm sure she'll turn up back at the resort. Okay . . ." There was the sound of Liz huffing and puffing. "I'm out by the parking lot now. I'm walking . . . I'm looking . . ." More sounds of heavy breathing. "Nope. I don't see her rent-a-car in the hospital lot. So I guess I'll see you back at the ranch. And I just wanted to say, well, sorry about all the fainting. This is so unlike me. I'm usually really, really strong. I never get all flustery. I mean, I'm an *accountant*. I am used to scary things—you know, like arithmetic. Anyway, later."

Liz was fine. That was certainly good news. I slid back into party-planner mode and checked off one more mental concern. All party guests were required to have fun if at all possible.

But something else didn't seem exactly right. Why had Holly left Liz all alone at the ER? I bet Liz insisted Holly go, not wanting to completely spoil the bride-to-be's weekend. Friendships are so complex. And between Liz's fainter's guilt and Holly's caretaker's instincts, who can say what feeling would win out when you had only a few more hours of daylight on an island holiday?

The third message was from Keniki Hicks.

"Madeline, you were so very very sweet to come by and see me this morning. My goodness, you are on your vacation, after all, and you still took the time to drive all the way out here to Hawi. I am really grateful for that, and thank you so much for dropping by the check, and, well, for everything. Also . . . I wanted to apologize to you for getting so . . . well, so upset. I am never like that. Never. It's just been . . . Well, Cynthia says we're all in shock."

I heard her sister's voice in the background, giving some gentle reminders.

"Oh," Keniki's voice continued, "and I also wanted you to know that some friends are putting on a small luau in honor of Kelly tonight. Everyone wanted to get together and we thought . . . well, we thought Kelly would like the idea of a luau. I know you are probably busy, but we would love to see you there. It's being held at a friend's house, over on the other side of the island. Near Hilo. And my cousin, Roddy, is helping out. He owns a helicopter tour company, and his heliport is pretty close to the Four Heavens. Roddy and his pilots are going to ferry all our friends over to Hilo and back. So you can see our beautiful island from above. That is, if you can make it. Starting at eight tonight and going on probably all night. Just go to Pele Helicopter Tours. You've probably seen their sign. They are right there off the highway just south of the resort, you know, toward Kona."

Poor Keniki. She had an awful lot to deal with, but she sounded like she was on her way to managing. What else can anyone do?

The last message was from Jennifer Sizemore, newly appointed president of the Four Heavens Resorts Division and, although we'd yet to see her, our hostess for the weekend. Oh, good. I'd left her a message yesterday, letting her know about the trouble Holly had checking into her room.

"Well, kiddo, hi." Jenn's voice sounded cheerful, and very much as I remembered it from our days together in Chef Louis's class on grilling techniques. Funny how well we recall the voices from our past. "I'm in my office in New York and I've got to say, I was surprised to hear from you. Look, I don't know anything about your trip to Hawaii. You are staying at one of our top properties, so I do hope you enjoy it, sweetie. But I was confused by your message. I never invited you or your friends to stay there. Is this your way of hinting I should have? Call me sometime soon and let's talk."

Not her guests? What the hell was that about? I redialed her office number in New York but only got weekend phone mail and left her another message.

I was annoyed, my typical Jennifer Sizemore reaction. Wait until Wes heard we were going to end up paying for all the rooms. How had this misunderstanding happened? I left our room and walked quickly over to the main resort building, the one that held the reception desk. I had dealt with billing issues a million times in my events business, and it wasn't unheard of for the costs that were projected before a party to suddenly balloon up after it was too late to change things.

"Hello," I said to the lady behind the front desk. "Can I please speak with Mr. Jasper Berger?"

"I'm sorry, Mr. Berger is gone for the weekend. Might I be of assistance?"

"Yes. There may be a misunderstanding. Would you be able to look up my room and see to whom the bill is being charged?"

"Didn't you leave a credit card imprint when you checked in with us?" she asked kindly.

"No. I did not. I was under the impression we'd been invited to be guests of the hotel."

"Oh, I see."

"Yes. And when I spoke with Mr. Berger yesterday, he concurred. Could you please look it up?"

"Of course. Your name?"

I told her and waited as she hit a few keys on her computer.

"Your party has four rooms for two nights, is that correct?"

"Right."

"Yes, Miss Bean. It's fine. Your room charges are being taken care of."

"By the Four Heavens, you mean?" I asked. "By Jennifer Sizemore?" I tried to remember Jenn's married name. "I mean, Jennifer Handley?"

"No," she said, her manner still most helpful and charming. "That's not what I have listed on your record."

"Then who is paying for us?"

She scrolled down the screen, her eyes darting back and forth as she read. "We are instructed to accept all charges made to those four rooms. It is noted that we received a cash deposit in advance, so you needn't worry at all, Ms. Bean."

But yes, in fact, I did.

"Cash? Who paid for us?"

"That I do not know. But the deposit was ten thousand dollars in advance, which should be quite enough to cover all your costs this weekend. So have no fear."

"Please," I asked, my concern mounting by the minute, "can you ask any of the others working here if they know who paid for us?"

"I'm afraid that information would only be held in the accounting office of the resort. And they do not work on the weekend. Perhaps you could inquire on Monday?"

"Thank you."

Someone had made sure we came to the Big Island of Hawaii this weekend and stayed at this resort. And if it hadn't been my old nemesis from culinary school, Jennifer Sizemore, who the hell had brought us here?

I was so lost in this new and disturbing thought that I almost forgot to inquire about my package. But just as I was leaving the lobby, I noticed another desk tucked into a corner which offered business center services to the resort's guests.

"I believe there's a package for Madeline Bean."

"Miss Bean?" The young man behind the light wood desk looked up. "Oh, yes. Would you please sign on this line?" He pushed across a receiving log, and I signed on the line indicated. "I have it right here," he said. "It was dropped off personally, by quite a fan of yours."

"Of mine?"

"Yes. A tall gentleman. Famous on our island."

"Really?"

The young man reached behind the desk, and I noticed for the first time there was a small refrigerator tucked away down there. He pulled up a lovely fresh flower lei, one made out of the most exotic orchids I'd ever seen.

"Wow."

"It's beautiful," he said, and then came around from behind the desk and said, "May I?"

I smiled like a big island goofball as he put the tricolored garland over my head. The creamy white interior of each orchid petal made a line up the center of the lush string of flowers, while the purply-pink edges of the petals and another outer row of deep burgundy orchids made the masterpiece complete.

"You see," the young man said, smiling, "this lei is the most special kind. Given only by very special friends to ones they care for." I think his eyes twinkled at me.

I looked closely at the beautiful lei. "How on earth do they make these?"

"Over seven hundred center petals of the orchid are meticulously sewn in the kui lau style, which is a back-and-forth pattern, creating an elegant flat lei like this one."

"Who is this gift from again?"

"Ah, the gentleman asked that we withhold his name," said the young man. "But I'm sure you can think of it."

I looked blank. I'm bad at guessing games. Wes? He was my special friend, but he was not someone the clerk would describe as famous around the resort. Could it have come from Berger, the manager who was trying to soothe us down yesterday? Um . . .

The young man took pity. "Maybe you should think of a dessert?"

I turned, barely able to keep the smile off my face, and suddenly memories of last night's luau came rushing back. Cake. And what had Holly just been saying not long ago. Seize the moment. Run free. I turned to leave.

"Oh, Miss Bean," the young man called. "Did you want to pick up your friend's package while you are here?"

"For which friend?"

"For Mr. Westcott."

"Oh, sure." The business center clerk flipped a page in his log and showed me where to sign. Then he rummaged around in the cooler, coming back up with a small box, which he handed across the desk.

"It's to be kept refrigerated," he explained as I felt the cool package, wrapped in white paper.

"No problem," I said as I signed Wesley's name. One of the lovely things about staying at the Four Heavens was that every guest room came with a small refrigerator. Now, these were not your average garden-variety minibars, those awkward, overstuffed units where you have to shove the tiny bottles of Michelob aside just to put in your own small carton of cream. No. At check-in, each guest is presented with a menu of delectable snack-type items from which to order. If we wanted Diet Coke, my own personal addiction, we simply ordered it by the six-pack and were charged the regular retail price. It was amazingly civilized. The six-pack or any other item desired (Wes had ordered about a case of guava juice) was delivered immediately and set up in one's refrigerator.

So I left the lobby and took a quick detour back to our room to leave Wesley's package and my new orchid lei to cool themselves in the elegant privacy of our room refrigerator. The Four Heavens, where even the snack food reclines in luxury.

It was ten minutes past three by the time I made my way back to the Four Heavens Sports Club and Spa. The atmosphere inside was—no big shock—state-of-the-art serene, but luckily, my own heebie-jeebies about being imprisoned in all that well-maintained serenity had disappeared completely since the morning.

I waited at the reception desk, but the woman who works at that counter was nowhere to be seen. I looked around and noticed a few magazines. I checked out the clock. My foot tapped. I thought for a moment about Cake, my Hawaiian Prince Charming. About how hot he looked on the beach the night before. About how romantic it was to receive flowers from a guy. About how I don't take the wild path in life enough, and maybe I should do it more often. I checked the clock again.

It is hard for me to wait. Very hard. I need to have something to do. In the serene dimness, I had a new thought. Where were all the Nichols girls right now? Were they having manicures or sugar scrubs or what? The master appointment book was sitting, closed, upon the reception desk. It couldn't really hurt for me to simply look up the appointment times and discover for myself where everyone was currently at, could it? After all, I had come here to talk to Wesley, and if ever a receptionist finally appeared at the desk, I would just have to bother her to look up this information anyway.

I pulled the green leather-bound book toward me and

then, looking back up one more time and peeking around—no one was here, no one was coming—flipped the book open.

Under three o'clock, I saw the following listing:

Ladies' Treatments:

✓ Jet Lag Rejuvenating Massage . . . D. Nichols . . . . . Room 2 . . . . Staff: David

  Reiki Therapy . . . . H. Nichols . . . . . Room 5 . . . . Staff: Liki

✓ Shiatsu Therapy . . . . M. Nichols . . . . Room 8 . . . . Staff: Haulili

✓ Coca-Cola Wrap . . . . D.A. Norris . . . . Room 3 . . . . Staff: Pualani

  Macadamia Nut Paka Facial . . . . . . M. Bean . . . . Room 12 . . . Staff: Nella

✓ Spirulina Body Mask . . . . G. Nichols . . . . . Room 1 . . . . Staff: Tod

✓ Ayurvedic Foot Treatment . . . . A. Nichols . . . . . Room 10 . . . Staff: ~~Cynthia~~ *Mimi*

  Chakra Healing Stone . . . . L. Mooney . . . . . Room 4 . . . . Staff: Mimi

There was no check mark next to Holly's name. Where was she? And Liz hadn't shown up either. She wasn't back from the hospital yet, I supposed. Or perhaps she'd gone straight to her room, skipping the rest of her spa appointments.

I looked down the list and felt a sudden pang to see no check mark next to my own name. I had missed my Macadamia Nut Paka Facial? Aw. How cool did that sound? But now was definitely not the time. When I get to working on a problem, I find it hard to slow down. And, truth to tell, I would rather make headway on solving a problem than take time off to get nuts rubbed into my pores.

And this problem I was trying to solve just kept getting tougher. I noticed that Keniki's sister, Cynthia Hicks, had originally been assigned to give an exotic foot treatment to Azalea. But of course Cynthia was home and wasn't coming to work today. Her name had been crossed off and replaced with Mimi's name, which was written in in pencil. Seemed to me the spa management was still playing musical chairs with the staff to keep all their appointments covered.

Since some time had gone by, and still no receptionist had shown up to reprimand me for snooping, I turned the page. The list of men's appointments under three o'clock contained fewer names. But before I could read even one, I heard the sound of my privacy evaporating.

"Thank goodness you're here," said the woman, a neat beauty with clear skin and hazel eyes. "Our receptionist is filling in as a facialist. Four of our aestheticians are gone. They just called me in on my day off! This is an impossible day to provide serenity to our guests, but we must try."

I turned.

"You like men?" she asked me briskly.

I blinked. "Of course."

"Good. Very good. We have Mr. Westcott patiently waiting in treatment room thirteen."

Lucky Wes.

"You go change immediately. The staff room is in the back down this hall. And you know Lomi Lomi, correct?"

She thought I was a substitute masseuse. What damn fun. I nodded. Heck, the receptionist had just told me all about Lomi Lomi, hadn't she? Elbows and forearms.

"Fine. The service told me your name but I've forgotten it. Barbie, is it?"

Barbie? Good grief. I just smiled, trying to look tranquil.

"I'm Paloma. Nice to meet you. Okay, scoot. Get into the sarong. You'll find one hanging in the closet in the staff lounge. And hurry. Mr. Westcott has been in his Hibiscus Herbal Wrap for seven minutes already, and I'm afraid the poor man may be beginning to shrivel."

I stifled a smile. Indeed.

"And I still haven't anyone to tend to room six and room seven. Not all our girls are comfortable working on men. I don't know why. They are always perfectly respectful here at the Four Heavens. We have simply never had an incident of any kind."

I hurried along the corridor to the staff room and found the proper Four Heavens sarong, the one with the pale pink and yellow hibiscus print that I'd seen all their spa staff wearing. I stripped out of my shorts and T-shirt and slipped the sarong over my head, figuring out how to tie it behind my neck. I looked in the mirror.

There was simply no way to wear a bra with one of these backless sarongs with halter-type ties. Off mine came, and I put my clothes into a spare locker. Wasn't Wesley just going to die laughing? There he was, shriveling up in some herbal wrap, and here I was about to waltz in. I hoped he'd have his eyes closed, the better for me to sneak in, serenely of course, and surprise the heck out of him.

I twisted my hair and pulled it neatly back, fixing the end with a flower from a fresh arrangement on the table. Good. Done. I left the staff room and spotted myself in one of the dozens of full-length mirrors in the spa, pleased at how even an L.A. girl could blend into the spirit of aloha when dressed appropriately. I turned and checked myself out. The thin sarong fabric seemed to cling in all the right places. Island women can teach us all a lesson.

Only one problem. I forgot Wesley's room number.

Quickly I skipped out to the reception area, but

Paloma was by then nowhere to be found. Never mind. I went back to my trusty appointment log and opened the green leather volume to the appropriate time and turned the page to look at the men's appointment list.

There were three names, all with Xs marking they had arrived. W. Westcott was in room 13—right! now I remembered—but wait. There was also another name that caught my eye. In treatment room 6, scheduled for a massage, was Ekeka. Cake? Oh, my. And in room 7, a Mr. M. Smith was also waiting for a treatment.

I was suddenly overcome with impish spirit. Standing there, in that resort-issue sexy sarong, to all the world nothing more than a temporary resort spa staffer, I felt it wouldn't be polite if I didn't go into room 6 and thank Mr. Cake for his flowery gift, that lovely string of orchids that was at that minute reviving itself in my hotel fridge.

I padded down the hallway in my flip-flops and found the door to room 6 unlocked. Heh.

I entered the treatment room to the sound of a flute duet piping lightly in the background. Several candles flickered softly, filling the small room with the scent of sandalwood.

"Ah," said Cake from the treatment table, responding to the slight whoosh as the door closed behind me, and the expectation of a delayed masseuse. "You're here? Lovely." He lay there completely relaxed, his eyes covered with slices of cucumber.

Still unseen, I walked up to the high treatment table. He was covered in only a large white sheet, and if all massage treatments were created equal, he had no clothes on at all underneath. No shorts. No nothing. It was a most erotic thought. I remembered Cake's tanned and well-muscled chest from the night before. My eyes had by this time adjusted to the dancing candlelight, and I confess, they wandered to check his entire, um, form.

"Sorry for the delay, sir," I said, acting the part a little longer, wondering if my voice would be easily recognized. Would he suddenly swipe off those cucumber slices and check out who was actually here with him?

"No trouble," he said lazily. "I've been having the best fantasy, just lying here dreaming."

"Of a young woman?" I asked, moving right up to the table, my body brushing up against one of his arms.

"How did you know?" he asked, his voice dusky and low.

"I had . . ." Oh, man. I couldn't stop myself. I was only barely able to resist a giggle. ". . . hoped." And before he could express any surprise at the forward nature of the conversation, I pushed a small stool up next to the table. With a quick gymnastic hop, I was on the table too.

That did it, of course. No matter how long you study the ten-page list of exotic treatments provided by the best luxury spa on the planet, you won't find one that includes the friendly aesthetician straddling you on the table. Not at the Four Heavens, anyway.

I had to hand it to Cake. He wasn't an easy guy to shock.

In an instant his eyes were open and he was laughing. "Can this be?" he asked, laughing even louder. "Madeline?"

"You like?" I asked, gesturing to the sarong.

"What the hell happened? No, don't tell me. You couldn't pay your room charge and they put you to work."

I was overwhelmed with my own craziness. What was in this island air? I couldn't stop laughing.

Cake pulled me down gently until my face was inches from his. "It's like my fantasy has come true."

"Lucky you." I couldn't help myself. He was such a good sport about it all. And so completely handsome, his thick long hair down around his shoulders, his dark eyes now on me. He smelled clean, and there was the scent of herbs and musk there too. I slowly lowered my face closer until my lips were not more than a quarter of an inch above his.

"What are you up to? Some new kind of resistance therapy?" he asked, breathing up at me. "Like spa . . . torture?"

I stretched myself slowly over the sheet across his body. From my on-top position, I had reassuring evidence of how exciting my improvised "treatment" actually was. "Are you comfortable, sir?" My lips were still only a fraction from his.

"Call me Cake," he said, his voice very low.

"Ah," I said, mimicking my best version of a concerned masseuse, "I think I feel a little tension and, um, stiffness . . . Cake."

"I'm sure you do," he said, slowly reaching his hands up to my hair, pulling me down just that quarter inch until our lips touched. It was a long, soft, most un-spa-like kiss.

"This treatment promotes relaxation," I whispered, pulling back just a bit.

"Says you," Cake said, shifting me a little, brushing his hands all the way down my back and up again, and pulling my hair out of its neat pins.

I kissed him again. And again. Each time very slowly

and very gently. As a good spa client, he let me take the lead and simply waited for the next kiss and the next. His lips were surprisingly soft, and they retained a hint of a smile. He tasted like a blend of smoke and herbs.

"Do you smoke?" I asked.

Cake reached up for the ties of the sarong. I knew I had to stop this impromptu spa treatment soon, or we would be at the point of asking personal questions about contraception. I smiled, wondering how it would feel to have a vacation fling, if I was free enough to allow the flirtation to go too far.

He must have been reading my thoughts. "Wouldn't it be fun?" he asked. "Wouldn't we have a memory?"

And how often does a young woman get to Hawaii? How often does she stumble across a man who sends her a flower necklace made out of seven hundred orchid petals? How many times would she have the chance to get impressively naughty on top of a massage table? It appealed to all my free-spirit desires.

Cake kissed me one more time, patiently offering one last persuasion.

But I never got a chance to decide how truly naughty I could be. There came a soft tap on the door to the treatment room. Then another.

"You locked it," Cake asked. "Right?"

The knob began to turn.

"Um." The door opened silently. Oops. "No."

"Barbie!" Paloma's voice rang out, more than shocked. "Barbie, *no*!"

Busted. Busted big-time. And I was pretty sure the pitch of Paloma's voice was at this point a few million decibels shriller than the staff handbook must recommend for optimum serenity.

"Keep calm thoughts, Paloma," I suggested.

Paloma caught herself, lowered her voice, but continued, just as exasperated as before. "We don't do this sort of massage here at the Four Heavens, Barbie! *Get down off our guest at once!*"

Nui Lumi Kuke
(Great Kitchen)

*T*he magic incantation that saved my butt from getting shipped straight to some aesthetician penal colony for spa-technicians of fallen virtue, or worse, enduring the outrage of a totally flipped-out supervisor was a word more powerful than abracadabra or hocus-pocus. It was that glorious five-letter word: *guest*. After only a few more *"No, Barbie! No!"*s, I quickly and loudly asserted that I was in fact really a (cue heavenly choir) *guest* of the Four Heavens. As soon as spa dominatrix Paloma realized she was not dealing with a freelancing employee, but instead, a couple of consensual, if overly hormonal, spa patrons, she calmed right down. After all, the guest is *always* to be indulged at the Four Heavens. Isn't that nice?

An hour after the spa fiasco, I filled Wesley in and tried not to leave out too many juicy details so he could get the chuckle. "Cake, of course, just kept smiling. I think he wanted to be banned from the spa for life."

Wes thought that one over. "Because of the mythic quality it would add to his romantic reputation on the island?"

Wes understood the competitive male thing. "You are a student of human nature, Mr. Westcott."

"Just figures," Wes said modestly. "That guy is pretty full of himself."

"I don't think so," I said, on the defensive.

"Here we go . . ." Wes gave me an affectionate look that I instantly detested. It was always this way. Wes always disapproved of the men to whom I was most attracted, although he never came right out and said so. The fact that his opinion so often turned out to be justified only made it worse. And it still did not make me particularly eager to follow his advice the next time. That I would keep ignoring his good sense was what drove him insane, which in turn was what I loved.

I decided to further goad him. "Cake said—"

"Cake. That name." Wes shuddered. "Isn't that ridiculous?"

I smiled and shook my head. "You ask that question of a woman who is known as 'Mad'?"

"Yes. I do," Wes said, refusing to be shut down. At present, he and I were in the kitchen of the Four Heavens' Presidential Bungalow, pulling out bowls and surveying the stockpots. "Mad is simply short for Maddie, which in turn, is short for Madeline. Perfectly proper name derivation. Cake, however, is the self-conscious nickname of a preening, ego-inflated, shifty, untrustworthy—"

". . . sweetie?" I asked.

"Maddie. This 'Cake' of yours just tried his hardest to get you in trouble. Even after the spa requested you both leave. He *asked* to be reprimanded."

I laughed. There I was, no way innocent in this scarlet affair, having pretended to be a spa pro and messing around in a treatment room with an incredibly sexy man I barely knew, but Wes only saw fit to blame the other guy. Never my fault, in his eyes. I took back all my grouchiness. I loved Wes.

"You laugh," he continued, returning my smile, "but think about it. You are a sweet, innocent girl, and he's a scoundrel. A story like this will make him an island sex legend." Wes shuddered again. "Cake."

"It's short for Ekeka," I reminded him. "A noble Hawaiian name. You know, deep respect for island culture. You have to admire that."

Wes shook his head at me but kept smiling. "I'm thankful, at least, the spa didn't decide to ban *all of your friends* for life. Imagine that."

"No more lotus wraps for my darling Wes!"

"That would be a true disaster."

Paloma had calmed down immediately once she realized I had nothing to do with the temporary agency she had called. Well, that, and once she saw the incredibly huge tip Cake handed her. In cash. But she did ask Cake and me to please take our private relationship somewhere private.

The thing was, every wild, spontaneous moment has a shelf life—the wilder, the shorter—and by the time Cake counted out two hundred dollars for her trouble, our wild moment had already expired.

We said good-bye, and then I got back to business. I had no time, really, for strange interludes with handsome strangers. I found Wes and told him about the memorial luau for Keniki's boyfriend, Kelly. And the two of us decided we needed to bring something to the luau that was our own and home-cooked. It was our way.

Wesley and I headed for the resort's premier restaurant, Ben A's, and introduced ourselves to the chef, Ben Anderson. It was standard procedure among us in the culinary biz, and we talked about whose new restaurants were taking off on the islands and in L.A., and with which chefs we had worked in common and other fun industry gossip.

"We are going to need some cooking space," Wes

said, looking around. But the kitchen at Ben A's was too crowded and busy to allow a couple of mainland cooks like us enough room in which to work.

However, Ben and his kitchen staff knew Keniki Hicks. Most had met her fiancé, and they all wanted to help out. In addition, there is a professional courtesy among the culinary community, and Ben, like all successful chefs, was a problem solver. A few minutes of conversation with the front desk was all it took for Chef Ben Anderson to clear our path, and soon we were invited to pick up the key card to the hotel's Presidential Bungalow.

Wesley and I just blinked when we saw it. And then melted. The Presidential Bungalow was an incredible residence, the ultimate Four Heavens extravagance, the most heart-stoppingly luxurious accommodations available at a super-top-end resort. And the front desk had just tossed us the key, gratis.

The five-bedroom mansion, complete with its own dipping pool, normally rents out for $5,000 per night, but as our luck had it, a rock-and-roll heartbreaker checked out early in the A.M., and a Silicon Valley half-a-billionaire had delayed his arrival until tomorrow, leaving the luxury dwelling free for just this evening.

The Presidential Bungalow was really a mini-mansion set apart from the rest of the guest rooms and suites. In addition to five enormous bedrooms, it had seven bathrooms, and a fully stocked library of over two thousand books. When we were looking around earlier, I had picked up several pristine volumes in awe.

"Looks like this is the only book anyone has actually read, though," said Wes, replacing *The Da Vinci Code* on a shelf.

Figured.

The Presidential Bungalow offered a stocked wine cellar, a koi pond, and a three-thousand-square-foot lanai. But the most desirable features to us by far were the two fully equipped gourmet kitchens, one indoors and one located out on the lanai. We were like Paris Hilton in a Prada factory-outlet store, Wesley and I, and we eagerly accepted the hotel's offer to use these kitchens as we wished.

"If we had the time," Wes mused, "I would love to make the honey garlic ribs recipe I got from those two fabulous guys I met in the bar. Those professional wrestlers. What were they called, again?"

"The Hawaiian Gods of Destruction," I reminded him.

"Ah, yes!"

"The H-Gods, for short." I shook my head at him, amused as always.

Wes liked to collect authentic local recipes wherever we traveled. He met folks. He talked food. He often wangled invitations to sample great regional dishes by proud home-cooks the world wide. These wrestlers, however, the Hawaiian Gods of Destruction, were an unusual source for culinary inspiration, even for Wesley.

"Exactly. Good fellows. Tiki and Bruiser." Wes had run into them at the resort bar late last night, after our luau. "You have got to meet them, Maddie. They have an authentic island . . ."

I looked up from the drawerful of brand-new spatulas I'd been rooting around in, in my survey of the kitchen's batterie de cuisine.

". . . charm," he finished.

"And you make fun of my new friend," I said. "So this Tiki and Bruiser can cook?"

"Oh yes. They are Food Channel junkies, apparently. Anyway, we got to trading recipes. You know how one thing leads to another . . ."

I nodded.

". . . and I thought these boys' ribs might be perfect for our gathering tonight. Unfortunately, the recipe calls for preboiling the ribs for three hours."

"It's not to be," I agreed. "If we had that much time, I would have loved to try preparing authentic laulau."

"The dish with the taro leaves?"

I nodded. Taro is the staple of the Hawaiian diet and gave the name laulau (which means "taro tops") to the traditional Hawaiian feast. "It sounds fabulous. You bake the taro leaves with coconut cream and octopus."

"But according to tradition, the leaf-wrapped bundles of laulau must bake and steam for six hours, right?" Wes asked.

"Right. And today we need something quick."

Wesley looked around the kitchen, pulling a large black platter from one of the cupboards. "Ben is great. I don't know how he got us into this bungalow."

I nodded. The executive chef at the Four Heavens on the Big Island carried a lot of weight.

Wes pulled out a second large black platter. "He said every one of the kitchen staff knows Keniki. The ones who have the night off tonight are going to the luau near Hilo. So whatever ingredients we need, they will provide."

"Very generous." I walked over and gave Wes a hug. "Let's make something special, Wes. It will do me a lot of good if I can cook something really magical for Keniki."

"So let's create a new recipe for her."

"That's perfect. I want this dish to remind her of the sweet things in life."

"Should we devise some sort of dessert? Using something . . . let's see, what's local? Coffee? Or pineapple?"

"How about an appetizer? Something to pass around and share when we arrive."

"Good thought."

"Hey," I said, looking up at Wes, inspired as I always was by getting together with my best friend over food talk, "I've got an idea. Let's use raw sugarcane."

"Sugarcane." Wes started a shopping list on his Palm Pilot.

"It's got that stiff texture, right? Maybe we can carve the cane?"

"Wow." Wes nodded, happily in thought. "I love that. But there is a time factor . . ."

"Okay, we carve the sugarcane into something fairly simple"—I made a few chopping gestures in the air—"like lollipop sticks."

"You go, Maddie."

Wes and I brainstormed for five more minutes and came up with an outrageously cool plan. We phoned over to the resort kitchen, and soon, thanks to Chef Ben, all the ingredients we asked for, even a pile of sugarcane stalks, came over on a motor cart, fresh and ready for us to prepare. A young man helped unload the items and brought them through the bungalow and out to the lanai kitchen where we had set up. I mean, if you could cook anywhere in the world, wouldn't you pick an outdoor patio right on the sand by the blue Pacific Ocean?

"Heck, Wes." I picked up a handful of fresh green stalks about two inches in diameter. "They even had the cane."

"Actually," the guy said, bringing the last box of provisions out to us, "I just stopped in our field out there and cut some down for you. If you need more, just let me know."

"Thanks."

"And," he said, laying down a silver tray holding two chilled mai tais in icy glasses, "compliments of the chef."

Heaven, I suspect, is most likely alcohol free, so I now had to figure we had one-upped even Paradise.

Wesley handed the young guy a large tip. Not, I noted, quite as glaringly large as the tip Cake handed over to Paloma, but sufficiently generous as to reward the fellow for hacking around in the cane fields for us.

"Let's do it," Wes said, smiling at me, clinking glasses.

I began to strip the individual sugarcane stalks of their outer leaves. Meanwhile, Wes walked over to the bungalow's impressive sound system and popped in a CD. Ukulele music. Fabulous uke music. I looked up, and Wes held up the CD case: *Tropical Swing*. Bill Tapia was the legendary, barely remembered ukulele jazz genius that had suddenly, brilliantly, been rediscovered and had improbably just recorded his first ever CD. At age ninety-six. I smiled. Perfect.

Wes and I carefully selected the right knives from a pretty impressive collection and, still sipping our drinks, got straight to work. Other tourists could lie about in the sun if they wished, or splash in the waves, but the two of us had our own kind of superb relaxation. Ocean view. Fabulous kitchen. "My Little Grass Shack (in Kealakekua, Hawaii)" on the CD player. And a brand-new recipe about to be born.

We began by trimming the leaves from the stalks and then slicing through the thick cane, carefully whittling each one down to a pile of four-inch-long sticks, one-quarter inch by one-quarter inch thick, making thin skewers out of the hard and fibrous sweet raw cane. We needed two hundred skewers, quite a lot of work, but then we couldn't resist sampling our booty, relishing the odd texture, noting how juicy the freshly cut cane was, and remarking on the tangy flavor that colored the pure sweetness.

"This could become addictive," I said, popping a second slender sliver of cane into my mouth and biting down.

For all his artistic flare, Wes was a kitchen workhorse. He carved up the cane so neatly and efficiently we were almost two-thirds through the pile before I began to tire. He hadn't even broken a sweat. While we worked, I told him about Keniki and her sister, Cynthia. I told him about Liz Mooney and Marigold. I told him about the HBA and their amazing plan to save Hawaii. I told him about Claudia Modlin and Earl Maffini. And I told him that our entire trip was being comped by some mysterious person who was *not* my old pal Jennifer Sizemore. He didn't say a word, just heard me out.

"You start the chicken," he offered, "I'll finish the carving."

Exactly. When in doubt, cook.

Our idea was to produce lemongrass chicken on sugarcane. I started with about eight pounds of chicken, which Ben's chefs had thoughtfully sent to us freshly ground up in the resort kitchen. It was much easier to prepare a large batch of food when one had the benefit of professional kitchen equipment. And I smiled when I saw the added gift Ben had sent out to us from the restaurant. I said a prayer of thanks for industrial-size Cuisinarts, and minced several small red onions and half a dozen peeled carrots. Then, by hand, I finely chopped two large bunches of lemongrass, about fifty stalks in all, along with a bunch of cilantro and a bunch of basil. The perfume of the herbs was intoxicating, bewitching. All the vegetables must have just been picked from the resort's own kitchen garden, because every chef knows that the freshness of one's ingredients makes all the difference in the glory of the final dish, and every great restaurant has access to the freshest produce.

Into the large mixing bowl, I added additional ingredients. I diced up half a dozen small jalapeño peppers, humming along to the divine musical combination of the steel guitar, double bass, and ukulele. From the excellent sound system, Bill Tapia strummed and sang "Hapa Haole Hula Girl," which of course made me think of Keniki once again.

I sighed, and Wes looked up. "Life," I explained. "Death."

He nodded, thoughtful, and added, "Food."

"Food." I looked at the harvest of ingredients on the vast outdoor counter and perked up.

Wesley was still hard at work. "I'm almost done with these freaking sugarcane sticks, you evil genius," he said, laying his knife down into a small puddle of sweet cane juice. "I'll make the sauce next."

While he moved over to the gas range, I crushed about a dozen cloves of garlic and added them to my bowl, stirring them together with all the other ingredients. I love, above all else, spicy flavors mixed in subtle relationship with sweet. It's all about balance. But in this creation, our new recipe for Keniki, more flavors were called for. I grated fresh ginger root until I had about four tablespoons, and then counted out half a dozen plump limes and began juicing them. The idea was to combine the tart and the sweet, the savory and the hot, together into the mild ground chicken base, and then finish the appetizer with the candy-treat zing of fresh sugarcane, until the entire concoction blew everyone's taste buds to smithereens. At least that was the goal.

As we worked, I asked Wes what he thought had been going on with Kelly Imo and his sudden death.

"What worries me," said Wes, a man who virtually never worries, "is the way in which Kelly died."

"In the ocean," I agreed. "I know. It doesn't make sense that a healthy young man could have such an accident."

"What," Wes asked gingerly, "if Holly hit him over the head so hard that she . . ."

"She what?" I asked, suddenly startled. A flood of scenes flashed quickly before me. Holly bashing Kelly with the lamp. The hotel maids removing his dead, lifeless body and cleaning up. Jasper Berger tossing Kelly's lifeless body into the sea in the dark of night. It was simply impossible to believe. "You think Holly may have accidentally killed him?"

"Not exactly."

"Wes. Be serious. She couldn't have hit him that hard. And what happened to his body? I know the Four Heavens has a reputation for customer service, but disposing of bodies has to be beyond even them."

"I'm not saying she killed him," he said, shocked at my suggestion. "But what if she hit him so hard he got a concussion. Maybe he was working out by the cliffs later that night and just got woozy for a moment. Maybe he lost his equilibrium."

I felt a little sick. What if Wes were right? "Don't tell your theory to Holly," I said quickly. "Let's wait to see what the coroner says."

It seemed even more important now that we get answers to what happened to Kelly Imo. Whatever strange business he had been mixed up with, whatever sent him to Holly's hotel room yesterday, whatever other troubles he had accumulated in his life, we needed to find out fast. That's the direction in which I was certain we should be looking for answers.

For the time being, though, I was grateful to have the cooking project to distract me. I cracked a dozen eggs—they would help the mixture bind together—before I added the last ingredients, some fish sauce and plenty of salt and pepper. Then it was just a matter of mixing the ground chicken into all the minced and chopped herbs and juice with my bare hands. This sort of finger mixing can be extremely therapeutic.

As I kneaded the lemongrass and spices into the ground chicken, Wes finished stirring up his impromptu sweet chile dipping sauce. He planned to transport it to the luau in a large ceramic bowl, and I watched as he put the covered bowl into the refrigerator. Then he came over to help me begin our huge construction project.

"Okay, then," I said, looking up at the prepared ingredients. "Some assembly required."

Wes waited for me to take the lead. With the tip of a teaspoon against my palm, I quickly rolled about one ounce of the chicken-lemongrass mixture into a ball, then molded that portion onto the top of a sugarcane stick, lollipop-style. It only took a second or two. Then I made another. Wes joined in. It was, of course, a race. Wesley Westcott, born competitor. Every culinary challenge an Olympic event.

We each had a large black platter beside us, and soon the mountain of four-inch-long sugarcane sticks became flatter and flatter as our neat rows of chicken appetizers materialized and grew, herringbone-patterned, around the rim of the large platters.

I looked up, certain I had finished ahead of Wes, only to discover him checking his watch, his platter completely full. How does he do that?

"It's almost five-thirty," he said, covering the trays with plastic wrap from a restaurant-size roll.

"We're great," I said. "Let's just toss these trays into the refrigerator and we'll pick them up on our way to the heliport." Our plan was to fry them fresh at the luau. We had borrowed an enormous wok from the hotel kitchen and had procured a huge jug of peanut oil for that purpose.

"Right. The thing is, I need to find Holly," Wes said. "Rather quickly."

"Yeah," I said, "where is our girl?" I picked up a cordless phone from the outdoor kitchen counter and dialed her room. No answer. I dialed each of her sisters' rooms, one after another. Again, nothing but automated offers to leave voice mail, which I ignored. I tried our room even, but of course no one was home. I called over to the spa, but a rather frosty-sounding Paloma said Holly had never returned to the spa that entire afternoon. And the rest of our gang, like Wes, had left long ago.

"Well," I said, getting off the phone, "they could all be in the bar, picking up Hawaiian wrestlers."

He smiled.

"Or maybe out by the pool," I said. "Or snorkeling. Or at the beach. Or in one of the cafés."

"I think I may need to write off my little gift for Holly."

"What? Your gift?"

He nodded. "It's time sensitive."

"What did you get her?"

"I made a reservation. This was months ago, back when we were home. I was meaning to tell her about it, thinking I'd have half a second with her alone, but we've been apart all day long. It was going to be my bridal shower gift."

"What was?"

"I made a reservation for Holly to go swimming with the dolphins over at the Grand Waikoloa. The reservation, however, is for six o'clock. Tonight. And she's not gonna make it, is she?"

"Oh, Wes. That sucks."

"Mad, it is the most amazing experience. You simply cannot imagine it. You remember, I swam with wild dolphins in the Red Sea and I'll never forget it."

That stopped my train of thought. "You swam with dolphins in the Red freaking Sea? I never heard about that."

"When I took that trip to Egypt. Anyway, I wanted our Holly to have a transcendental spiritual encounter while she was here this weekend. That's what I wanted to give to her before she got married. Oh, well."

"Can you reschedule?" I asked.

"No. These dolphin encounter sessions are booked up months in advance, and it's too late to—"

"Wait!" I had the solution. "Why don't *you* go? You can go and take that spot."

"No," he said, looking up at me, finding his own solution by the look of him. "*You* go."

"What?"

"Yes, Mad. You go. It will be great. I've already swum with dolphins. In the wild."

In other words, swimming around in a tank with a couple of tame hotel dolphins wouldn't extend Wesley's list of world adventures. But it would mine.

"But I have so much on my mind, Wes. So much more to figure out."

"You'd be doing me a favor," Wes said, knowing how to get my attention. "Please."

"You know what? I think I will," I said, feeling that giddy, I'm-a-free-spirit zing.

"This is perfect," Wes said, happy again. "The Grand Waikoloa is just down the beach. Five minutes to get there in the car. You better get going."

"Okay!" I was in Hawaii and I was about to swim with dolphins. What could possibly be cooler?

"Oh, but wait." He looked annoyed. "They may have a cancellation policy and a waiting list. If you tell them you have come in Holly's place, they may tell you to leave and take the first person that's waiting on standby. Shoot."

"It's okay," I said, as agreeable as a large mai tai and a happy bout of cooking can make a girl. "I'll be Holly Nichols for an hour and go swim with some nice old dolphins."

Hana me a Nai'a
(Affair with a Dolphin)

Wes waved good-bye. He was perched on a chaise longue, his feet up, out on the lanai of the Presidential Bungalow. He was speaking quickly into the cordless phone as I left, busy calling all over the place, leaving voice messages for our gang. He was spreading the word that they all had a free night on the island, dinner wherever and whenever they chose, and of course they were welcome to join us at Kelly Imo's memorial luau if they wished. We would all meet up at midnight at a little club called Breeze back in Kona, where we intended to pick up the party pace once again. We'd toast our bride-to-be and shower her with bachelorette party gifts. That was the plan.

Meanwhile, I ducked out of the Presidential Bungalow and dashed over to our room, which suddenly appeared much smaller than it had. Slumming around in that five-thousand-bucks-a-night palace down the beach had already turned my head. Ah, well. A small slice of the fine life was still sweet. I quickly changed into a yellow bikini, a tiny thing I'd been dieting for a month to make "work," and then covered it up again with a pair of hip-hugging blue board shorts and a cropped tee. What the outfit lacked in subtlety, it made up for in beach chic, as

I was once again all about expressing my newly unveiled wild inner child.

Okay. Keys. Altoids. I looked about the room one last time. My cell phone winked at me from the corner of the desk where I'd left it perched in its charger. A message had come in while I'd been out all day. Maybe Holly? I dialed the message number and heard Chuck Honnett's voice. Chuck. Oh, yes. The reality show that I was about to return to tomorrow—my real life—had not simply vanished. Damn.

But I was being unkind. Harsh. Honnett was not calling to guilt-trip me for running off and kissing some almost naked Hawaiian stranger. Naturally, he didn't know anything about Cake. But my own conscience was making my stomach feel a little twisted, just thinking about Honnett and Cake at the same time. Some wild child I turned out to be. I breathed in and out, trying to think calm thoughts, and listened to the message playing back as Honnett made apologies for bothering me on my weekend away. Like he had any reason to feel apologetic this particular weekend. Oh, man. But then he started saying he'd found the information I'd asked him for, how he'd gathered some stuff on his end about Holly's maybe-husband, Marvin Dubinsky.

"Mad, I know you're on your holiday, but I wanted to get this out to you, in case it makes a difference. I wouldn't have troubled you, but when you hear what I found out, you may want to know the details as soon as possible."

What was this? So I sat on the edge of my bed, listening to Honnett, his voice all Texas twang but yes-officer serious as he gave his report.

"Dubinsky is a pretty successful fellow. You hadn't told me that part. He owns a couple of decent-size companies that are traded over the counter, which is broker-speak for damned important. You know what that means? He's loaded. All the companies have something to do with biogenetics, improving plant genetics, stuff like that. That's the best I can tell you now. Here's the thing. There is no mention of a wife in any of the biographies filed with his businesses, but we did turn up a valid marriage license from Nevada. He married Hollyhock Miranda Nichols. We're still checking on annulment or divorce records, but nothing has turned up yet. So that's that. I also think you should hear about where Dubinsky is currently located."

I hooked the small cell phone between my shoulder and ear and looked around the room for anything I'd need when I swam with the dolphins. I grabbed my large canvas beach bag and tucked in a tube of sunscreen, a darling mini-shampoo from the bathroom, and a wide-tooth hairbrush for after.

"Here's the thing," Honnett's voice continued. "Dubinsky moved over there a few years ago. To Hawaii."

I dropped the mini-conditioner.

"Odd, ain't it?" the message continued. "That's where he's headquartered now, as a matter of fact. Has a company called BotaniTech." He spelled it out. "Out there on the island of Hawaii, which as best I can understand it must be the same damned island you are on right now. Don't that beat all? Say, you call me if you need anything else."

Honnett was good. I was bad. I got it. But there was suddenly much more to think about than that.

Marvin Dubinsky on the Big Island. Hadn't I called that one? And of course Holly had mentioned to me that Marvin had been some sort of plant genius. So it seemed extraordinarily coincidental that we had become mixed up with another plant expert, Kelly Imo. Not to mention Claudia and the rest of the Bamboo herd. How did they all connect? But I couldn't take the time to process it all right now. I looked at my watch and upped my pace. I had a date with a dolphin.

I flip-flopped down the sidewalk on the way to my parking space, knocking at each Nichols sister's door absentmindedly, thinking mostly now of Honnett's bombshell of a message. Liz Mooney and the Nichols gals were just not home, so I scrambled into the rented convertible and hit the road. What was Marvin Dubinsky doing, anyway, winding up so damned close to us here on this island? How had all roads led back to Holly?

At the Grand Waikoloa Village, I let the valet park my Mustang and literally ran down to the dolphin enclosure, located out near one of the vast manmade lagoons all the way around at the back of the resort. The architectural style of this hotel was unlike the subdued opulence and authentic low bungalows of the Four Heavens. Here, luxury was of the megasize man-made variety, from huge man-made waterfalls to huge man-made trams to huge man-made snorkel bays.

I arrived at the Dolphin Excitement office a little breathless and gave the name on the reservation: "Holly Nichols."

"Hey there, Holly." Another waiting dolphin-besotted adventurer, a sunburned young man, saluted me with two fingers to his forehead. "I'm Gabriel Swan. From San Francisco. Nice to meet you." His swim trunks were covered in a pattern of green and orange angelfish. "That's kind of a private joke," he said, noticing my gaze. "Are you an angel person?"

"A what?"

"Angels. They are everywhere." He winked at me. "'Course you know that."

The athletic young woman who was leading our group encounter with the dolphins looked up from her clipboard. "There will be three of you with us this afternoon. We are awaiting the arrival of just one more guest." In the meantime, she had us sign a few forms, which held the dolphin group free from liability no matter what happened to us in their lagoon. I signed merrily away. Holly Nichols. Holly Nichols. Holly Nichols. If this were the extent of my bad-girl behavior, I could hardly balk at a little forgery!

"You know someone named Denise?" Gabriel asked me, looking startled.

"I beg your pardon?"

"Denise? That name mean something to you, Holly?"

I almost giggled. Holly. "Well, I don't think so. Should it?"

"I should say so," he told me solemnly. "I think there is someone named Denise who needs your help very badly."

I looked up at him again. "Why do you say that?"

"It's coming through loud and clear. From the other plane."

"It is? How do you . . . ?"

"Just something your fairy told me," Gabriel said, his demeanor perfectly sane despite the conversation.

"My fairy."

"We've all got them, you know. Buzzing around, sitting on our shoulders. I have always been sensitive to fairies. I can see them. That's my gift." His deep red face broke into a bashful smile, large overbite revealed by rather chapped lips.

I shaded my eyes and asked straight out, "You mean you see fairies flying around me?"

"Oh, of course I do. That one there"—he pointed to an area near my left breast—"is very worried, though. She's the one who told me about Denise."

I swear, I know absolutely no one named Denise. I thought about it a bit harder. No. No Denises whatsoever. It's not that I believe in any of this stuff about fairies and angels and what-all. Of course I don't. But I like to keep an open mind. What can that hurt? The Big Island is the New Age Mecca, drawing believers in crystals, angels, and dolphins by the hundred. I like to give every spiritual group respect, whatever strange thing they believe, just for showing the optimism to believe in *anything* in our weary world.

"Oh, hey!" said our dolphin guide, looking up. Our guide was a very fit young woman in her early twenties with long blond hair tied back in a ponytail. Her name badge said: MEG. "Here she comes now, I think." She was looking across the lawn at a lovely elderly woman who was approaching our shed at a trot.

"I'm here!" the woman called out to us. "Don't worry. I made it."

Meg checked her clipboard. "You must be Millie Reisch."

"Yes. That's right. It's me. I'm late, but that's my husband's fault. I told him to wake me from my nap at four-thirty. But did he wake me? Oy."

Millie had to be in her seventies, a woman with quite a substantial bosom trussed into a daringly low-cut one-piece swimsuit with a skirt, and she looked damned good in it. Her voice gave a hint of New York.

I glanced over at Gabriel. "Gabe, do you see Millie's angels?"

"What's that?" Millie asked, her eyes shining. "You should forgive me, darlings, but angels, schmangels. What I want to see are the dolphins." And then Millie turned to me. "Be careful, young lady. You know these dolphins have amazing powers. They can tell if a person is pregnant. Yes. They have some special perception. I mention this," she said, giving me a gentle dig in the ribs, "just in case you're trying to keep any secrets from your husband here."

"Mrs. Reisch," I said, instantly dizzy from the sheer number of misconceptions. "It's a pleasure to meet you. But I think you must be mistaken! I'm not married. In fact, I just met Gabriel here a few minutes ago. And I am not in any danger of setting off the dolphin pregnancy police."

Millie chuckled as she signed on the dotted line of the liability forms. "I'm kidding. I'm kidding. And call me Millie. Only my boyfriends call me Mrs. Reisch."

"I'm Madeline," I said, and we smiled at each other.

"I thought you were Holly," Gabriel blurted out, suddenly concerned.

"Yes. That, um, too," I said very casually, as if I hadn't just made a hysterically huge mistake my very first minute of assuming Holly's identity. Some undercover spy I would make. Right. Sheesh. "Madeline Holly Nichols. But everyone calls me Holly."

"Oh, yes?" Gabe asked. The angels must have been telling Gabe a different tale, because he looked completely unconvinced.

Millie, on the other hand, instantly launched into a story about her oldest grandson, Adam, who was an honor student at Rutgers. His girlfriend back in high school was named Madison, which was almost like Madeline. What a small world.

And then before we could get any more of Millie's

family's history, Meg told us it was time to go swimming with the dolphins, and we followed her out to the man-made dolphin pools.

With Meg, we waded knee-deep into the shallow water of the pool, while another of the Dolphin Excitement staff members opened the gate, which allowed the animals to swim out into the enclosed dolphin lagoon in which we were waiting. Three dolphins joined us, circling around in the warm water with ease.

"I'd like to introduce you," Meg said, "to Romeo and Juliet, and their grown-up son, Little Willie."

We couldn't hold back on the oohs and ahhs. It was impossible not to be amazed by the beauty of the dolphins and their power in the water as they swam swiftly around us.

Meg held a special trainer's whistle in her teeth and gave it a toot. The dolphins circled nearer, and the female named Juliet came to Meg and rolled over onto her side in the water, allowing Meg to hold Juliet's flipper and stroke her neck.

Meg kept up a constant patter, telling us everything we'd ever need to know about dolphin behavior and the wonderful care these dolphins in particular were getting. I noticed a number of hotel guests had gathered near the edge of the deck on a bridge over the lagoon, watching us and the dolphins playing in the water. We were, after all, just a few more players in this resort's never-ending mega-man-made show. I heard a child ask his mother why he couldn't swim in this lagoon right now and heard her valiantly try to explain about costs and reservation policies to a seven-year-old.

"Here's Little Willie," Meg said, standing next to me in deeper water now. "Let him roll over and you may pet him. He likes that."

I'm sure. Why should he be different from any other male? I smirked to myself and patted Little Willie.

"He's really taken with you," Meg said approvingly. "Look," she called to Millie, who was having a fine time getting to know Romeo. "Look how much Little Willie likes Holly."

It was true. Little Willie looked at me deeply with one of his glassy eyes. And although he was a large gray rubbery-skinned sea creature, I felt he was saying something to me with his long deep gaze. Gadzooks. Little Willie was tying to communicate.

Gabriel called to me from a few yards away, where he was getting to know Juliet. "Say, Holly, listen to Little Willie."

This was almost too hilarious. But then, of course, I was torn between wanting to laugh and wanting to ask Gabe to translate for me. See, this is where irony will get a girl.

"Okay, Gabriel," I said, giving in. "What is Little Willie saying?"

"Oh, only that he loves you, Holly. And he's a little worried. He thinks you are in danger."

Just then the large dolphin turned over and submerged below me, coming up gently underneath so that I was astride him and then taking off, not too fast, and giving me a ride. It was the most amazing thing ever.

"Oh, I want to do that," called Millie, looking for a way to hop onto Romeo.

"No, no," said Meg, swimming over to us. "We are not to ride the animals. I don't know what got into Little Willie. But it is not our policy to force the animals into acting like playthings. Sorry, Millie. I think Little Willie has just really taken a shine to Holly."

The crowd standing by the gate applauded when I

came by on my slippery steed. All except a band of intense Japanese tourists, men in suits, who just stared and pointed cameras.

"That's it, I'm afraid," said Meg. "The dolphins need their rest."

How had our half hour gone so swiftly by?

Little Willie swam by for one last longing look before he disappeared with his parents into the holding tank beyond the lagoon.

"That animal was in love with you at first sight," Millie said as we walked back to the little shack where we'd left our things. "Must be that bikini. I used to wear bikinis all the time. Still could, you know. I've got the goods. But I don't want to be a distraction to the lifeguards."

We both laughed.

"I felt tremendous healing energy," said Gabriel, his sunburned face aglow. "Did you feel it, Holly?"

"It was thrilling," I said. "Just being so close to such beautiful creatures, so large and so gentle."

"And that Little Willie," he went on. "He kept talking about knowing you in a former life. You had been lovers."

I stared at Gabe.

"Well, that's what he said."

"To you?" I asked him, point-blank.

"No, of course not." He looked at me as if I must be crazy. "He told your fairy and she told me."

Of course.

We all used the outdoor shower, and then I toweled off and climbed into my little T-shirt and shorts. By the time I left the Dolphin Excitement shack, a fresh photo of Little Willie and me ordered from the kiosk, the sky was already showing signs of darkening as the sun was setting somewhere offshore.

I cut behind the lagoon and took a path I suspected might be a shortcut around the resort. It was deserted, and I picked up my pace as I skirted around a stand of huge man-made jungle.

As I continued, the path arced, and I soon realized I was no longer alone but approaching the group of Japanese gentlemen I'd earlier noticed had been observing our Dolphin Excitement session from the deck. I smiled and moved to the side to let them pass.

The four men stopped and quickly surrounded me, speaking only a command or two in what I imagined must be Japanese.

"What is going on?"

Another hurried word, but I couldn't tell what the man said, and still he wouldn't move.

I thought of Little Willie's warning. But then I chided myself. All that was impossible. Here I was with the glorious sun setting against the backdrop of giant ferns, just a little off the beaten path at a freaking luxury resort. What sort of danger could there be?

I asked, "Can I help you?" I just felt uncomfortable being surrounded, was all. I supposed the men might have been in need of directions and didn't realize they were swarming me. I tried to back up and away, but it seemed another short man in a suit always moved in my way.

"Stop." The man who spoke looked very serious.

"Excuse me," I said. "I am in a hurry to meet a friend."

"Look at me," he said, his voice dull and urgent at the same time.

That's when I first realized the short man in the ugliest of the suits was actually pointing a gun at my stomach, only I hadn't noticed it before. Typical me to have to be reminded that I was being threatened.

"What is this?" I asked, almost put out. I'd just had a mystical experience with a young dolphin who claimed to be my lover in a former life. Did I really have any consciousness left to waste on four shortish thugs? I thought not. "What do you want?"

"We want your husband."

Quick-thinking time. Husband. We knew someone had been looking for Marvin Dubinsky, and I was Holly Nichols over here at the Grand Waikoloa. So it didn't take Nancy Drew to figure out that these men must be connected to all that.

"Look. Guys. I am not in contact with Marvin Dubinsky. That's the truth. I don't know where you can find him. Honestly. Now, please leave me alone."

"Oh, no. You are coming with us now. We will hold on to you until your husband must come and find you. He is a terrible man, you know. He deserves much worse to happen. He steals from us, so it is fair that we steal from him."

"No, no, no." I couldn't believe it. Was I being kidnapped in daylight from the overly landscaped grounds of a luxury resort? Tell me it wasn't happening.

"Yes, yes, yes, Mrs. Dubinsky," the guy holding the gun said. "Move." They all nudged me down the path and around the hotel and farther away from anyplace populated. Hands grabbed me so hard I knew I was going to be black and blue. We came to a small private road. Down the long drive came a car, rolling fast. A valet was bringing it around to the front. Of course he didn't slow down to gawk at our group of four men in dark business suits surrounding one outraged redheaded girl. Nothing out of the ordinary about us. Much. Did these men actually mean to kidnap me while waiting for a valet to bring around the car? I mean, really.

"Get a grip," I told the men. "There are witnesses! You'll never get away with this. Let me go."

"Nobody see nothing." Well, eloquence was not one of their virtues.

"What's to stop me from screaming my head off?" I asked the gang of men, furious as they herded me farther and farther from the front of the hotel entrance.

"You make one sound," the man told me, tapping his pocket where his hand was still gripping his gun.

"Yo!" A man's voice. "Holly!"

All of us turned at once toward the voice.

Gabriel Swan, wet angelfish swim trunks clinging to sunburned thighs, came hightailing it down the path behind us at a fast clip.

"Tell him go!" ordered the man with the gun roughly. "Or I shoot him too."

But you know, I really didn't buy it.

"Nope."

They stared at me.

It's not that I'm reckless. It's not that I'm brave. And hold on—it's not that I was getting a special delivery message from my fairy. No. It was logic. It simply was not going to get these Japanese dudes any closer to Marvin Dubinsky if they shot any of us in public.

I pulled away from the two men who were holding my arms, and they struggled to hold on.

"Let go of me!" I yelled.

"Holly! Who are these fellows? Their auras are—"

It was at that point that one of the men rushed up to Gabriel and attempted to smash him on the head with the side of his pistol. And at that moment, I pushed even harder on the one guy who still had me in his grip, and I broke free.

Luckily, Gabe is a tallish guy, and his head was rather

out of range for the short Asian man who was trying to swipe at him. "Hell's bells!" Gabriel cursed, shocking any number of invisible heavenly creatures and disturbing our myriad angels all to glory. "Get away from these men, Holly. I'm all right."

The thing was, every time someone called me Holly, I hesitated just a second, not recognizing it was me they were calling.

"She comes with us," muttered the man who had scuffled with Gabriel, and short of bashing him in the head, instead wrestled him now to the grass.

Gabriel kept up his end of the fight, but he kept looking toward me. Well, more accurate to say, he was looking at my left breast. "No, I shouldn't," he said to my chest area. And then he hauled off and slugged his assailant, knocking him back down to the grass.

Two men, carrying golf bags on their shoulders, could now be seen across the private drive, far down the path. "HEY!" I yelled, trying to wave both arms.

They were too far away to hear me well, but they looked up sharply.

"LET GO!" I raged at the two men still grabbing at me, and they finally did.

The four men spoke furious Japanese to one another, and then three of them dashed away down the drive.

The one who remained was the one with the gun. "You be smart," he said, his mouth pressed close to my ear. "You keep your mouth shut. You go to the police and you will for sure see me again. The next time I pick a quiet place where no one will interrupt us. Then not only your husband going to die, Mrs. Dubinsky. You understand me? You tell nobody about this and maybe you can stay alive."

And then he left us, jumping into a rented Lincoln that his buddies had pulled up to the curb.

I spun around and rushed over to Gabriel Swan, lying dazed on the ground.

"Are you all right?"

"Me? I'm fine," he said, his voice just a little shaky. "Thank the lights and the crystals that Sally came to me and told me you were in trouble."

"My fairy?"

Gabriel Swan gave me a beautiful smile. "She is really looking out for you today, I'll tell you. So who the heck were those jerks, Holly?"

Now that was exactly what I wanted to know.

Holoholona Kuko
(Animal Lust)

I jumped into the Mustang convertible and drove as fast as I could back to the Four Heavens, leaving Gabriel, shaken but unhurt, as he made his way to the Grand Waikoloa security office. He was off to report the attack, but I had to leave, had to find Wesley and Holly.

As I drove, I thought I saw a dark car parked just out of sight behind a tangle of bushes. Did it pull out on the road behind me? I studied my rearview mirror and saw a car turn left and disappear. Not a Lincoln, though. No. Probably not. I shook it off.

Reporting this incident to some bored policeman was not going to make it go away. They said they'd retaliate. What if they made it their mission to hurt us? I didn't doubt they could do it the second time. The adrenaline rush was wearing off, and I began to shiver. What the hell had I been thinking back there, pulling away so hard from a man who was holding a gun on me? Was I insane?

I looked back in the rearview mirror. Who knew how many men in suits were gunning for Marvin Dubinsky? Arresting those four wouldn't protect us. Others would come. And, damn it, they knew what I looked like now. They'd be better prepared. I noticed I was driving sixty on a thirty mph road and took my foot off the accelerator. What had that poor plant dweeb, Marvin, done to them? He stole something, they said. But what?

I needed more information. If I could find Dubinsky—he was apparently somewhere on this island—then at least I would have something to deal with. And that meant I absolutely had to speak with Holly. And warn her we were still in trouble.

I thought back. The last time Holly had been seen was at the North Shore Medical Center, where Liz had been taken in for tests. And then, Liz said, Holly suddenly left. It seemed unlikely to me that Holly would have walked out on her closest friend while she was in the midst of being treated.

What had really happened?

And then something clicked. Not two plus two, clean and simple, but like a long line of twos that suddenly become sixteen. And don't go getting all woo-woo and telling me that it must have been my little fairy "Sally" flying around, buzzing with ideas, who sent me a message. No, it was a small remark Millie Reisch had made that suddenly came back to me.

I parked my car near the main lobby at the Four Heavens and rushed up to the lobby bar to use one of the house phones. The hotel operator patched me through to the Medical Center.

"Hello," I said. "I need to talk to a nurse in the ER, please."

A few moments of Gloria Estefan later and I was connected.

"ER, can I help you?"

"Yes. Hi. This is Liz Mooney," I said. "I was a patient in your ER this morning. Did I meet you?" Heck, I'd been a bamboo worshiper, a temporary masseuse, Holly

Nichols, and now Liz. It was positively getting easier, no question about it, for me to be someone else.

"What time did you leave the ER, hon?"

"Early afternoon."

"Then we probably didn't meet. I'm on the evening shift," said the voice. "Is something still wrong, hon?"

"No, no. I was just a little dazed when I left the Medical Center and I don't actually remember all the advice the doctor gave me. And I thought it was probably important."

"Which of our doctors did you see?"

"I can't remember."

"Didn't you keep the copy of your discharge instructions?" she asked, surprised.

"The discharge instructions, right. Well, I can't find them," I said, giving my best version of regret-filled embarrassment.

"Never mind," she said. "We keep a copy in your files. I can look them up for you."

"That would be just great," I said. "Elizabeth Mooney."

"Just a second, Miss Mooney."

I waited happily, humming right along to the Miami Sound Machine. And then she was back on the line again. "Here it is. I found it. Now, what did you need to know?"

"Well . . . anything on that sheet."

"Not much here, hon. I just see a note that you were advised to consult your doctor at home," she said.

Oh, hell. I had this woman convinced I was Liz and still I was getting nowhere. It was time to take my chances. "To see my ob-gyn, you mean?" I asked.

There was a pause. "Wait a sec," the voice said, and

immediately I was back to Gloria Estefan singing about the "Conga."

She was on to me. I could feel it. There were goose bumps along my scalp. Why had she placed me on hold so long? Was she having the authorities trace the phone call? What law had I actually broken—impersonating a patient? And if the cops burst through the double doors of the Four Hea—

The music abruptly ended and the nurse was back on the line. "Oh, here it is. I couldn't find all the tests. Right. Here it is. *Congratulations!*"

"Thanks." My scalp settled down. My stomach settled, too. "Thanks very much." I hung up the receiver and leaned back on the cushion of the lobby bar settee.

So that was that. Liz Mooney was pregnant.

No wonder she was fainting right and left. And maybe, just maybe, Holly heard the test results, hanging out as she probably had been in the curtained waiting area. Didn't all those ERs have curtained waiting areas? And maybe this pregnancy news upset Holly. Upset Holly enough to prompt her to drive right away. Now why would her friend's unexpected pregnancy do that to Holly?

"Hi, Mad."

I looked up. Marigold Nichols was walking over. It appeared she was just coming through the lobby and had veered over in my direction when she spotted me seated at a deep wicker sofa in the lobby bar using the house phone.

"Hey," I said back. "Have you seen Holly?"

Marigold shook her head, and I noticed her eyes were red.

"Sit down for a minute. Let's talk a bit," I suggested.

Marigold was the second sister, twenty-four years old, coming right after Holly in the progression of Nichols girls. Since she was only two years behind Holly at school, I figured she knew all of Holly's old schoolmates.

"Look," I said, "Marigold, I'm worried about your sister."

"Holly always turns out all right," she said. "Say, Maddie. I'm really having a great time in Hawaii. I was just out on a nature walk. The animal life here is, like, profound. I can't wait to look up some of the species I've observed when I get back home to my work computer."

That's right. Marigold worked with animals. "You like working for the zoo?"

"God, yes! It's the most fascinating work," she said, warming up.

"Tell me," I said, always curious about what turned other people on, "you must have an area of specialization."

"Sex."

"Ah."

She grinned. "I'm the resident expert on mating."

"Wow."

"Specifically, animal mating ritual behavior. I can tell you how over two thousand individual species do it."

"That must be the official zoological term."

Marigold smiled. "When I see people, I can't help but think of the animals they resemble, behavior-wise. For instance, have you heard of a species of bird called the Jacana?"

I shook my head.

"Well, in that species, traditional sex roles are reversed."

"Really?"

"Yes. In fact, there are twenty species of birds in which that's the case. The female Jacana is pretty much superior to the male in every way."

I smiled back at Marigold.

"In the bird world, female Jacanas kind of rule. They take many lovers. And later the males must raise the babies. Pretty socially evolved of them, don't you think?"

"Yes I do."

"I thought you would. You remind me of a Jacana, Maddie."

Oh. Oh, my. "So . . . anything else I need to know about them, Marigold?"

"When a Jacana female decides she wants another female's mate, she goes after the male and pretty much forces him to have sex with her."

I couldn't help but think of Honnett and me. And Honnett's ex-wife. And while I guess I had flirted with him awful hard when we first met, I hadn't realized he had another female flying around. Really. I had to give Marigold props. Either she was more perceptive than I realized, or she was taking a bizarrely lucky guess. I swallowed. "You mean the male tries to fight her off?"

"Yep." She smiled broadly, enjoying watching me squirm under her anthropomorphic microscope. "But how can a guy refuse an offer of sex? He usually gives in."

"Oh, man. I need a Diet Coke." I looked around the lobby for a waitress and signaled her over. Both of us ordered, and then she left us.

"What do you know about dolphins?" I asked, still feeling a little warm.

"Oh, be careful with dolphins, Maddie. I mean, really. Male dolphins can be very . . . um . . . experimental."

"Sexually?"

"To say the least," Marigold said, grabbing a handful of macadamia nuts from a small bowl on the table. "Bottle-nosed dolphins, the kind people love to swim with, are sexually aggressive."

I thought of my dear soul mate, Little Willie. Say it wasn't so. "All of them?"

"Well, they are charming and intelligent. They are mammals, of course. But the males like to poke themselves into all sorts of other creatures."

"No."

"Yes. They stimulate themselves by having simulated sex with eels, sharks, turtles, other male bottle-nosed dolphins, honey you name it."

"Go on!"

"True. They are indiscriminate players, all right."

"Kind of reminds me of some of the animals I've met in Hollywood."

She smiled. "But only the alpha males. Most of the other males in the herd have such low testosterone levels they are mostly just nonsexual."

"So what animal does Holly remind you of?" I asked.

"Holly? Let me think." Marigold paused for a moment. "Maybe Holly is a blue jay."

"Very pretty." Holly did like to dress up.

"I was thinking about their mating rituals," Marigold said. "Female jays love to eat. And male blue jays always bring a nut or a sunflower seed when they are looking for romance."

"Holly does love food," I agreed.

"Not to mention," Marigold said pointedly, "men bearing gifts."

Not the most romantic assessment of her sister.

But she was hot on her topic now and continued. "Now the one I am most intrigued by is Liz."

Our Diet Cokes were delivered, and we both took deep sips. "Liz," I said, taking another sip, "intrigues me too."

"Liz is a thirteen-lined ground squirrel."

I giggled.

"Hear me out," Marigold said. "The female thirteen-lined ground squirrel is a little uptight."

"An uptight squirrel?"

"She avoids sex. Almost completely."

I knew Liz kept a very quiet profile—the shy account-ant—but I now had proof positive that she was not en-tirely abstinent. Marigold looked at my expression and read the skepticism.

"Wait!" She held up a hand. "Except for one after-noon a year."

"Really?"

"For that entire afternoon the female thirteen-lined ground squirrel just whoops it up and has nothing but sex, sex, sex."

"And you think that's Liz?"

"Well, she has never had a real boyfriend. Not really. Holly and Liz are a strange pair of friends, aren't they? Holly dates about a hundred guys a year, and Liz is al-ways alone on Saturday nights. But about once a year, just when we are least expecting it, Liz brings a guy around to a party. We're always so shocked and hopeful. But then she never mentions the guy again, and she comes to parties alone the rest of the time. So I figure . . . thirteen-lined ground squirrel."

"You remember the last guy she brought around?"

"Of course, silly," Marigold said, putting down her empty glass. "It was Donald."

I looked up, startled down to my flip-flops.

"Donald," she repeated. "Donald Lake."

"*Holly's* Donald?"

"Yes. Didn't you know? That's how Holly and Donald met for the first time. He came to a party with Liz."

Now I was completely confused. Earlier in the day, I had thought I heard Marigold saying she was in love with Donald. Yet by her tone of voice, it didn't seem like that was so. "What about you, Marigold?" I asked. "I thought you were interested in Donald."

"Me? Good grief, no! He's not my type at all. Too tall, for one thing. I like the short ones. And I've never been into all that movie business nonsense. I like the very intellectual, scientific guys. Big brains turn me on."

"But you're sure that Liz used to like Donald?"

"Yep."

Donald Lake? My goodness. I'd had no idea Liz Mooney had at one point in time dated Holly's fiancé. And now one had to ask: had the thirteen-lined ground squirrel remained attached to her once-a-year flame?

My head began to swim. If Liz was pregnant and if Holly heard the news and fled, did that have something to do with Donald?

Makana
(A Gift)

*B*ack in our original room at the Four Heavens, I showered quickly and put on the dressiest outfit I'd packed: navy blue linen pants and a little white top with spaghetti straps. Then I stepped into high-heeled sandals and was ready to walk out the door, all in a matter of fifteen minutes. My makeup kit, cell phone, jewelry, all got tossed into a large navy shoulder bag. I opened our little refrigerator, looking for the last can of Diet Coke, hoping to keep my caffeine high going a little longer, and noticed the white-paper-wrapped box I'd picked up from the front desk earlier in the day and had completely forgotten about. Might as well take that along and give it to Wes now. And while I was at it, I decided to wear my orchid lei while it was still fresh and beautiful.

The soft evening air began to dry my damp curls as soon as I stepped outside our room, and I hurried over to the Presidential Bungalow, my heels clicking on the sidewalks, to meet up with Wesley. While I had been getting ready, Wes had packed up the food supplies, wok, and serving platters, and loaded them all into our second rented Mustang, the black one. We decided to leave the red Mustang, the one I'd been driving around in all day, behind in case one of the girls might want to use it later.

Wes was already outside, waiting for me in the private driveway of the Presidential Bungalow, standing next to the Mustang, its top down, its rear seat filled with the accoutrements of our cooking project. His black jeans and black button-down shirt actually looked pressed, quite a remarkable sartorial feat in this island humidity, but Wesley had a way with his wardrobe. He greeted me with a kiss on the cheek and a quick head-to-toe appraisal. "You look wonderful. Like you got some sun. How were the dolphins?"

"They were amazing," I said, smiling at him. "Amazing and incredibly strange. I've got so much to tell you about, Wes, you have no idea. Just don't ask me about my past love affair with Little Willie because frankly I forgot to ask him what species we were at the time."

Wes raised an eyebrow and then backed the Mustang out of its parking spot. "We're going to the Pele Helicopter Tours Heliport, right?"

"Right. You know how to find it?"

"No problem," he said and changed gears, leaving the fabulous Presidential Bungalow behind as he drove slowly through the maze of small streets on the Four Heavens property.

"Oh, and I forgot to show you this," I said, dipping down into my navy bag and coming up with the box wrapped in white paper. "It came this morning. The guy at the front desk said to keep it refrigerated."

"What's that?" he asked, steering the car past the front entrance of the resort.

I tugged off the white string and unfolded the wrapping paper. "Hey." There was a message written on the inside of the paper. "Look at this," I said, turning the paper upside down and reading: "'To my new friends with very good taste.'" I smiled. "It's from Mori. The sushi chef from our luau."

"I hope that isn't some leftover sushi," Wes said.

"No." I had opened the cardboard box and found a water-filled plastic Tupperware container inside, about three inches high and wide by eight inches long. And inside that was a six-inch-long, bumpy, ugly, raw, greenish-blackish pickle-shaped object. "How, um, phallic," I commented.

Wes took a quick look and said, "Whoa! That's hon-wasabi. True raw wasabi, I think."

Using my thumbnail, I scraped a tiny bit off the side of the root and tasted it. The complex sweet/hot flavor I remembered from last night spread over my tongue. "You're right."

Wes looked extremely perplexed. "They do not grow wasabi outside of Japan. Not anything of this quality. Where did Mori come up with it?"

"Maybe he imports it?" I guessed, putting the slightly obscene-looking rhizome back in its Tupperware home.

"No one ships whole rhizomes from Japan that I've heard of. And if they did, do you have any idea what one that size would cost?"

I shook my head.

"A lot. They cost about seventy dollars a kilo in Japan. So that little fellow would go for about thirty dollars here. If you could get it, which you can't. Nice gift from Mr. Mori. We need to find him and thank him."

"Oh, Wes," I said, looking around as we turned onto the main highway. "Look at that." Along the road here were miles of bumpy black volcanic rocks as far as one could see. "This island is so eerie. In one section it's a rain forest with waterfalls that fall straight into the ocean, in another it's like the surface of the moon."

"Hey, look there," Wes said. He slowed the car down so I could read what he was pointing at. Not only was the Kona highway bordered by these striking black lava beds, but these flat, plant-free fields had also attracted hundreds of graffiti writers. Instead of using spray paint, however, they were much more Hawaiian about it. They used pure white coral rocks, lining them up neatly and spelling out their messages, white against black, all along the side of the road. "Can you read that one?"

The white stones were formed into the words: "David Voron 2004." I read them aloud.

"No, Mad." Wes stopped the car alongside the road. "Right above that one, over there."

There were dozens of messages neatly written out of stones right here. I followed his finger, looking where he was pointing. "Doc Robin Loves Cake." Oh.

"And that one," he pointed out, chuckling. "And that one!"

"Karen D Loves Cake." "Corkie Loves Cake." "Ann Theis Loves Cake."

"And there's another one," Wes said, laughing out loud.

"Joseph Loves Cake."

"Very funny," I said, smiling graciously in defeat. "Maybe they're from a sect of dessert lovers, did you think of that?"

Wes took his foot off the brake and eased back into traffic, laughing his damned head off.

"Never mind. I have more important things to worry about than him," I said.

"Good for you," said Wes, unable to let it go. "Let them all eat Cake, eh?"

I didn't even dignify that with a reaction. I'd get him. Sooner or later I'd get him back. Instead, I launched into a quick review of what had been going on that afternoon since I'd left him. I told Wes about Liz Mooney and Donald. About Marigold and animal sex. And about the men who were trying to grab me—well, Holly—in order to find Marvin Dubinsky. He was just as worried about that one as I was.

Wes said, "The good news is, I did finally find Holly."

"You did?"

"Yep. She and some of the sisters have been taking the afternoon to the limit, tourist-wise."

"And she's okay?" I asked, suddenly more relieved than I realized.

"Perfectly," he said as we passed a large billboard planted in the black lava rocks beside the road that promised Pele Helicopter Tours Heliport was coming up one-half mile ahead on the left.

"You saw that sign?" I asked, making sure Wes was on track.

"You mean the one that said the entire University of Wisconsin Class of 2001 Loves Cake?" he asked innocently.

"Okay. Shut up. Tell me about Holly."

Turns out, Holly had been out and about. She left the Medical Center early in the afternoon and decided to cruise around some of the other resorts nearby and sightsee. She went snorkeling and ended up swimming with a pair of sea turtles. Meanwhile, the twins, Daisy and Azalea, went into Kona, shopping for crystals and hula skirts and estate-grown coffee. And Gladdie signed herself up for surfing lessons and hit the waves. Liz, apparently, had come back and taken a nap.

"Well, at least they are all having a good time," I said,

my event-planner hat on once again. "And what have you been doing?"

"I've been up to my eyebrows dealing with the neighbor from hell."

"Elmer. What's up with that?"

"I got a call from Rachel. She got an offer on the Hightower house. The guy who wants it directed all these old sci-fi films from the sixties. Blake Wither-spoon, do you remember that name?"

I nodded. It sounded vaguely familiar.

"He's a single guy, and Rachel says he loves the house to death. The only thing he'd like to do is move the entry gate."

"That's what Elmer didn't care for," I said, getting excited.

"I know. And he wants everything, all the furniture, the works."

"Really?"

"And his offer is . . ."

I looked at Wes, excited.

". . . incredible. Huge. I don't even want to think about that much money."

"Oh, Wes. Are you going to sell?"

"I have to think about Elmer. So I just called him."

"How'd he take it?"

"He didn't pick up, but I know he was home. Hell, he never goes anywhere. So I just left my nicest, most polite message. We'll see what happens."

"You are incredibly sweet, Wesley."

"I don't want Elmer to have a stroke. I want everyone to be happy."

"That's all either of us wants," I agreed.

"Here we are," said Wes, turning off the highway into the driveway of Pele Helicopter Tours. Off on the tarmac beyond the fence were three helicopters, and Wes pointed out to me that they were the new superluxurious Eco-Star models. He had been excited all afternoon about this helicopter ride. There were three or four cars parked over on the far side of the lot. "Thought there might be more people. Maybe we're early."

It was seven forty-five. Right on time, I thought. We pulled up next to one of the parked cars.

"Aloha, folks." A cute guy in his late thirties holding a clipboard approached us.

"Hey," said Wes, opening the door.

"You here for Kelly's luau?" The guy wore his blond hair short, and like everyone on the island had a killer tan.

"I'm Wes and this is Madeline." He stepped out of the Mustang and the guys shook hands.

"Hi. I'm Vance. Good to meet you. Roddy just stepped away," he said, "but I'm here to let everyone know we've had a change in plans."

"What's up?" Wes asked.

"The luau has been moved to a different site. We're not going to Hilo anymore."

I looked at Wes. I knew he was disappointed.

"What was going to be a small luau has turned into a much bigger deal," Vance explained. "It just kept growing, you know? Keniki is now expecting over two hundred guests. So there was no way Roddy and Tom and I could ferry that many guests over to the other side of the island and back. We were thinking we could do maybe twenty, you know?"

"Of course," I said.

"And another friend of Kelly's has a huge ranch not too far from here. He's offered to have the luau there. And this guy has bucks, so there is no problem there. Much better for Keniki, you know?"

"So no Eco-Star?" Wes was having a hard time with this one.

"You like the Eco-Star?" Vance asked Wes, lighting up. "Man, aren't they awesome?"

"Amazing," Wes said, a trace of wistfulness in his voice. "I had been hoping we might see some live lava flow, but that's probably too much to have expected. I know the volcano has been active, but you don't always see the flow activity on the surface, do you?"

"Oh, you won't believe this," Vance said, getting into it. "We've had the most spectacular live sightings today, better than we've seen in weeks. There's fiery lava flow at one location. I mean, not just the smoke and areas of tubing under the surface, but the real deal, man. I've been taking tours up all day, and it's been breathtaking."

Wes smiled. "I should have made a reservation for the tour. I'll remember that, next time."

"Come on," Vance said, looking deep into Wesley's eyes. "You never know about tomorrow, right? Let's go up tonight. I'll take you for a private ride."

"Wow," I said. It seemed like Wes had made a new friend.

"I've got to help Maddie set up some food at the luau," Wes said, "But thanks anyway. Very nice of you."

"I'll be here all night, Wes," Vance said. "Come on back and I'll take you up for thirty minutes. Just over to the flow and back again. It's the best at night. You won't believe it."

"I'll see how it goes," Wes said. "Thanks."

Vance handed Wesley a map with the directions to the new location of Kelly's memorial luau. "Come on back, okay?" he asked. "I'll be looking for you."

Kekahi Lu-'au
(Another Luau)

Wes and I were back on the highway, continuing south.

"Mad, look at the size of these estates. This is the pricey side of the island." By this point in the terrain, the eerie lava fields had given way to bushy coconut palms and tall grass. "The Kohala Coast is not cheap. But wouldn't it be a lark to have your own house here? The weather is the best on the island. There!" he said, getting animated. "That one looks like me." He was pointing off to a run-down old house on a large overgrown piece of land.

I tried to keep up with Wesley's real estate tour, but I was busy looking for landmarks in the dark. "This must be it up here," I said, checking back with the map on my lap. "Turn here, Wes."

Wes took the turn toward the Pacific Ocean, and we followed a small road almost all the way to the beach. Ahead of us was a long row of brake lights, as many other cars had arrived here for Kelly's luau just ahead of us.

"They have parking attendants," I said, checking out the scene up ahead. With the top down it was easy to see the entire property. Off another few hundred yards closer to the ocean was a large house several stories high, built in the old Hawaiian plantation style with deep porches.

"Hi, folks," said an enormous Hawaiian man, built like a Volkswagen Beetle. "Your name needs to be on da list, bra."

"Madeline Bean," Wes said.

The big fellow took a long time getting through the list and then grunted. "Yep. Okay. We're taking cars here, Madeline," he said to Wes. We both kept straight faces. "I'm gonna park it off the property. You can get out here, okay, and walk down to da house." He gestured the way, and I could see two other big guys giving the same directions to the people in the cars ahead of ours.

I looked around. Bright security lights were blazing all the way to the house. Tall fences surrounded the property for as far off as we could see, and they were topped with a particularly hideous-looking razor wire. "Is that fence to keep cattle in?" I whispered to Wes.

"Hardly," he said. "That's the sort of fence they use in prisons or mental hospitals. And that's an electrified gate," Wes pointed out ahead.

"Nice touch," I said, looking at the forbidding fencing.

"You can leave it right here," said the giant.

"We need to drive up to the house," Wes said pleasantly.

"No way, no how," said the man without a smile. "Absolutely no one drives up onto the property. Orders of the owner. Now give me da keys."

"We've got food," I said, gesturing to the backseat. "For the luau."

He noticed the seat filled with coolers and platters and a three-gallon jug of peanut oil. He stared at Wes in his button-down shirt. "You da caterers?" he asked.

We both nodded. Why annoy this three-hundred-pound lug with the literal truth when our tried-and-true methods always worked?

"Nobody told me nothing," he said, growling. "Okay, take it all the way down there to the left and pull around to the back of da building. That's the kitchen entrance."

"Thanks," Wes said, giving a short wave.

Other guests who had arrived ahead of us were relinquishing their vehicles to the behemoths that were demanding their keys, and we had to wait a few minutes as those cars and trucks were pulled around and taken back up the drive. Wes slowly inched the Mustang up to the large electric gate, which our own security fellow opened by pushing a button on a remote control device. As Wes pulled ahead, he carefully dodged the luau guests who were walking up to the house ahead of us on the private road.

Soon we'd found a nice, tucked-away spot to park the Mustang, and Wes and I began unloading our goodies. In the kitchen, we met the housekeeper, who was happy to show us where to put the giant wok and other items.

"Should I go move our car?" Wes asked her when we were through unloading our supplies.

"No need," she said. "You stay. Maybe you need to load your things up at the end of the luau?"

"Right," he said.

"So you stay there. We keep it quiet," she said, and then she winked.

"Lots of security here," I commented.

"Mr. doesn't like a lot of people. I don't know why he let everybody come here tonight. Must be because he was such a good friend."

"Of Kelly Imo?" I asked.

"That's the one," she said. "He was a very nice man, that one."

Wes had already begun to heat up the oil in the wok,

and I started opening our large coolers, but the house-keeper shooed me away. "I can do this thing," she said, smiling at me. "You don't need to do all this work."

"But we are friends of Keniki's," I explained, "and we are caterers too. So we wanted to cook something special."

"This look good," said the housekeeper, getting close to Wes, watching him stir-fry the lemongrass-chicken lollipops.

"Thank you," Wes said.

"I make all the food for the luau," she said. "I made the kulua pig in the imu. I make laulau. All the tradi-tional things. But nothing like your lollipops chickens. You go check out the table, miss. You tell me what you think."

"I'll be fine here," Wes called to me.

A door on hinges led from the kitchen to the dining room, a huge space lit by a fabulous chandelier. The chairs had been removed to another room, but the enor-mous koa wood table was gleaming. Atop the polished table, lauhala mats were rolled out and a beautiful cen-terpiece made of ti leaves, ferns, and an array of multi-colored orchids was laid the length of the mat. Bowls filled with poi and platters of taro-wrapped laulau and grilled pork were set out along with sweet potatoes, steamed fish, and steak covered in leaves, which were laid directly on the clean mat.

The housekeeper had followed me to the dining room, and she was smiling now, looking pleased with my reaction.

"This is amazing," I said. "It looks so authentic."

"Exactly right. You know about the history of luau?" she asked.

I shook my head.

"In ancient Hawaii, men and woman ate their meals apart. Commoners and all women were also forbidden by the ancient Hawaiian religion to eat certain delicacies."

"That's rough," I said.

"This all changed in 1819, when King Kamehameha II abolished the traditional religious practices. So what did they do, miss? They had a great feast and invited the womenfolk. That feast where the king ate with women was the symbolic act which ended our island's religious taboos."

"And the luau was born?" I asked. So partying here in Hawaii was a feminist act. I knew I liked this state.

"Now I go back and help your friend," she said and disappeared back into the kitchen.

The house was filling up fast with Kelly's friends and associates, who were entering at the open front door. I made my way out of the less crowded dining room and edged into the large living room, hoping to catch a glimpse of Keniki or her sister, Cynthia Hicks.

"Madeline."

I looked up to see Claudia Modlin, the lady from the bamboo club, coming toward me. "Hi, Claudia."

"Have you heard about Kelly?" she whispered when she had gotten closer.

"No. What?"

She pulled me a little to the side, away from the crush of entering guests. "His death was no accident. The police released some information to the press. I heard it on the radio when we were driving here."

"What happened?" I had an instant when my stomach knotted, thinking of Holly and the lamp.

"He was shot. They had kept that quiet up until now,

but it's true. He was shot, and then his body was dumped into the ocean."

"Oh my god."

"I knew you would want to know," said Claudia. "And I think his girlfriend, Keniki, has been at the police station most of the afternoon, answering questions from what I understand. This is now a murder investigation. Poor girl."

"Who would have done it?" I asked Claudia.

"How would I know?" she asked me, surprised. "You don't believe the rumors that he was seeing the sister on the side, do you? I certainly don't. It's completely preposterous."

What was this? Was she implying Keniki might have had reason to doubt Kelly's love, might have been jealous of her own sister, might have had a motive for murder? Or perhaps her sister, Cynthia, had a motive? Impossible. I hate rumors. I hate the damage lies can do. But how does one stop them? Only by finding out the truth. And the truth wasn't always as neat and clean as I would wish it to be. I had to admit, once I calmed myself down again, I had no idea how solid Keniki and Kelly's relationship had been.

"Please tell me what you know about it, Claudia. You said he was close to your family."

"Yes, he was," she said. "Those are my two boys there." She looked off toward two tall handsome teenagers who were standing awkwardly near the front door.

"But you didn't tell me Kelly had worked for you too." I watched closely for her reaction. "Was that something you wanted to keep a secret, Claudia?"

"Not at all," she said smoothly. "My husband and I

were trying to do a little real estate transaction. Nothing more. Kelly was surveying some land for us, drawing up likely parcels. But that project was over months ago."

"So you have no idea why Kelly would have been shot?"

"None at all. Will you excuse me, Madeline? I see someone I need to talk with."

I watched her walk away, thin and beautifully dressed, certain she wasn't telling me everything she knew. But hearing the news that Kelly had been shot to death had me now more worried about the thing that I did know. Those men who had stopped me at the Grand Waikoloa had threatened me with a gun. If Kelly had been shot, I really had to get to the police and tell them. Gabriel Swan had been planning to complain to the Grand Waikoloa security office, but I had to make sure that information got all the way to the cops.

Wesley appeared in the living room, holding a platter of freshly fried lemongrass-chicken sugarcane lollipops along with a bowl of his sweet chili dipping sauce, and I could see the swirls of guests as they gathered around him. My cue to help out.

I swiftly returned to the kitchen and smiled at the housekeeper, who was now working on the appetizers, expertly tossing them in the wok. I decorated my own large platter with a batch of freshly prepared lollipops and headed back for the party.

It was heartwarming to see the expressions of gustatory appreciation as the guests sampled our brand-new recipe. In fact, I stopped and tried one of the lollipops myself, something I should have done earlier. The delicate but kicky spices in the chicken "pop" bounced beautifully off the juicy sweetness of the sugarcane sticks. And for extra dash, the sweet chili sauce was amazing.

Just then I finally spotted Keniki's sister, Cynthia Hicks, amid the throng and made my way over to her side of the room. She turned to me, noticed the tray of food I was passing, and met my eyes.

"Oh, Madeline," she said. "This is so sweet. You cooked this yourself?"

"I worked on it with my partner, Wes," I said. "Cynthia, I just heard the news. I was told that Kelly had been shot. Is that true?"

"Yes," she said, her face going pale. "It's true. But we cannot believe it. They don't have any idea who might have done this thing. And Keniki is also shocked. She cannot even guess what happened to Kelly. Maybe he discovered some sort of burglar and was shot when he tried to stop him?"

"Maybe," I said.

"This is killing my sister," Cynthia whispered. "The answer must be found. She will get no peace until this matter is resolved."

"I'm so sorry."

"I try to comfort her," Cynthia said, a tear escaping even as the luau swirled around us, guests greeting old friends warmly here and there. "But I can do nothing for Denise. She is tearing herself apart."

"For *Denise*?" I stopped offering my tray around and concentrated on what Cynthia had just said.

"My sister. Keniki is her Hawaiian name. It's Hawaiian for Denise."

Denise. What was it again that Gabriel Swan mentioned that my fairy said that the dolphins had told her?

Denise needs your help.

I avoided looking down in the region of my left breast and tried not to think about my fairy. I tried very, very hard. But it wasn't working.

Ohe Eha-
(Bamboo Four)

*O*kay," I whispered, "I'm on it."

I was whispering to *myself*, naturally, just strengthening my resolve, but I suppose an argument could be made that *if* my fairy happened to be hanging about and listening, she could hear my pledge as well.

Over in a far corner of the living room, I thought I saw a familiar face. I looked closer and recognized the wild Hawaiian-print shirt covering the middle-age spread on the rather short torso of Earl Maffini, the president of the Hawaiian Bamboo Association. He appeared deep in conversation with another fellow. The crowd was such that I couldn't get a clear shot, so I worked my way over to Earl's side of the room, detouring left and right to offer chicken lollipops to whomever I caught hungrily eyeing my tray. I stopped to serve a small group of somber young people near a grand piano, turning my back to Earl's corner of the room, but close enough to overhear some of his conversation.

". . . or I'll lose another friend. Is that what you want?"

A familiar masculine voice answered him. "Of course not. But no one flies low over my property. I've taken care of all that."

The dour young man in front of me, whom I had momentarily forgotten, removed two lemongrass-chicken appetizers and said a baleful "Thanks."

I nodded but kept my ear on the conversation behind me.

"You are taking a terrible risk!" Earl said, his voice now lower, but I was following every word. "Look, all four of us have got to hang together if we are going to pull this off. And Claudia isn't a fool. If she knows about your crop, that will only give her more power."

The crowd parted a bit and I turned. And as I expected, it was Cake whose voice I'd just heard talking to Earl. Cake was standing with Earl, looking fabulous as always. "A man has to make money on this island, right?" he was saying, smiling. "You worry too much, Earl."

They both recognized me at the same time.

"Hi," I said, almost shy now in Cake's presence. It was such a girly emotion, this flush of excitement I felt. And I fought the weakness in my knees.

"Ms. Bean," Earl called out, his tone of voice instantly hearty.

Cake's eyes filled with surprise. "Maddie?"

"Care for an hors d'oeuvre?"

He looked me up and down, not missing the sheerness of my linen top, the tightness of my slacks, the tray I was carrying. "Every time I see you, you're working."

I blushed. "Well . . ."

"What an industrious spirit you have."

"You two know each other?" Earl asked. "Why am I not surprised, Cake. I suppose you'd like your privacy. Well, I've got to go talk to some of the others. I see Ike has finally made it."

"Could I have a word with you, Earl?" I asked quickly before he could get away.

"With me? Well, of course."

"In private?" I asked, indicating he might follow me off to the side of the room where there was an open door to an office.

He smiled at me and then turned and gave a cheery little victory wave to Cake.

"I'll see you later, then," Cake said to me, his hand on my bare arm, his expression puzzled. "Right, Maddie?"

"We'll see."

A smile played on his full lips as he watched me walk away. "We'll see," he echoed.

For one thing, I needed to be rational now. This present knees-a'buckle feeling, caused by mere proximity to a dangerously handsome man with whom I'd shared a semi-intimate encounter, was ludicrous. And for another, I was certain the conversation I'd just overheard between Earl Maffini and Cake couldn't be good news. Whatever Earl had been warning Cake about, it seemed mixed up with the Bamboo Four, whoever they were. And what sort of crop had Earl implied could get Cake in trouble if he wasn't careful?

Earl followed me all the way to the office, his eyebrows raised.

"Thanks for giving me a minute," I said, resting my empty platter on the desk, smiling at the fifty-year-old guy.

"Now that's got to be the first time in history the pretty lady asked *Cake* to get lost so she could spend some private time with *me*."

"I can't believe that, Earl."

But flattery only worked on some of the men some of the time. And a few minutes of private conversation was as far as it was going to get me. He said, "So why don't you tell me to what I owe this pleasure?"

Alas, he was not quite the fool I'd hoped he'd be. "Did

you hear about Kelly?" I asked. "They say it was murder. That he was shot."

"That's what I heard too, but I can't believe it," Earl said. "Kelly was a wonderful boy, wonderful. I can't imagine what happened. We don't get this kind of crime on our island. It makes no sense."

He sounded completely sincere. But I knew he worked as a lobbyist in his previous career. He was a professional wheel-greaser. How hard was it for Earl to sound concerned when he really wasn't? I tried another topic. "Earl, who are the Bamboo Four?"

"What?"

"You. Cake. Claudia." I ticked three fingers.

"Who told you about the Bamboo Four?" he asked, amused.

"Keniki Hicks. She said Kelly was having trouble with the Bamboo Four."

"Not at all. I explained this to you after the HBA meeting. Keniki was upset and she doesn't understand. We were all, including Kelly, on the same page, just that Kelly wanted to read a little too fast for the rest of us."

"So who is the fourth member of the Four?"

"That's not something I'm at liberty to say," Earl said in a gentlemanly way.

"You know I can find out from Keniki, if you insist."

"Now, now, Ms. Bean. No one wants to go disturbing that poor gal today."

I had to know. "The fourth member of the Bamboo Four, is it Marvin Dubinsky?" It all made sense to me. Dubinsky was the missing link. Dubinsky was living on the Big Island, involved in botanical research, and remained the elusive quantity throughout the entire weekend. It had to be.

Earl's pleasant face instantly lost its jolly, politicking sheen. "You know Marvin?"

"Yes," I said, certain I was right. "He's married to my best girlfriend."

"Marvin is married?" asked Earl. "I never heard anything about that."

"So," I continued before he decided to stop talking, "Marvin Dubinsky is part of the Bamboo Four."

Earl cast his glance around, but no one was near the entrance to the office where we stood. "He likes to keep an extremely low profile, Ms. Bean. I can't really confirm your suggestion. I think we understand each other."

I understood nothing. "I've got to find him," I said quickly. "My friend may be in danger. Please. I know you must have his address."

"I do," he said, his expression becoming totally mystified.

"Will you give it to me?" I pressed, no longer working the flirty angle at all. "Please."

"You've got it."

"What?"

"You're here."

I stared at him.

"This is Marvin's home," Earl said, speaking slowly, perhaps so I could comprehend what he was saying. "Right here. You're in it."

"I can't believe this." The shock of the news sapped me of words. And just then I noticed on the wall of the office there was a framed print featuring the Japanese kanji symbols for Mountain Hollyhock. Well, duh. I leaned against the desk to keep from falling.

"I told you you got it all wrong," Earl explained patiently. "We were all Kelly's friends. That's why we're here tonight, paying our respects at his final luau. Look here, Marvin even came forward in the pinch to offer his home. You may not have heard, but this whole shindig had to be relocated because Kelly had so many friends who wanted to come. I called Marvin, and he didn't hesitate to offer the plantation house here. So don't get any crazy ideas about who his friends really are."

"I didn't know," I said, still in shock. "So, okay. I better go find him. Thanks."

"Well, that's the thing. He's not here, of course. Marv avoids parties. His property holdings here are pretty vast. He's somewhere out there." He gestured out the window toward the darkness beyond. "This property is bigger than you might imagine."

And that one comment triggered an entirely new train of thought. What had I heard about each of the Bamboo Four? Earl, Claudia, Cake, and Marvin were not only horticulture freaks, they were also wealthy individuals who shared a compelling interest in land. Claudia had been secretive at first, but she finally admitted she had plans to acquire land, and that she had employed Kelly to help draw up likely parcels. Earl, I recalled from his business card, was also into real estate. And Cake and Marvin were both large landholders on the Big Island.

And this suddenly tied into what I'd learned at the HBA meeting this afternoon. The Four were opposed to the immediate announcement of Kelly's big idea: his cockamamie scheme to transform the Hawaiian Islands from a sketchy tourist-dependent economy into some mythical filthy-rich bamboo empire. They were fighting for a delay.

It was suddenly clear. They needed time to lock up more land.

Land that was now worthless for agriculture might become a gold mine in the future, and the Bamboo Four wanted more time to get their hands on it cheap. But could they ever pull this agricultural revolution off? Their whole plan seemed so completely nuts to me, but then they were the bamboo experts, and I could barely grow a houseplant. I also happen to believe that the distinction between crackpots and visionaries is nonexistent, so no matter how far-fetched their scheme seemed to me, I had to take their own resolve very seriously.

With just the right property acquisitions, these would-be bamboo barons must have figured they could control a potentially explosive new industry. Like the missionaries that came to Hawaii almost two hundred years before and controlled the sugar plantations.

"Whoa," I said, suddenly groggy with insight. I had to ride this train to the end of its logical tracks. Kelly loved the plants, loved the people of Hawaii. But Claudia and Earl? What did they love most? What about Cake and Marvin? Was it money? Did one of the Bamboo Four kill Kelly Imo? Did someone shoot Kelly and dump his body in the bay in order to keep the lid on these bamboo pipe dreams just a little while longer, while these monopoly-crazed bamboozlers got their hands on more land?

I didn't have a shred of evidence to support nine-tenths of my theory, but at least some of that had to be true. I felt certain of it.

"Earl," I said, suddenly feeling ill, "did Marvin agree with Kelly's plans for bamboo farming?"

"Oh, heck, no," Earl said, looking at me weird. Could he read my thoughts? "Marvin thought we were all a bunch of morons!" He laughed.

"What?" I was totally thrown. "Didn't he love bamboo just as much as the rest of you?"

"Marvin? Oh, he likes the stuff for landscaping.

That's about it. He thought Kelly was off his rocker about introducing the construction industry to using bamboo products."

"But I thought Marvin was a big plant genius."

"He is," Earl agreed. "He is. But he couldn't care less about farming. He's more into immuno-whatzits. Using plants for medical research, all that sort of fancy stuff."

"So he didn't want to grow bamboo?" I felt my entire theory deflate.

"Not really, no. Why?"

"I've got to talk to him," I said urgently. "Right away."

"He's probably out at his foreman's house, back on the property," Earl said. "His foreman doesn't live there anyway, so Marvin sometimes uses that old house when he wants some privacy to think."

"Where is it?"

Earl explained how to get there, following the private drive about two miles along the coast.

I ran out of the office and scanned the huge crowd, searching for Wesley. He wasn't in the dining room or living room, and the housekeeper told me he hadn't been in the kitchen for fifteen minutes at least. I ended up taking out my cell phone and calling Wes's cell. I listened to the ringing and then heard his voice mail announcement. I described my discovery, that Marvin Dubinsky was not far away, and how important I felt it was to contact Dubinsky in order to protect Holly from any further threats.

Then I called the police. It was almost nine-thirty on Saturday night, so there weren't any detectives available, but I left a message about my encounter with the gunman at the Grand Waikoloa.

Finally, I tried calling Chuck Honnett, but again, there was no answer. Why was no one ever near their phones when you needed them? And what was Honnett up to? It was half past midnight in Los Angeles. Why was he out so late on a Saturday night? I felt the true pang of jealousy over some unknown woman he was probably sharing a drink with. But I had no right. Hadn't I been pushing Honnett away for weeks? Hadn't he given me every chance in the world to start over?

"Madeline, hello. Here you are!" said Keniki, reaching her arms out, letting me give her a comforting hug. Her long hair had the gentle scent of coconut. "Look who's here," she said to the big yellow dog by her side. Dr. Margolis's tail thumped the glossy hardwood floor.

"Dr. Margolis," I said, bending down to pat his square head. "How are you?"

"He's well," said Keniki. "But I'm falling apart. Have you heard?"

I nodded. Kelly's death was no accident. It was murder. I could see it was wearing her down. "Try not to think about it too much," I said. "Things will get clearer as the days go by. The police will sort it out."

"But what if the police suspect *me*?" Her eyes had a glassy appearance.

"I'll help you, Denise," I whispered, concerned about her.

"You are so sweet," she said and attempted a half smile. "The doctor gave me a pill. I can hardly feel anything now. Don't worry, Madeline."

I didn't know what to say, so I just hugged her again.

"And I like it how you called me Denise," she said, moving away to greet other guests. "Not everyone knows how much I like that name. That's what my mother used to call me."

Score another point for the dolphins.

I opened the door and looked up the road. It was more than past time I jumped in the Mustang and took a little trip looking for Marvin Dubinsky.

Malawina
(Marvin)

I started up the Mustang and slowly pulled away from the large plantation house onto the back path, hearing the crunch of lava rock gravel under my tires.

The top was down, of course, and the night sky was brilliant, filled with billions of stars. The farther I drove away from the main house with its huge floodlights out in front, the more breathtaking the sky became. The moon was full tonight, but at the moment he was hiding behind clouds, like a self-confident hero allowing his astral rivals their chance to shine.

The private road skirted along the coast, permitting glimpses now and then of the night-black Pacific beyond. The road was only one lane wide and meandered, weaving along the contour of the coast; thick roadside foliage masked what was coming around each bend. I had checked the Mustang's odometer when I got into the car, keeping watch that I not go too far. Earl had said two or three miles from the house. It would be a long walk, too long for anyone dressed in high heels like me, but no trouble for the only guest at the party who had managed to sneak her car inside the security perimeter. I was pretty proud of myself.

The Mustang turned a bend, and I saw light up ahead in the distance. Soon I could see a house—the foreman's house. It looked like your average San Fernando Valley ranch home, nondescript and low. The lights were a good sign. Marvin must be home.

The terrain was markedly different up here. Outcroppings of brush petered out abruptly, and vast fields of black lava rock spread in most directions away from the shore. However, down closer to the ocean, a large system of PVC pipes crisscrossed neat semi-submerged fields. A dense leafy crop was growing behind an additional barrier of razor-wire fencing.

The road eventually brought me to the backside of the foreman's house, and still crunching on black gravel, I parked the Mustang near the back door. However, I felt it was only respectful to walk around and approach the dwelling from the front. The sidewalk took me past a neatly swept rock garden, where masterful designs were arranged out of coral, to a sliding glass door. The interior of the house was illuminated but masked from view by a closed curtain. I stepped up and pressed the doorbell, which I could hear ringing throughout the house in the night's silence.

"Hello," a voice called.

"Hello," I called back. "I'm Madeline Bean. Holly Nichols's friend. May I come in and speak to you?"

The floor-length white curtain was pushed aside, and standing behind the sliding glass door was Marvin Dubinsky. Marvin Dubinsky, found at last.

"You're Holly's boss," Marvin said, beaming at me. "Wow. What are you doing out here? I mean, wow. This is blowing my mind. But wait. I mean, come on in."

First hurdle jumped. He remembered who Holly was.

I had no idea what her name might mean to him after all the years that had passed, but I suppose a wife is hard to forget.

And, second thought, he knew who I was too. Now that was unexpected.

I walked into the house and turned to take a good look at my host in the strong light. In no way did he now resemble the Marvin Dubinsky that Holly described.

For one thing, a growth spurt had obviously come to a very last-minute rescue. Marvin stood a towering six foot four, if I could guess from standing next to him. He was also attractively free of any skin problems or braces. The Marvin Dubinsky before me now was an extremely tall, messy-haired, deep-voiced, cute geeky-god.

"You look nothing like I was expecting, Marvin," I said, still checking the guy out rather closely.

"Holly told you about me?" he asked eagerly, his voice getting an excited bounce.

"She did." He still seemed to have some feelings for Holly—go figure?—so I figured I'd better let him down softly. "Well, you have been on her mind ever since she began to get these threatening e-mails. And she began to worry that someone might try to kill her if she didn't tell them everything she knew about where to find you. Which, of course, she had no freaking idea."

"Damn those idiots," Marvin said, abruptly losing his temper. "They had no right to upset Hollyhock."

"What idiots?"

He sighed and pulled his hand through his thick hair. "It's a long story. Say, where are my manners?" he asked, startled at himself. "Sit down. Here." He moved a notebook computer from a cushion on the yellow sofa. "I'm doing some research on the Internet. Just love the Internet," he said.

I sat down. "So just what is all this stuff about Mountain Hollyhock, anyway?" I asked more directly. "Are you still in love with Holly?"

"What?" he asked, again looking startled. "Oh, that. Oh, yes. Of course." He looked embarrassed. "I've always loved Holly."

"This is seriously strange, Marvin," I said. "You haven't talked to her in, like, eight years! If you loved her, why did you just disappear off the face of the earth?"

"I'm . . ." He looked at me, an appealing man without much experience socially, by the look of him. "I'm just shy," he said. "Too shy. I know. But when I left town after graduation, Holly was already on her way, dating another guy." He stuck his hands in the pockets of his khakis. "Look. Hollyhock was the most popular girl in our class. I knew I was lucky to have had that one perfect night with her. I just sort of crept away. Off to college. You know."

"And then?"

"Then? Well, I expected I'd hear from her. Every week I just knew she would get in touch. To annul our marriage. You know. Or get a divorce. I expected she would be getting in touch very soon. But she never did. So I kept hanging on to the hope that she had some feelings for me after all."

"But you never called? You never came over to see her?"

"I wrote her letters," he explained. "I told her I loved her in the letters. I sent her poems. But I told her of course I would sign any papers she wanted me to in order to let her out of our marriage. After all, it was just a mistake to her. I understood. But she never answered the letters. I figured she would when she was ready, so I didn't want to rush her."

"Marvin," I said, a little lost, "whoa. Stop. I don't

think Holly has ever gotten your letters. She would have mentioned them to me. I'm positive. Were they e-mails?"

"No. I sent real, regular mail letters."

"Where did you address them?"

"To her home. I mean her parents' home."

I wondered if Holly's parents had conveniently forgotten to deliver them to Holly. I would have to check with Holl to see if her parents approved of Marvin way back when.

"And you never just picked up the *phone,* Marvin?"

He looked uncomfortable. "And said . . . what?"

I could think of a million things. But the point was, of course, this lovesick dweeb couldn't. "So that's why you call this place Mountain Hollyhock? Why you have the kanji for Mountain Hollyhock on your wall. And on T-shirts."

"Well, yes and no," Marvin answered, taking a seat opposite me in one of those odd rocking chairs that have gliders on the bottom. "See, I became fascinated with a certain plant when I was away at school."

"Where did you go to college?"

"Berkeley first," he said. "They were eager to let me design my own major."

"Which was?"

"I wanted to combine ethnobotany and phytomedicinal prospecting, actually."

"Oh. Right." This guy was either crazy-smart or just crazy. "What's that?"

"Okay, well, ethnobotany is studying the historic uses of plants as medicines. Mostly it's digging into the medicinal traditions of Europeans, Chinese, Egyptians, American Indians, and like that. I was intrigued at first by what could be learned from more recently discovered cultures. I did field studies with shamans in Amazonia and Belize, for instance, but then I suddenly got interested in Japanese culture and took a different route."

"And phytomedicinal prospecting?"

"Good retentive memory," Marvin said, flashing a quick smile. "See, once you discover the plants that have been used as medicines by primitive cultures, you need to screen the plants for biological activity."

"Okay," I said. "I can follow that."

"Huge projects are currently under way by such organizations as INBio, Costa Rica's National Institute of Biodiversity. INBio is cataloging all species of plants and animals in the country—estimated to be around five hundred thousand! I spent some time down in Costa Rica helping them train what we called 'community taxonomists' to identify plants and animals."

"Sure," I said, almost keeping up.

"Anyway, I had some laughs, made a few discoveries, started a few companies, and turned them over to doctors to run—you know, the usual postadolescent fun."

"Marvin, you are one strange dude," I said, marveling at the guy my Holly had married.

"Yeah, well," he said bashfully. "Anyway, I had theorized there was a class of medicinal roots that were like the antibiotics of the plant kingdom, with healing properties like no other. I'd been doing the biological activity studies on a class of plant found in Asia, and I suddenly fell in love with my first root. The specific variety I needed was only grown in Japan, a semiaquatic member of the cabbage family, but the medicinal properties of this plant are phenomenal. Anticarcinogenic. Antitoxin. It was, like, absurd, this root was so wonderful. The only problem was, the Japanese growers refused to let me have samples to grow in my lab so I could continue my studies."

Somehow, as Marvin Dubinsky waxed rhapsodic about roots, I was certain I knew where it was all heading.

"Marvin, are you talking about wasabi?"

"Of course," he said, looking incredibly happy with me. "*Wasabia japonica*. You know it's been served with raw fish for centuries, not simply because the taste is pleasing. Because it actually counteracts food poisoning."

I shook my head. Imagine that.

"Mountain Hollyhock! That's the kanji for wasabi. Don't you see how perfect it all is? I fall in love with a girl in high school named Mountain Hollyhock, and years later I discover the most medicinally significant plant known to humankind, and its historical Japanese kanji from the tenth century translates as Mountain Hollyhock. How could I not leave my postdoc position at Harvard then? This was more than fate, Miss Bean. It was about destiny, I think."

"So what happened?"

"I still had this problem with the Japanese growers. They were becoming more and more suspicious. I tried to buy larger quantities of their finest specimens of wasabi, but they balked. They traditionally sell in only very small quantities to a set list of buyers, mostly up-scale restaurants in Asia, and they couldn't make an exception for me, the guy who was about to cure bloody cancer. I mean, really! I wanted to grow my own, but of course they wouldn't let me."

"So you stole some specimens. You stole them from the Japanese farms and began growing your own wasabi here in Hawaii."

"Well," Marvin said, sheepishly. "Yeah."

That explained a lot. The razor-wire security fencing and electronic gates. The enormous security guards. The secrecy. The crop fields I had just seen. The perfect specimen of fresh raw wasabi our sushi chef, Mori, had produced. I guessed Mori must be connected to this ranch in some way and was slipping out his own samples for less-than-medicinal purposes.

I was pretty upset. I stood up. "And now some angry hairy-fisted goons have been sent from Japan to retaliate because you stole their precious plants, the secrets about which they have been protecting for ten centuries."

Marvin looked completely forlorn. "That's about it, yes."

"This just sucks."

"Look, I'll take care of it," Marvin said, trying to calm me down a bit. "I'd never let anything happen to my Hollyhock."

I glared at him. Men. They think they are invincible. But he hadn't had to stare down the barrel of a gun, like I had. And what had happened to Kelly? I had been sure Kelly's death was wrapped up with some deep dark bamboo plot, but now I was no longer so sure.

"What happened to Kelly?" I asked.

"Please sit down, Miss Bean," Marvin pleaded. "I'll tell you everything I know."

I sat back down and waited.

"Now this first part is the difficult part. I'm going to ask you to just hear me out and not scream or get freaky, okay?"

I tried to keep my cool. If it turned out that Marvin was about to confess that he had murdered Kelly Imo, I did not know what I could do. I put my hand nonchalantly into my navy bag and found my cell phone, resting my hand around it. Just in case I ever had the chance to use it again, at least I had it near.

"Look, this isn't as bad as it's going to sound," Marvin said, his hand going through the motions again, finger combing through his bushy black hair. "I already told you I'm in love with Holly. I always have been. I always will be. It's my destiny. I told you that."

"Yes."

"So I just couldn't go on living without her. I know what you are going to say. I'd written to her, and she rejected me. I needed to give up. But I couldn't. I just couldn't. I needed to see her in person one more time. To plead with her for another try."

Oh my God. I suddenly saw it all. Marvin was the one who "arranged" to have us throw our party for Holly on the Big Island. He's the one who put ten thousand dollars in cash down to cover the cost of our stay at the Four Heavens.

"Marvin, did you arrange our entire trip?"

He nodded and hung his head. "I had been keeping tabs on Holly. I hired someone to let me know if she was doing okay. I travel a lot. I just wanted to get word every so often that she was fine. He told me Holly was going to get married again. And I just needed to see her one more time before then. I mean, either she would look at me and not even remember me, or she might need to get that annulment, so she wouldn't mind, I thought."

"Or maybe she'd still have feelings for you?" I could imagine what he had dreamed; it was clear in his sad eyes.

"I could have come to the mainland, but I had the idea I might look a little better to Hollyhock if she saw me here." He gestured beyond the window, to the large compound he owned.

"You brought us all to the Big Island."

He nodded, looking horribly sorry about it.

"How?"

"I am really good on the Internet," he said. "Really good. I play a lot of MMO games, and some of my online buddies are extremely good at hacking around. Anyway, I found out you went to school with the woman who is running the Four Heavens resorts. It's in both of your Web site bios. And I just hacked an e-mail hoax to you inviting you and your friends to stay at the Four Heavens."

"And you know that manager fellow, Jasper Berger?"

"I gave him a sufficient tip, that's all. Anyway, no harm done, right? I was paying for a luxury vacation for friends anonymously. He had no trouble with it."

"Oh, Marvin. It's creepy, that's what it is. Almost like stalking, only well, like reverse-stalking."

"I never approached Holly! I haven't even seen her. I just wanted to let her know I was here if she wanted to talk."

"So," I said, just figuring it out, "you sent your buddy Kelly Imo to Holly's room to invite her to see you."

"Yes. I wanted to see her. Desperately. But in the clutch, I panicked. I couldn't do it. Holly was so close, but I didn't have the courage to face her. Kelly thought I was a riot. He said he'd go and talk to her. He had no trouble talking to women, so I said yes. I was grateful."

"And Berger let him into the room?"

"Yes."

"And then what?"

"I have no idea," Marvin said, miserably. "I never heard back from Kelly. I had my housekeeper make a very special dinner last night, but Holly didn't show up, and Kelly was supposed to invite her here. It just never worked out. And then this morning, we learned that Kelly had somehow fallen into the ocean and died."

"So you never heard from him after he met with Holly?"

"No. As I said, he didn't get back in touch with me. I figured he just didn't want to hurt my feelings. But then when they said his death wasn't an accident, I didn't know what to think."

"What happened," I said, relaxing just a little as I realized that while Marvin Dubinsky might be the most romantically mixed-up young man on the planet, at least, thank god, he wasn't homicidal, "is that your friends from the wasabi fields of Japan are on the island and they have a gun, Marvin."

"Shit!"

"Yes. And . . ."

Before I could tell him "and . . ." *what,* a terrible, terrible thing occurred. Every single light in that little house suddenly went out.

I let out a little yelp. "What's happening? What's happening?"

Marvin's voice came out of the complete pitch-darkness. "I don't know. Our power must be down."

"What?" I asked, nervous. "Does that happen often out here?"

"No. Never," he said. "The power out here comes from the main house."

"So you mean the electricity is off at the main house too?" I tried to imagine two hundred guests bumping around in the dark, about three miles up the road, knocking into one another, spilling their kalua pork. Maybe yelling and jostling. It wasn't a pleasant mental picture.

"This isn't good, Madeline," Marvin said, his voice tense. "I've got a backup generator. If the lights don't go back on in another second or two, I think the power has been sabotaged."

We sat there, Marvin and I, in the absolutely silent

darkness, willing the lights to come back on. Another second went by. Then another. My breathing became much more shallow. Thirty seconds later and I figured the lights weren't going to be working anytime soon.

."Look," Marvin's voice said, still tense. "You've got to get away. If those men have been trying to get to me, they may have figured a way to do it. They're probably outside right now, on their way down the road right this minute. You've got to get away."

"We can both go," I said. "I've got my car out back."

In the far distance we could just barely hear the sound of a car's engine. It was getting closer.

"No, they'll just find a way to run us off that little road. I don't want you to get hurt."

"But, Marvin!" My voice was anxious and I stood up, trying to figure my way to the door. From outside I could hear the car's engine growing louder by the second. "Let's get out of here, now. Please."

"Don't open the front door," he said, hearing me bump into a table. "They'll see you. Look, I've got another idea. There's a crawl space under this house. Come toward my voice." I heard some shuffling of furniture and walked straight toward his voice, my chin bumping into his outreached hand.

The night was still, but we could hear the unmistakable thump of a car door slam, then another. And feet scuffling on gravel.

"Look," I said, "let's both go. Promise?"

"Sure," he whispered. "Now feel down here on the floor. I've lifted the hatch on the crawl space. Just ease yourself down. It's about a two-foot drop. And get away from here, Maddie."

Two small beams, as from flashlights, suddenly flicked on outside and immediately began tracing impatient patterns of light across the sliding glass doors. The curtains were drawn, thank God, but the faint illumination of the flashlights filtered into the room enough for me to make out Marvin's face in the darkness. "You're coming, right?" I whispered. I felt along the floor and found the opening, about two feet by three feet, and lowered myself down. Then I scrambled onto my stomach and edged away to make room for Marvin to follow.

The hatch quietly closed above me. Marvin had stayed to face his foes.

Iwakālua Mua Kenekulia 'O-hule
(Twenty-first-Century Nerd)

I had no great plan, no inspiration at all. I crouched low outside the house beside the back bedroom, leaning against the coolness of the exterior siding, trying to catch my breath, and took stock: I was alive at the moment, unharmed, unseen, unlooked for. That was the good news. The bad news was, there was an unknown number of angry men, probably armed, probably willing to kill, pinning us down at a little house in the middle of nowhere on the island of Hawaii, and they weren't there to share recipes.

I always had this vision of myself that I did my most creative thinking under pressure. I was better at whipping up a startlingly good impromptu meal out of leftover ingredients than some chefs made out of a limitless larder. I was far happier when called upon to improvise than I was just plodding through some well-thought-out elaborate plan. So at this particular harrowing moment, I should have shined. I should have soared. I should have thought up something brilliant. The fact was, I didn't.

All I could think of was reaching Wesley. I had taken my purse with me, and I opened my bag very slowly and very quietly and pulled out my cell phone. Before I flipped it open, I said a little prayer. But that was one prayer wasted. No cell coverage out here. None. Not even one bar. Well, that was that. I needed a plan. I needed a plan.

I slipped my shoes off—high-heeled sandals were not going to figure into my plan, that was one thing I was sure of—and tucked them neatly near the house. I was crouching by a spiky shrub in the large rock garden, where, unfortunately, the sharp coral scratched my bare feet. Not my biggest worry now, however.

There were too many things I didn't know. I didn't know how bad the situation really was. Maybe Marvin would give these men their wasabi roots back, allow them to dig up his fields, pay for any damage he might have done to their business. Maybe there was still a hope in hell that reason could prevail.

Right. What was I thinking? Marvin's wasabi fiasco had gone far past that point. For a thousand years, farmers had kept the secrets of cultivating their precious root, only to now be done in by this twenty-first-century nerd. They had lost the battle to some freaking phytomedicinal prospector, and they weren't being gentlemanly about their loss. They had sent these horrible, violent men—men who used tactics that marked them as thugs and enforcers—out here to teach Marvin a lesson. They didn't care about science or logic or the potential new uses for an ancient crop.

So, basically, we were screwed. Could I make it to my car, was the question.

It wasn't far. The black Mustang sat tantalizingly close, with its top down, only a hundred feet away from where I was now sitting. I had my purse. I had the key. If I could make it to the car before anyone inside the house heard me, I might have a chance to drive out of here and get away.

But what if someone did hear me? In the stillness of

this absurdly quiet night, the roar of the engine turning over would alert them instantly. What if someone came running out of the house, gun drawn, to stop me? Who would hear gunshots out here? And another shiny new doubt cropped up: What if they had prepared for trouble, and had left other cars filled with other gunmen farther down the private road in order to prevent anyone from escaping? My heart was beating out of my chest, the more I envisioned fleeing in the Mustang and being chased off a cliff to die in the rocky water below. Like Kelly, I thought, and my heart beat even faster.

Maybe I should just stay low and hide by this little bush. Forever. Well, not really forever. These gangsters had to leave sometime, and fairly soon. Marvin's security men had their hands full right now, true. I could picture the scene only a few miles away, with a house full of disturbed luau guests being led out of the dark house, demanding their cars, scurrying to leave. It would take some time for the security men to bring around all the cars and evacuate the main house. But then, in an hour or so, Marvin's security team would certainly come to check out the foreman's house. The men inside must know this and would not stay any longer than necessary.

If I could stay quiet for just an hour, the men inside might leave without ever knowing I was out here at all. Maybe by just hiding quietly, I could survive this night. That was, if I was willing to listen to whatever awful things were going on inside. From where I sat I heard muffled yelling coming from the direction of the living room. Were they hurting Marvin? Torturing him? Would they kill him? Could I sit here and wait quietly for Marvin Dubinsky to be murdered?

And then, right in the middle of my intensely quiet panic, up sprang an idea. It wasn't a fabulous idea, but who could be choosy at a time like this? I worked as silently as I could, praying the moon would stay behind the clouds a little longer, moving farther away from the house, toward the fields of black lava rock. And when I was finished, I had to congratulate myself. I had managed to survive for fifteen more minutes, and I was not yet dead.

The bottom of my feet were bloody, though, having scraped them against the rocks, but I barely felt the pain as I tiptoed to the Mustang and back to the house, and still no one came to stop me.

I had been in a worry spiral, thinking every sort of bad thing, and was now exhausted with worry. I had been worried about Marvin, worried that at any second I would hear a gunshot ring out from inside that house, and worried I would go crazy if I did. I was back against the house now and figured I should hear a little more of what was going on inside. I crept around the corner and found a spot under a dining room window that had been left open. Inside, the house was not completely dark. They had left their flashlights on as they interrogated Marvin Dubinsky.

The voices inside could be heard quite clearly in the nighttime silence. I couldn't tell how many men were inside with Marvin, but it appeared that one man, at least, had stayed behind in their car. I could just peek out from my position and see the familiar late-model Lincoln, the same car the men had been driving when they threatened me at the Grand Waikoloa. It was now parked near the front door of the foreman's house, with a man sitting inside, bored at the wheel.

It was only the merest fluke of good luck, I realized, that that sentry hadn't taken the time to walk around to the back side of the house and make sure all was quiet.

None of these men had expected Marvin to have a guest with him tonight. None of them thought to check out the silent night. That's what saved me.

I peeked out again. The man in the Lincoln hadn't moved, and by the hang of his head, he might be sleeping. His eyes seemed closed. Another stroke of luck, and my heart continued to race as I ducked back down again and tried to make out what the men inside were saying.

"How you do it?" asked one of the men.

"I figured out the system of cooling the mountain water," Marvin was saying. "I told you about this already."

"Listen to me. You will tell again. And again. No one can do what you have done. Wasabi is very difficult to grow. Tell again."

That was why they had come to Hawaii. They were angry this guy stole their precious wasabi plants, sure, but there was more to it than that. Men had probably stolen live plants in the past, but nothing had come of it. They were truly furious that Marvin had gone one better. He had figured out how to grow their famously temperamental wasabi outside of their tiny province in Japan. If they could learn how Marvin had done it, they might be able to stop other wasabi marauders in the future.

"Look," Marvin said, "I told you I'm not trying to harm your business. You grow about five thousand tons of wasabi a year, right? My little garden here is nothing, my man."

"How you know so much?" another man's voice rang out, belligerent.

"I don't want to get into your line at all. I'm not really into sushi," Marvin said, his voice still sounding rational. "Look, it's the phytochemicals I'm concerned with."

"The what? You tell us everything now."

"Okay. *Wasabia japonica* is part of the cabbage family, right? So of course, its pungency is due to isothiocyanates. But I've identified two glucosinolates in the root: sinigrin, which is also the characteristic aroma compound of black mustard and horseradish, and traces of glucocochlearin."

"Enough!" said the first man who was interrogating Marvin. And then I realized, as long as Marvin Dubinsky had information they needed, they wouldn't kill him. I was filled with relief.

Marvin continued, "See, the tasteless compounds are enzymatically hydrolyzed to the pungent mustard oils, allyl isothiocyanate . . ."

Oh my God! Marvin had a plan of his own. As long as he kept up his chemical blather (in the background, now, I could hear him saying: "[CH_2 equals $CH\text{-}CH_2\text{-}NCS$] and sec-butyl isothiocyanate—[$CH_3\text{-}CH_2\text{-}CH(CH_3)\text{-}NCS$], respectively . . ."), he could delay the inevitable. His execution. Geek-speak might save Marvin's life. Marvin was a genius after all.

"Stop that! Why you waste our time?" asked the man. "You steal our plants. You pay for that."

"You've got to hear me," Marvin pleaded. I didn't like the sound of his voice, though. It was much more strained. Were they hurting him? I couldn't take the chance to turn around and try to look through the open window. What if the man in the car opened his eyes? I couldn't even see him from where I was sitting, but if I stood up again, he might spot me.

Marvin didn't stop his spiel, no matter what they were doing to him. "Look, I'm just saying that what I'm finding out is amazing stuff. The chemicals natural to wasabi work faster than aspirin to prevent blood clots. And it's insane, but they also show protective properties against osteoporoses, diarrhea, and asthma. It's like a whole new class of drugs, only better than drugs. Don't you understand?"

"You leave me no choice, Mr. Dubinsky. I have to kill you now."

I couldn't tell when I'd started shaking. Probably just at that very minute.

"Shut up!" yelled one of the other men. Then he said, "First Mr. Dubinsky is going to tell us how he grow the wasabi outside Japan. Many men tried that. No one else can do that. You tell now."

"It's got to do with the water," he said. "For wasabi to thrive it must be constantly bathed in pristine, chilly water with just the right mineral balance. Apparently the melted snows that trickle through the volcanic soil of both Izu and Nagano are ideal for this. I've studied your setup, and there has to be rushing water to flow past the roots. Just like you have in the mountains of Japan. That's why they call wasabi Mountain Hollyhock. You probably know that already."

"Go on."

"Well, the water has to be the right temperature. Cold. Izu grows wasabi on terraced fields carved into sloping hills, while Nagano's Azumino plain boasts flat beds with wide streams between the mounds of earth—both provide a water temperature of about forty-five to forty-eight degrees Fahrenheit year-round. And to get the mineral balance just right, it has to filter through volcanic rock. Like in Japan."

So that's why Marvin had relocated to the Big Island. He needed the volcanic rock to grow his illicit crop of wasabi.

"So that's all? Cold water?" asked the man.

"No, of course not. It's so much more complicated than that," Marvin said.

Good for you, Marvin. Keep them talking.

In the quiet stillness of the night, I heard a very low roaring sound. Not a car. What was it? Possibly an airplane?

"Good evening!" A flashlight glared; a rough hand grabbed my shoulder, shocking me. "You stand up now!"

And that was the end of my secret little hideout.

The man who had been stationed in the Lincoln Town Car had apparently woken up and taken a stroll. In his hands he was holding a strappy pair of high-heeled sandals. My abandoned sandals. Shoot! Busted by fashion.

"Get up," he said and pulled me to my feet.

"Ouch!" I yelped. My feet were scratched and bleeding. And now I could feel them hurt.

"Go inside with your husband," said the man.

Right. They were still all about that.

"What's that?" cried a man's voice from inside the house. And when I was brought into the living room, two more flashlights were instantly trained on my face.

"Madeline!" Marvin yelled, horrified to see me. "I told you to run. Damn it. I was doing everything I could to give you time. I almost recited my entire doctoral dissertation for these imbeciles. What happened?"

"I didn't want to leave you," I said.

"Silence," the man with the gun called.

And, of course, it was exactly as I had expected. We were being held hostage by the same merry band of pranksters I'd run up against at the Grand Waikoloa. "Hello again."

"You think this is a joke?" he asked us, furious. "You

find out it's no joke. I already kill one man on this island. I don't mind killing more."

My head reeled. Kelly Imo. He was admitting to killing Kelly. I had watched enough television to know that the murderer never admits to killing anyone unless he's damned sure he's going to leave those witnesses dead too.

"Why did you kill Kelly?" Marvin asked, anguish in his voice. "What did he have to do with you?"

"He work here with you, right? He know how you grow the wasabi, but he doesn't tell us. I give him two chances. Number three and I shoot him. He tell me one good thing. He tell me your wife is here on the island now."

They caught up with Kelly some time after he left the Four Heavens on Friday afternoon and his mixed-up encounter with Holly. And when he wouldn't give them the secrets to Marvin's success at growing wasabi, they shot him and threw him into the Pacific. Horrible.

"So you see, I'm a serious man. Now your wife will die with you," said the gunman. "Unless you tell us what we need to know."

"They think I'm Holly," I told Marvin. "And they found out that Holly and you are still legally married."

"You have to love the irony," said Marvin to me, dazed. "The only people in the world who recognize that I'm married to Hollyhock are about to kill me."

"Marvin," I hissed, "just stay focused. We'll get out of this."

"How?" he asked me, his voice reckless and angry. "How are we going to get out of this? We're in a bloody abandoned house out in the middle of nowhere, Madeline. And there is no one on earth out looking for us."

Just then, the loud *chop-chop-chop* of helicopter blades roared loudly overhead.

"Well," I said, just short of fainting from relief, "that's not exactly true."

"What's that?" cried the gunman. One of his goons ran to the window to look.

"Police," yelled back the goon. "The police are above us." The sound of a second helicopter roared in.

"I had a plan," I explained calmly to Marvin as the Japanese thugs ran around the room, looking for escape possibilities.

Before they could think up their own plan of escape, the front door broke down and several of Hawaii's finest officers came crashing in on us, guns drawn. "Down on the floor!" they yelled. "Right now!"

The perfect ending to a perfect luau night.

Ahe
(Breeze)

Graffiti saved us; I'd been telling the story all night long.

It was just past midnight at Club Breeze, a funky nightspot in Kailua-Kona on the Kona Coast of the Big Island. Outside, a few couples clustered around Formica-topped tables, nursing mai tais in the warm night air, the muffled sounds of dance music wafting out from the club each time the door opened. Inside, the DJ was spinning "Let's Get This Party Started" as a disco ball spangled the crowd with specks of light and Saturday turned into Sunday. And the gang was all there.

Holly's four sisters were bumping and spinning on the little dance floor near the front of the nightclub, singing along to the tune. Liz Mooney was also there, sipping club soda and talking to a bartender. Wesley was sitting with his arm around me on the black leatherette bench of the club's back booth as we watched the scenesters having fun. On the booth seat across from us was a pile of snazzy gift boxes.

Holly had just that second arrived at the club. On her way back through the bar she was stopped by a number of our friends. By her expression, I figured she was hearing snips and snaps about Wes's and my thrilling luau romp from a variety of folks who had already heard

quickie versions of the tale. By the time Holly got bac
to our booth, her mouth was a circle.

"Tell me every single detail," she said, sliding her si
ver leather miniskirt into the booth seat across from u
"I can't stand it already. Tell."

"I saved Madeline's life," Wes said, a smile on h
face. "What's to tell? After all, I am the senior partner.

"Wes saved you!" she squealed, turning to me.

"Yes. True," I admitted. "But that was only becaus
he followed my directions."

"You left him directions?" Holly asked, totally en
thralled. "But I just now heard from Gladdie that yo
were being held at freaking gunpoint, Maddie."

"True. But before that, I left him a note."

"Graffiti," Wes explained. "I was up in the air on
little private helicopter tour, just a quick trip to see th
lava flow."

"Oooh," Holly interjected. "I've heard that's amaz
ing!"

"Amazing!" Wes said, enthused. "It's alive! The K
lauea Volcano has been spewing liquid rock from th
Mauna Ulu area off and on since 1983. At night, Holly
it's like a stream of pure liquid fire on black velvet. I'
never seen anything like it before."

"Hey," I said, "let's get back to me, please. The res
cue?"

"Right," Holly said, returning to the important topi
of me. "Tell."

Wes shrugged his shoulders. "Okay. Well, we wer
coming back from the volcano, flying back along th
Kohala Coast, and we started checking out prime rea
estate from the air."

"You're kidding me!" Holly said.

Wes nodded. "It's fantastic from up there. The only way to shop."

"Get on with the 'me' part, Wes," I prompted.

"Anyway," Wes continued, "we were not far from the house, the one where they were holding Kelly's luau, and suddenly all the lights below us just blinked completely off. From the air, it's a pretty dramatic sight. All the buildings on the property and the exterior lighting just blacked out."

"Go on," Holly said. "I didn't hear this part."

"Vance wanted to fly closer and see what we could see. And then we noticed a crazy thing. Deep onto the property, away from the main house, bordering the lava rock fields, there was light. And we realized we were seeing headlights. But they weren't moving. They were the headlights of a parked car. And the closer we flew, I began to realize it was our Mustang—the one Mad and I had arrived in earlier. That was odd enough. But when we got closer, we saw the headlights were illuminating graffiti."

"What?" Holly looked enthralled. "Where?"

"On the black lava field right next to a small house."

"It was Hawaiian graffiti, Holly," I explained. "Letters made out of white coral rocks. You know, the sort of thing you see all around here from the highway."

Wes said, "It was amazing. Maddie wrote out a special graffiti message just for me."

"You didn't!" Holly said, always the best audience ever. She ordered a drink from the waiter—a blue Hawaiian, which, she explained quickly, matched her nail polish tonight—and then turned back to me, rapt.

"I prayed he was still up there somewhere, flying around," I explained. "The heliport was so close by, it seemed possible."

"She's either a genius or a witch," Wes said. "I can't tell which one I'm partial to."

I ignored him. "But it made sense to me at the time. They would have to notice how dark the property had suddenly gone, wouldn't they? From the air, that had to be damn alarming. I thought there was about one chance in hell that they'd fly over and take a closer look. So I spelled a message out of white coral. And then turned on the headlights of the Mustang."

"Oh," Holly said, shivering in approval. "That's good."

"Well, it sounds clever now," Wes acknowledged. "But I'm sure it was pure desperation. Our poor Maddie."

"What did the message say?"

Wes smirked. "I believe she used her last minutes on earth to leave the vital message: Mad Loves Cake." He turned to me. "Wasn't that it?"

"Oh, Wesley!" I punched his shoulder.

Holly giggled.

"It did not," I pointed out in a little bit of a huff. "I wrote: WES HELP! And then I made an arrow pointing toward the house."

Wes finished the story. "Vance radioed the police helicopter, and the rest was easy."

"Right," I said, thinking again of how "easy" it had all been a couple of hours ago, talking to the police, explaining a thousand details, giving a statement, watching them lock up Kelly Imo's killers.

"Maddie," Holly said, "not to change the subject . . ."

Of course not. I nearly get killed and orchestrate my own fabulous rescue and my posse can only give me about three minutes of attention at best. Right. Gotta love them.

". . . but I need to have a heart-to-heart with you right now," she said.

The waiter arrived with Holly's blue Hawaiian, a sapphire-colored concoction of white rum, blue curaçao, pineapple juice, and cream of coconut, decorated with a paper umbrella, and suddenly smitten, I asked for one too. Wes stood up and excused himself so Holly and I could talk privately, but I noticed Vance had arrived at Club Breeze and was standing near the dance floor. The guys probably had volcano news to discuss.

"Hey!" I said, remembering a party detail, "let's open your bridal shower gifts. The girls brought these. Aren't you excited?"

Holly looked at the tower of boxes beside her. "Are you sure . . . ?"

"Of course. The girls are all over the club, having a blast. Open them now!"

I thought this would be the highlight of Holly's night, but she was rather subdued as she untied the ribbon on the first slender box.

"Oh!" I said as she lifted the lid. "Hot pink! One of your favorite colors."

She had pulled out the slinkiest, sexiest little silk thong and tiny matching satin bra.

"This is cool," she said wistfully.

"It's not cool," I said, trying to perk her up. "It's hot!"

She quickly opened the rest of the boxes. More deliciously outrageous lingerie followed. Some even featured feathers. But it didn't appear that Holly's heart was in her underwear.

"Holly?" I asked as Holly put the new duds back into their shiny boxes and cleared the wrapping paper and bows.

"Maddie," Holly said, "it's about Donald."

"Oh, yeah," I said. How ridiculous of me! In all the tumult of the night, I had momentarily forgotten about the possibility that Donald was involved with Liz. And frankly, there had to be a better word than "involved" when referring to one's fiancé fathering a child by one's best friend.

"What's up, sweetie?" I asked her gently.

"I am not going to marry him, Maddie," she said. "And I feel like I should have told you about this way way earlier. Except, you totally surprised me with this cool flaming bachelorette luau getaway trip. And you had gone to such amazing lengths to make this party great, I didn't want to be the one to dampen your fun."

"*My* fun?" I was shocked.

"Yes, Mad. I know I work for you guys and all, but I have to tell you, seriously, you and Wes are the best event-planners in the universe. And, well, aside from the murder and mayhem parts, this whole entire weekend has been totally awesome fun! Really. The best bachelorette party ever. So how could I be the buzz-kill of the century and tell you I'm having big doubts about the wedding?"

"You're having doubts?" I asked.

"Yep. Donald is a terrific guy. He is. But I have been wondering if we were going to go on battling with each other all our lives, you know? We have always been rocky. And then when I heard Marvin's name again after all these years, something happened. The oddest damn thing. I got kind of misty for Marvin."

"You did?" I stared at Holly.

"Weird, huh? But I can't stop thinking about him. He was the one guy I ever knew who just simply worshipped me, Maddie. I know it's a silly concept, but that's how I felt back then. Like I was worshipped. And he was such a smart guy. I started wondering if a smart guy like Marvin could love me, maybe he knew more about love than I did back then. I mean, I never know what's right. I just go with my gut."

"So you've been thinking these thoughts about Marvin," I said, trying to get my brain around this new development. It is, frankly, a bizarre enough story for a bride-to-be to discover she's in love with her former prom date just on the brink of her wedding, eight years later, to an entirely different guy. But then one had to factor in the equally unusual fact that Holly was actually still married to this former prom date. Which made the entire thing a little more convenient, if no less romantically complicated as hell.

"So you see," she continued, sipping her blue drink, "it just wouldn't be right for me to consider marrying Donald now, while I'm feeling all confused."

The waiter brought me my own blue Hawaiian, and I sipped it thoughtfully. I then told Holly all she needed to know about Marvin Dubinsky, today's version. I told her about his elaborate plans to bring us here to the Big Island, and his hope to see her one more time. I told her also about Kelly Imo's role in the affair. How Marvin had sent Kelly to talk to Holly on his behalf.

"That," I gently explained, "is why Kelly had been waiting in your hotel room."

"Oh, no!" she said, her face crumpling. "Oh, my God. I hit him, Maddie. I thought I was defending myself. Oh, no. I attacked the very guy who was bringing me news of my Marvin!" Tears popped into Holly's pale blue eyes. "And now it's too late. I can't apologize to him. I mean, the guy is dead, Mad. I can never make it up to him. I feel awful."

"You made a mistake. It was a strange situation. It's okay," I said, knowing how bad she must feel. "But you had nothing at all to do with his death, Holly." Then I proceeded to recount the rest of the terrible story.

"So poor, poor Keniki loses her love," Holly said, a tear dropping into her blue Hawaiian, "and I gain back my old love. How is that fair?" She looked up at me. "I'm so confused."

"I know all about confused," I said, agreeing. "That's how I've been feeling, too."

Holly looked at me. "Honnett?" she asked, right as always.

"Yep. I've been running away from him, Holly. I just don't know how he and I can forget about our past junk. And even planning this trip and coming over to Hawaii seemed like a way to avoid Honnett for a bit longer."

"Maybe you're trying to fight your natural feelings," she said.

"You think?"

"Maybe you totally care about that dude, but you were hurt, Mad. He lied to you and you hate that. So it's a pride thing. That's why you're getting all these little flirtations out of your system. You can't admit you fell hard for a man who wasn't honest with you."

"He wasn't honest about the fact that he still had a wife," I said, defending my stupid position. "That wasn't an insignificant detail."

"All right," she agreed. "But men are kind of idiots. If they turn out to be the good-hearted idiots, we have to just forgive them."

I smiled.

"Over and over again," Holly said.

I laughed. "True."

"Like I am gonna do with Marvin," she said. "Even

though the way he brought us here is weird-city, it shows how much he still cares."

"You have a big heart," I said, admiring Holly.

"And I don't think your story is finished with Honnett yet."

"I don't know," I said, my eyes burning. "I don't know. Maybe I'll just consult my fairy and see what she advises."

"Good idea," Holly said, completely serious. I love Holly.

"So you're breaking off your engagement with Donald. You're sure."

"Right," she said, sounding relieved.

"Right," I said slowly. "And then there's Liz."

"Oh." Holly looked up at me, caught. "How do you know about Liz?"

"Holly, sweetie. You are talking to a woman who wrote the word *HELP* out of white coral rocks in the middle of the night. I think figuring out that Liz is pregnant and Donald may be the father is rather the easier trick of the two."

"Right. Right. You know everything. That's why I always come to you for help, Maddie." She smiled. "Anyway, I thought something was up with Liz and all those fainting spells. Liz may be tiny, but she's usually strong as a horse. At the hospital, I heard she was pregnant. Well. I had my suspicions about Donald and Lizzie too. Marigold has been warning me about them for two years."

"Thirteen-lined ground squirrel?"

"Exactly," Holly said, sighing. "But if they can be happy together, I say God bless."

"You are a good soul, Holl." I toasted her with my blue Hawaiian.

"Thanks, Mad."

"And you can forgive Liz?" I asked, making sure Holly was really okay.

"Well," she said, taking another sip and sounding pretty optimistic and philosophical, "why not? I mean, she's been my best friend for twenty years. And since I've known her, let's face it, I've had like a million boyfriends. And Lizzie only had this one. It sucks that he's the one I was engaged to, but what the hell? How can I hold it against her that she fell so hard?"

"But can you forgive her choice in shower gifts?"

Holly laughed out loud. "Man!"

Liz had been the only friend who hadn't brought flimsy underwear. Liz brought a book. A volume of IRS tax tips. Ouch.

"Think of it from her side," Holly said. "She was in love with a guy who was marrying me. I think it was brave of her to even come to my bachelorette weekend."

"And you don't hold this against Donald?"

"Hell, Maddie." She giggled. "He's a man." 'Nuff said.

"So," I said, watching Holly drain her drink, judging whether she could handle one more shock. "With this new turn of events, you aren't going to freak out on me when I tell you I invited Marvin to meet us here tonight. When he's finished talking to the police. Should be pretty soon."

"Marvin?" Holly's voice squeaked up half an octave. "Here?"

I was sure she and Marvin would have plenty to talk about.

"Say, look," Holly said, pointing to the door of Club Breeze. "Isn't that your cute friend Cake?"

I looked. It was. "Yes," I said. "But I'm not sure I'm

going to hang around with Cake tonight. You better keep your distance too."

"See? Talking about Honnett got to you, didn't it?"

I smiled. "I heard something disturbing when I was at the police station tonight. The cops were talking about going to Cake's house." I looked at my watch. "They're probably there right about now. When they don't find him there, they'll probably track him down here."

"You're kidding," she said. "What for?"

"He's been growing illegal plants on his estate. Hiding a nice healthy cannabis crop beneath the cover of bamboo. That's why Cake was part of the island bamboo society, Holly. He was learning tips on how to grow bamboo in order to shelter his pot farm. He figured it would make the stuff harder to see from the air, from the police helicopters."

"Do you really believe Cake would do something illegal?"

"I overheard this guy Earl warning Cake to be careful. And Cake said a guy has to make money on this island somehow. Isn't that odd, Holl? I mean, Kelly Imo and Claudia Modlin and Earl all had dreams of growing bamboo here on this island, and Marvin wanted to save the world by growing wasabi here, but Cake was the practical one. He grew a tried-and-true cash crop, marijuana."

"Oh, Mad. What a bunch of losers-in-love we've turned out to be."

"Then why do I feel so good?" I asked.

"You're a born party planner and we're still having a party?" Holly suggested.

"Cheers!" I clinked glasses with her again. And then I saw the latest arrival to our party at Club Breeze.

"Holly, I can't believe this. But your fiancé has shown up."

"My husband?"

"No, hon. Your future former-fiancé."

"What?" She looked up and scanned the nightclub. Standing near the jukebox was Donald Lake, with the appropriate anguished look on his boyish face.

"Oh, man. What the hell is he doing here?" Holly asked, grabbing my glass and chugging the rest of my drink. "Okay, I'm about to set a man free."

"Like the catch-and-release program," I said, giving her encouragement. "Let him go swim free with the other fishes."

Holly got up and smoothed her silver mini, then walked away, ready and willing to call the wedding off.

Marigold came up to the booth and took the seat Holly had just left vacant. "Can we talk?" she asked.

"Of course. What's up?"

"I've got a confession. I've been a real fool."

"Like a scarlet-bodied wasp moth?" I asked, unable to resist.

"More like a frog," she said, hanging her head. "Frogs get insatiable frog lust. When frog hormones go into overdrive they can't think straight."

"And that's you?"

"I have had a crush on Marvin Dubinsky ever since I was thirteen. But he was always crazy about Holly. Here I am, the scientist, like Marvin. The brain, like Marvin. And he preferred Holly. Go figure."

"Indeed. Love is strange."

"You don't have to tell me about that," said Marigold. "I'm the expert."

"True."

"Anyway, I need to confess something to Holly, but I

don't know how to do it. I think I may have sabotaged her love life a little."

"Really?"

"I was living at home while I went to college. And Holly got one letter every year from Marvin. He mailed it to the house."

"And you stole the letters. Marigold, how could you!"

"I didn't read them or anything. I just burned them."

"Marigold!"

"I know. I can't explain it, Madeline. I think it was just some form of blind, raving frog lust."

"But you have to let your sister run her own life," I said, exasperated. I could never have survived having sisters. I really couldn't have.

"I know. And the truth is, I haven't seen Marvin in all these years. So while I've been pining away for him, sort of building him up in my mind, I didn't realize how much the guy might have changed."

"Really."

"Yes. I just saw him again, Maddie. He's actually here. At Breeze."

So Marvin had shown up at last. How interesting. "What do you think? Did you talk to him?"

"I didn't recognize him at all. He's changed. Liz Mooney spotted him first, and he recognized Liz right away. She introduced us. I couldn't believe what he looks like now. He's lost every ounce of cuteness. He's just some average tall guy now. And I just don't go for tall guys."

"You don't?"

"No. I don't. And so in one quick poof, my frog-lust obsession just evaporated. And I need to tell Holly. How should I do that?"

"I wouldn't worry about it right now, Marigold," I counseled. "You're sisters. She'll understand."

"Cool. Thanks, Maddie. This is the most rocking party I've ever been to. Ever. It has been a hell of a weekend."

"Glad you're having fun," I said. And I was. It was one of my primary goals to make sure all our guests were enjoying themselves, and it warmed my heart to hear her say she was.

"Look, I'm going to go over there and check out that guy by the door," she said, straining to see through the dancers. "That hot older guy in the Hawaiian shirt. Now that I'm finally over my obsession about Marvin, maybe I'll get lucky."

"See you later." I watched Marigold, tall and gorgeous, walk through the crowd, aiming all her charms at her new prey. And really, to each his or her own. Wasn't that the basic premise of Marigold's work at the zoo, after all?

Now in need of another blue Hawaiian, I looked around for the waiter, and instead caught the eye of our favorite tall thin genius, Marvin Dubinsky.

"Hey," he said, smiling shyly at me. "There you are."

"Have a seat," I offered, and Marvin took the spot across the booth.

"It's pretty crowded in here," he said, looking with mild alarm at people dancing.

"It's fun," I suggested. "Do you good to get out once in a while, Marvin."

"Look. I never really got to thank you, Madeline," he said as he scooted into the booth seat. "And I mean, I owe you so much."

"Oh, don't be silly," I said by habit. People are always thanking me, and I'm always putting them at ease like that.

"You saved my life," he said, staring at me.

Oh, yes. That. I suppose that was something.

He met my eyes and held them. "Thank you so much," he said again, with deep heartfelt emphasis.

"You're welcome, Marvin." I smiled at him. He was pretty cute in a nerdy way. "What was happening with the police after I left?"

"It's a pretty big mess. The four men they arrested are Japanese nationals. The police have contacted the Japanese embassy in Washington. But everything is fine for us. They caught those guys with the weapon that killed Kelly. They are holding them, pending arrest. I think they'll have no problem proceeding against them from here on."

"Good."

"Look," Marvin said, "I have been unable to think about anything but Holly since we had our talk tonight. None of the rest of this stuff has really even touched me. Is she here?"

"Of course. Haven't you seen Holly yet?"

He shook his head no. "Well, if you don't mind, I'm going to go and look for her. I'm, like, shaking, I'm so nervous. But I have to face her. I have to know."

Wes plopped down in the booth, sliding next to me once more. He brought with him two fresh blue Hawaiians and set one down in front of me.

"My hero," I said, taking the drink. "You saved me yet again."

"I live to please." We clinked glasses.

"What a night!"

"Don't we always say good parties are filled with surprises?" he asked me, chuckling.

"Did you see that *Donald* is here?" I asked, still stunned.

"Yep. Amazing. Surprise guests are great for a party.

He came in on the evening flight from Burbank, I heard," Wes said. "Couldn't stay away, apparently. Ain't love grand?"

I looked over at Wes, opened my mouth, and then shut it again. I could tell him what was really going on another time.

"Did you see who else flew out on that flight?" Wes asked.

I looked over the crowd and could see no one else I recognized. Then I looked again. Seated at a small table was Elmer Minty. Wesley's grouchy neighbor, Elmer.

"What the hell is he doing here?" I said, laughing.

"I had him flown out here," Wes said proudly.

"Oh, Wes!"

"Actually, I got Blake Witherspoon to fly Elmer out. They're both here. See the guy with the purple beret sitting at that table with Elmer? That's Witherspoon, the one who wants to buy my house."

"You're brilliant," I said, suddenly guessing Wesley's master plan.

"I told Rachel the only way I'd agree to sell the Hightower property was if my neighbor was happy with the new owner. And Mr. Witherspoon agreed to fly them both out here so we could all three discuss it and settle it tonight. He brought the escrow papers along, just in case it all works out."

"And he paid for Elmer too?"

"I put that into my counteroffer. Elmer is on his first vacation in fifty-seven years. And he's loving it. Amazing."

"Amazing."

"And the two old guys seem to be hitting it off, so I expect I have just sold my Hightower house, Maddie."

"Cheers, Wes!" We clinked glasses.

"Cheers!"

"Well, it seems everyone has had an event-filled evening," I said.

"Extreme-sport event-filled."

"And now I could use a vacation."

"What?" Wes looked at me with affection, but he clearly didn't believe a word I was saying. "You never really relax. You've been nonstop party planning and cooking since we arrived here. Even when I tried to get you massaged into oblivion, you found a way to sneak out of the spa and solve a few crimes on your off-party hours."

"Well, someone had to do that," I said, joking. "But now I just want to drink a few more blue Hawaiians and totally relax. I think everyone we know on the island has been by the booth tonight, talking to me about their problems, Wes. I think I'm ready to put up a 'closed' sign and get smashed."

Wes leaned over and put his arm around me and whispered in my ear, "Sorry, Mad. It's not over quite yet. Somebody wants to talk to you. Outside."

I groaned.

Just then we were joined at the booth by two towering, enormously built men.

"Oh, hey!" Wes said, smiling up at them. "Mad, let me introduce you to my good buddies. Tiki and Bruiser."

"Hello," I said. I got out of the booth and they sat down. So these were the Hawaiian Gods of Destruction. "The wrestlers, right?"

"Pleasure to meet you," said Tiki.

"Woof!" growled Bruiser. I just barely escaped.

Someone was waiting to talk to me. Maybe it was the cops with more questions. Then I worried for a moment it might be Cake. Perhaps he hoped to get me alone so we could pick up where we had left off. But by now I was so over Cake, I couldn't believe I had ever taken a guy who called himself a dessert name seriously.

But when I walked through the dance floor, Cake was there swaying to the music. The DJ was spinning a funky old ABBA disc, and Cake had each arm tightly wrapped around one of Holly's twin sisters. As the record wailed on about "Waterloo," Cake spotted me while Daisy and Azalea laughed at his jokes. He smiled, as if to say, I'd had my chance and blown it. And I just smiled back, happy to be walking on by, going to meet just about anyone other than Cake outside.

Also spotted on the dance floor, arms around each other, was the stealth couple of Liz Mooney and Donald Lake. I had never seen Liz look happier. Donald seemed dazed, but not really unhappily so. Well, I guess some things manage to work out.

At the bar, I noticed another old buddy of mine. Gabriel Swan was talking to Gladiola Nichols. He was pointing to Gladdie's chest, and she was shaking her head no. I figured with what Gladdie had been drinking at the bar, even her fairies must be tipsy by this hour.

And that's when I spotted Holly. She was seated in a little booth halfway up toward the entrance. And she wasn't alone. Holly was locking lips with an ecstatic Marvin Dubinsky. Their passionate embrace might be considered vulgar, I suppose, if one didn't take into consideration the fact that man and wife had been separated for eight years. They looked divine together. And now Holly would actually have some fun with her shower gifts. Good for Holly.

The club was hopping, and many of the people were locals, enjoying a fine Saturday night. I scanned the crowd at the front of the club, and that's when I saw Earl Maffini talking to Marigold. Good old Earl. My lord, was he the new frog-lust of Marigold's dreams? I'd never understand Holly's sisters. Never.

But I felt a little pang of guilt about Earl. I had misjudged him when I'd suspected he might have been involved in the death of Kelly Imo, and for that I was sorry. But I was not convinced I'd been wrong about his other activities. I still wondered if Claudia and he were trying to get rich on bamboo futures. But, after all, what was the harm in a little capitalism? If their efforts to realize Kelly Imo's dream could help hundreds of islanders find good-paying jobs, I would just keep my nose out of the bamboo.

I pushed my way through the crowd toward Earl. Perhaps he was the one who had been waiting to talk to me. He might have become impatient and come indoors. But no. Now that I was closer, I saw that Earl had his arm around Marigold. They were so deep in conversation he barely looked up as I approached.

I heard Marigold telling him about the American black slug. "A pair of slugs will circle around each other on a tree for an hour or so," she was saying as I passed, "creating enough slime to make a rope. Then they both jump in the air at each other and dangle from the rope."

"Sounds like fun," Earl said earnestly.

I was soon out of earshot. Thank God.

I pushed open the door and walked out into the soft night air. The tables were deserted now, all the action of the club going on indoors at this hour. However, leaning against the building I discovered another recent island arrival.

"Hi, Maddie."

It was my guy Honnett. Here in Hawaii. It took me a few seconds to let it sink in.

"Honnett. You're supposed to be in L.A. What on earth are you doing here?"

"Hey," he said, looking wonderful, sounding wonderful. "You invited me, remember?"

"I did?"

"Yeah. Last night. You said I should really come to Hawaii sometime."

"Chuck! I meant, like, some time *in your life*," I said, almost laughing.

"This is some time in my life," he drawled. "Are you happy to see me?"

"I sure am," I said, and in a step I was in his arms.

"Who says I can't be spontaneous?" he asked, nuzzling the top of my head.

"Not me."

We held on to each other for quite a while, comfortable in the way that two bodies that know each other well can find instant alignment. The most perfect fit.

"Say," I asked, "have you been on the island long enough to hear any of the local news?"

"What sort of news?" he asked, totally oblivious.

"Nothing," I said. There would be plenty of time for Honnett to hear about the activities I'd gotten myself involved with. Tomorrow.

"Thing is, all this spontaneity comes at a price," Honnett said. "I just hopped on a plane. But I don't have a reservation for a room."

"You are so in luck," I said, hugging him hard. "Big spontaneous men like you get all the breaks. I happen to have the keys to a modest little bungalow for the night."

"You must have forgiven me," he said, letting out his

breath slowly. He said it lightly enough, but he waited to hear my response.

"Yes. Yes, I did. I think we're back, Honnett."

He pushed my hair off my face and looked in my eyes. I waited for what he had to say about it all.

"Think I can maybe find a strong cup of coffee before we head off?" he asked.

"Don't bother. I'll make you a pot of coffee in our very own bungalow." I kept holding on to him, my eyes closed.

"You'd do that for me, Mad?"

"That, and much much more."

"Will you show me that hula dance you learned?"

I opened my eyes. "Don't push it, Honnett."

The catering/event-planning business has been very, very good to Madeline Bean, but even so, it's not as good as the real estate biz. So what would Maddie do to acquire a killer apartment in LA? Pump the elderly landlady for hints as to her favorite culinary treats—and then bribe her with her own inspired gourmet version? Yup. Indulge the old woman in reminiscences of her film days? Yup. Knock off the competition for a piece of prime real estate? Now wait a minute . . .

Madeline Bean finds big trouble at a certain historic penthouse. So what does a savvy, determined, crime-solving foodie do?

Please join Madeline Bean as she hits the ground running—boldly looking for a killer, craftily avoiding becoming the next victim, and

DESPERATELY SEEKING SUSHI

Available Winter 2006 in hardcover from
William Morrow

A girl's got to eat, after all . . .

*T*he back streets of Hollywood. Not glittery. Not glamorous. Not at all. Not when you're on the ground floor of some out-of-the-way historic old building at nighttime. Not when you're supposed to be all alone and you distinctly hear the sound of stealthy footsteps.

Footsteps?

I stopped moving, stopped breathing. My eyes strained in the dim hallway. I listened, but my ears were now filled with the pounding of my heart. All else was silence. Adrenaline jolted me into a suspended state, hyper-alert to every tiny detail in the hall around me—the grime-muted picture of an orange grove hanging on the wall; the pattern of huge dark-green spiky plant leaves on the faded vintage wallpaper; the faint sound of wailing sirens filtering in from Selma Street—but I worked hard to resist the tug of panic.

I put a hand out to steady myself against the wall, tried to calm myself down to a state just north of cautious alarm. Think it through. Review the facts. There had been a noise. A definite shuffling noise. Had I really heard footsteps? Could it have been, instead, only the sounds of . . . what? Well, rats. It might have been rats scurrying away out of sight. But, come to think of it, would that make my situation any less frightening?

"Mrs. Gillespie?" My voice sounded whiney and tentative. Ridiculous. "Hello?" I was satisfied to hear my register drop an octave, the volume increase to hearty. "Mrs. Gillespie, is that you?"

Silence. More silence.

Edith Gillespie had been quite clear. I was to come at eight and we would meet in her "penthouse" on the fourteenth floor. Mrs. Gillespie never came downstairs anymore, she assured me. She had given me the combination to the lock she kept on the building's outer front door, and she had just a few minutes ago buzzed me in from the building's tiny lobby through the inner security door that led into the main part of the building. And here, at the end of this long hallway I would find the service elevator. I had visited Mrs. Gillespie several times before, so I knew the routine.

But I had only ever been here at the Edithwood Palms during the daytime, when her young valet, Bo, had been around to let me in and walk me to the elevator. At night this old gem of a building was much different.

In the few minutes that passed, there had been no more shuffling noises. My pulse was beginning to get back to its normal steady rhythm but my senses were still on active alert, taking in every detail. Pale green paint flaked from the ceiling, lit only weakly by the occasional working wall fixture—but what magnificent lighting fixtures they were! Chrome-plated ziggurats with tool-cut piercings. Pure art deco gorgeousness. Still, from a practical perspective they were part of the problem. Without enough wattage, I could see only seven feet or so ahead of me. But at least I had come prepared.

So there I stood. Listening to nothing more than the muffled sound of sirens from the street outside. Holding a powerful flashlight in one hand and a basket of freshly baked cherry tarts in the other. If only I'd been wearing a red-hooded cloak, you could make your little jokes with impunity.

I suppose I shouldn't have come to the Edithwood Palms that night but I was desperate. I was engaged in a war and that meant pressing every advantage, didn't it? I had had an impetuous impulse. Mrs. Gillespie had a sweet tooth and very little will power. This one secret could be my key to the kingdom!

I am a professional baker and all-around trained chef and, wonder of wonders, Mrs. Gillespie had found this fact most delightful. My name is Madeline Bean and I co-own a successful event-planning company called Mad Bean Events, but she had no interest in parties so wasn't wowed by that little fact. No, it was baked goods that lit up her world. I had already scored big points by bringing her a fabulous key-lime pie (one of her favorite childhood memories) and a tin of home-baked apricot macaroons (her late husband's favorite treats). As she sampled my high-calorie offerings, she let her guard down a little and reminisced about the good old days.

"Do you know what Mr. Berkeley called me?" Edith Gillespie had asked, selecting a perfect macaroon from the box of goodies I'd delivered.

"You mean Busby Berkeley, the great director?" Okay. I was laying it on thick. Forgive me. I wanted this damned apartment.

"Yes, Madeline, dear. The wonderful Mr. Berkeley. He had an eye for talent. A great, great eye. What a perfectionist he was! He called me 'Gilly'. For Gillespie, you know. He said I had the perfect figure. Perfect, he said. For a dancer. All Mr. Berkeley's girls were beautiful, you know. You've seen my work?"

"You appeared in the big Busby Berkeley musicals. How wonderful is that!" My partner Wes and I have a great fondness for the big splashy MGM musicals from the thirties and forties, so I'd seen a lot of Busby Berkeley movies. Naturally, I couldn't be expected to remember one face out of a chorus of hundreds, even if I could guess what Edith had looked like as a young woman, but I nodded and smiled and Edith took another macaroon.

"Wonderful, yes," Edith said, but then her expression changed. "Poor Mr. Berkeley. His life took such a tragic turn."

It did? I didn't really know much about him. Just that he had an amazing gift for choreographing long lines of dancing girls.

"Tragic?"

"Oh yes. All that booze, for one thing. That wasn't good for him."

I supposed not, but urged Mrs. Gillespie to go ahead and have another macaroon.

"My dear Madeline, the poor man would sit in his daily bath and simply guzzle martinis."

I looked duly shocked.

"It was a shame. He never recovered from his dear mother's death," she explained, "He had been devoted to her. Simply devoted." Mrs. G had a chatty way with her, never bothering to fill in all the details, leaving many tantalizing threads unpulled. But she had such first-hand knowledge of all the movie stars of the past, I loved hearing the insider gossip, even if we were dishing about a man who had been dead and gone for over thirty years.

"Was Mr. Gillespie in the movies, too?" I asked her.

This new topic allowed her to dip once more into the box of macaroons.

"Oh, goodness no," she said, and I thought I could detect a few dimples joining the rather deep creases already in place in her still-lovely face as she smiled at me. "My Walter was a man of business. His family had money, you see. They never approved when Walter decided to marry a chorus girl from the pictures. Oh, there was a great big fuss over that, I'll tell you. But Walter knew what he wanted and he wanted me."

As she talked about the past, I stole a few glances around her apartment on the top floor of the Edithwood Palms. It took up the entire floor and measured over six thousand square feet. It had very high walls, maybe twelve feet, which curved up to the ceiling, and all the doorways were long and arched. This was the only floor in the entire structure with windows and they were glorious, tall and wide with arches that matched the other arched features of the interior. Each magnificent window was surrounded by carved wood frames done in gold leaf. Her late husband, Mr. Gillespie, must have been a darn good businessman.

"When Walter came courting me," she was saying, "he always brought me something sweet! Chocolate or marzipan. Simply decadent! And my favorite of all were cherry tarts. We both loved those."

Aha! I made a mental note to stop by the farmer's market on my way home and pick up a few pints of fresh cherries. Of course, I tucked this exciting tidbit from Mrs. G's culinary past away. I had to use what little advantage I had, didn't I, if I was to secure the apartment of my dreams?

The problem was, others were after the penthouse. They wanted it badly. Well, so did I.

I moved my flashlight so I could see a little further down the hallway. The building was fourteen stories high, but all the bottom floors had no windows. This might make perfect sense for a grain silo. Or an insane asylum. Or a storage warehouse, which was the purpose for which this building had been built eighty years ago.

I hadn't heard any more footsteps or sounds of any kind so I stepped up the pace and jogged up the hall. About thirty feet from where I had stopped, the hall dead ended at a pair of elevators. Service elevators. Of course, the old Edithwood Palms had at one time had working elevators off of the lobby, but Mrs. Gillespie had the working mechanism for them shut down years ago since she never used them. Instead, what few visitors she had these days were obliged to find their way to the back of the building and use the service elevators. I pushed the call button and looked up at the car signal display, noting both elevators seemed to be resting on floor fourteen.

Only one of the pair of elevators faced the interior of the building. The other one was huge and opened to the exterior. It was used as a loading dock to bring large items up to the higher floors. The Edithwood Palms had been built to house storage lockers, large rooms which were leased over the years to individuals who needed extra room to hold their belongings. Only the top floor had ever been residential, the home to the proprietor, Walter Henning Gillespie and his wife.

I waited for the elevator to descend, feeling exposed and alone.

From the street again I heard muffled sirens. This section of Hollywood was like chipped china. But of such a dear old pattern I forgave it its flaws.

The elevator appeared to be stalled on fourteen. I couldn't stand still, couldn't wait any longer.

Instead, I pushed open the door to the service stairs. Fourteen stories. It would be good for me.

I began to climb and felt some relief. I would be upstairs in no time. It occurred to me that I might have to negotiate with Mrs. Gillespie to allow me to repair the guest elevator at the front of the building. At first, I'd found the entire scheme charming—Mrs. G told me I could park my car as she has always done. Right up on the fourteenth floor! She doesn't drive herself now, of course, but she has her valet drive her old car. He pulls it right into the large service elevator that opens on the loading dock in the back alley. He rides up to the fourteenth floor and then locks the elevator there until he's ready to go out again. On those occasions when Mrs. G wants to be taken on an outing, she has only to walk up to the elevator and enter her car.

I was up to the eighth floor and had begun to slow down. I had always thought I'd been in pretty good shape. Maybe I needed to reevaluate.

As I drew up to the twelfth floor I stopped at the landing. I was breathing hard. I admit it. I had definitely got to do something about working out. I got a lot of exercise running my parties, always on my feet, always running around, but I realize that twenty-nine years old isn't sixteen anymore. I would have to face this reality. I was slowing down. Damn it. I huffed. Actually huffed. Only twelve stories. I was pathetic.

That's when I heard the woman cry out from up above. That's when I heard the loudish thumps and then the silence.

Without thinking, I bounded up the staircase again. I turned at the half-flight and raced to the top landing. I had expected two more stories to go, four more half-flights until the penthouse, but of course, the building must have employed the art of faux-floor numbering. There was no official "thirteenth" floor in these old buildings. Therefore, the penthouse was not on the four-teenth floor at all. It was on thirteen.

I stopped on the final landing. The stairwell door was closed, but the floor number was displayed. Fourteen. Yeah. Right.

I raised my heavy flashlight, more out of some primitive need for a weapon than for light, and opened the door.

It led to a little entry hall outside of the penthouse. Across the entry were the doors to the two service elevators. They stood open, both still stuck on this top floor. Inside the larger one, I could see Edith's pristine Rolls Royce. Gleaming white and silver. In the smaller one was something else entirely.

The crumpled bodies of two men. Dead. As soon as I saw them I knew it.

And what made the surreal scene even worse: I recognized them both immediately.

A feast of funny, savory, and delectable murder from

JERRILYN FARMER

The Madeline Bean Novels

THE FLAMING LUAU OF DEATH

0-06-058731-8
$6.99 US/$9.99 Can
Madeline throws a getaway luau for her ditzy assistant, blushing bride-to-be Holly Nichols.

MUMBO GUMBO

0-380-81719-5
$6.99 US/$9.99 Can
When Madeline fills in as a writer for a hot TV game show featuring a dishy celebrity chef she finds herself face-to-face with a murderer.

PERFECT SAX

0-380-81720-9
$6.99 US/$9.99 Can
Just as Madeline is wondering what else can go wrong at the prestigious Jazz Ball, the hip event planner arrives home to discover a dead body in her bedroom.

A KILLER WEDDING

0-380-79598-1
$6.99 US/$9.99 Can
When a corpse turns up at a glittering wedding party in the Nature Museum's Hall of Dinosaurs, Maddie just may be the next species to become extinct . . .

DIM SUM DEAD

0-380-81718-7
$5.99 US/$7.99 Can
Madeline and Wesley are determined to throw a gonzo Chinese New Year banquet. Until one of the mah-jongg players turns up dead.

SYMPATHY FOR THE DEVIL

0-380-79596-5
$5.99 US/$7.99 Can
Madeline and her partner Wesley have successfully pulled off Hollywood's most outrageous A-list Halloween party when a notorious producer is poisoned to death.

IMMACULATE RECEPTION

0-380-79597-3
$6.50 US/$8.99 Can
Things quickly go from serene to sinister when a young priest turns up dead in the bed of an uninhibited Hollywood star.

JF 0905

PERENNIAL DARK ALLEY

PERENNIAL
DARK
ALLEY
An Imprint of HarperCollins*Publishers*
www.harpercollins.com

DKA 0905

Investigate the Hottest New Mysteries!

Sign up for the FREE HarperCollins monthly mystery newsletter,

The Scene of the Crime,

and get to know your favorite authors, win free books, and be the first to learn about the best new mysteries going on sale.

To register, simply go to www.HarperCollins.com, visit our mystery channel page, and at the bottom of the page, enter your email address where it states "Sign up for our mystery newsletter." Then you can tap into monthly Hot Reads, check out our award nominees, sneak a peek at upcoming titles, and discover the best whodunits each and every month.

Get to know the magnificent mystery authors of HarperCollins and sign up today!